CONTENT WARNING

The Take Me To Church Series Contains:

This series is a dark contemporary romance and may be disturbing to some readers so discretion is advised. On the following page is a more comprehensive list of trauma reminders. Small spoilers may be present.

This is your chance to turn the page
Turned it yet?
No... well you still have time
Last chance....
Okay, here we go!

Explicit sexual situations, strong language, graphic violence, self-harm, suicidal thoughts/ attempt, homophobia, internalized homophobia, anxiety/panic attacks, character injury, religious trauma/guilt, and recreational drug use (marijuana).

1

"Luka! It's almost time for breakfast!" his mom yells from downstairs, and Luka ignores her. Instead, he sighs as he looks in the mirror, debating about whether or not he should change his outfit for a third time. The first day of school is always nerve-wracking but adding the extra stress of it being his first day at a new school *and* his senior year, it's downright nauseating. Being an Army brat, he should be used to this by now, but he isn't. It never gets easier. He has been to five different high schools alone, not to mention all of the various middle schools he has attended.

He remembers when his mom married Matt. He was happy for her. She seemed happy, and it meant he was getting a new dad. He had no idea at the time that he would be ripped away from all of his friends and everything he held dear. All of the schools and faces over the years have just kind of blended together, no one really standing out. He quickly learned not to allow himself to even get attached to anyone. He is so excited to go to college next fall so that maybe, just maybe, he can finally lay down some roots. Have actual friends that he won't have to leave after a couple of months. He can dream.

He takes a deep breath, checking out his appearance again. He glances at the clock, knowing his mother will call him down to breakfast any minute now. He tugs at his shirt, not knowing what exactly the kids at his new school would be wearing. He then runs small fingers through his brown hair, going for a somewhat messy look.

"Luka! I told you it's time for breakfast!" she shouts, again. He has to be down to breakfast at exactly the same time every single day. He hates it. His mom and stepdad are somewhat controlling. Well, his stepdad really, his mom just tries to keep the peace. He stares at his reflection again, hoping that he won't stand out at this new school. He just wants to blend in until he is forced to move to the next location by Matt's job. Who knows, maybe this time he will get to stay an entire school year.

"Luka William Thomas, don't make your mother ask you again!" Matt's booming voice travels up the stairs and into his room, making Luka wince.

"Yeah, sorry! I'm coming," he calls back, turning and leaving his room then going down the stairs. He walks into the kitchen, where they always eat breakfast, to find his four sisters, mother, and Matt already sitting around the table.

"'Bout time, Lu. You know we aren't allowed to eat until everyone is down here and we say grace. I'm starving," Lizzie moans. If Luka wasn't in front of their parents, he would flip her off, but instead he just rolls his eyes and plops down in the open chair, avoiding Matt's glare.

Everyone holds hands as Matt begins, "Heavenly Father, thank you for allowing us to wake up this morning, and thank you for this meal. We thank you for our health and happiness. In Jesus' name we pray. Amen."

It's the same every morning, so Luka mumbles his 'Amen' and starts eating right away, trying to avoid the small talk with his family if at all possible. No such luck, though.

"I signed you up for football," his mom starts, glancing in his direction. He barely stops himself from rolling his eyes, knowing Matt would chastise him for it.

"Why?" Luka asks, through gritted teeth. He kind of likes the sport itself, being an active person, but he hates having to leave his team once Matt gets relocated. He would rather just avoid it all together.

"Because it is a good way to make friends, and it is a safe after-school activity for you to take part in," his mom answers easily, her tone leaving no room for argument.

"Fine," Luka grumbles, looking down at his plate of half-eaten food, suddenly not feeling hungry.

"First practice is today, after school. Your father talked to the coach yesterday since you already missed two-a-days, but he is willing to let you play, given you prove your skills. Don't forget about it. We expect you home right after," she says, and Luka *knows*. Of course, he knows, he has had the same rule since he was a child. How dare he try to do anything fun after school that isn't school-sponsored? He has never even been to a school dance because his parents fear that he may get drunk or lose his virginity. Their stupid rules didn't do them any good, though, because he has already lost his virginity and been drunk.

"I know, Mom," Luka tells her, suppressing yet another eye roll. Jesus, he will be lucky to make it through breakfast without getting grounded.

"Oh, and join your school's Bible Club," Matt adds, pointing one chubby finger at Luka.

"Sure," Luka answers robotically because he is just done with this already, and he hasn't even made it to school yet. He manages to evade the rest of the conversation, his parent's attention turning to that of his little sisters. After he forces down enough food to appease his mother, he practically runs out the door and to his car, silently praying that no one from his family stops him. He lets out a sigh of relief when he is safely in his car, the door slamming behind him.

He pulls out his school schedule, glancing over it to see what he has first period. Choir. *Fuck.* Must be one of those stupid general courses every high school student has to take. Why couldn't it be art or something? The rest of the classes seem fine. It looks like he is in Honors courses at this high school. His eyes rove down the list of courses: Physics, Chemistry, Pre-Calculus, Spanish, English, Creative Writing, and a free period.

He takes a deep breath before he puts the car into gear, making his way toward the location of the high school. It is a very small town, so the high school is equally as small. Hick-town, USA, it seems. When his mom enrolled him, she had said he would only have about 100 people in his entire class. That almost makes this worse. In bigger schools, it's easy to blend in. Smaller schools are a whole different universe. Everyone knows everyone, so when a new kid comes along, that person is easily identifiable. This thought makes Luka feel sick all over again.

He parks his car in the student parking section of the lot and takes a few more calming breaths, trying to slow his racing heart before he steps out onto the pavement. As he typically does with all new schools, once he leaves the safety of his vehicle, he keeps his eyes down and starts walking, not wanting to be met with the staring and pointing that inevitably happens when people notice 'the new kid'. He only glances up long enough to follow the signs for the main office, which is where he was told to go.

"Hi. I'm a new student here," Luka tells the older lady at the front desk. She is wearing red, thick-rimmed glasses with lipstick to match. She smiles, and Luka notices a few lipstick stains on her teeth. Her hair is also red and teased up. The higher the hair, the closer to heaven, he supposes. She looks like she just strolled out of the 80s.

"Lukas Thomas?" she asks, her thick southern accent prominent as she types something into a computer that looks about as old as her. Well, maybe not *that* old, but still not as high tech as it could be.

"It's actually Luka," he corrects, rolling his eyes. He is so used to people getting his name wrong, but it will always annoy him just a bit.

"Oh, I'm sorry, darlin'," she apologizes, smiling again, her yellow teeth looking even more stained against the red dots of lipstick.

"It's okay, ma'am," he answers politely, beginning to tap his fingers on the surface of her desk, needing a release for his nervous energy.

"Okay," she says as she stands up from her desk, and for the first time, Luka notices she is also wearing something that looks like it is from the 80s. Jesus, he loves the decade, but this is a bit much. She walks around her desk and uses one long bony finger to motion for someone to come in. Luka turns to see a student with longish dark brown hair and deep brown eyes make his way through the glass door of the office, smiling at him. He returns the smile because at least this boy isn't looking at him curiously like everyone else.

"Luka. This is Ezra Carter. He is going to show you around a bit, then take you to your first class," the woman says, gesturing towards the other boy.

"Hiya. Nice to meetcha," Ezra greets, eyes crinkling with his smile. He grabs Luka's outstretched hand for a shake, and Luka instantly likes him. Something about him seems warm and caring. Maybe they will be friends. Well, that is if Luka allows it. He hates the thought of leaving yet another person behind.

"Hi. Nice to meet you, too," Luka returns, smiling as well.

"Come on. I'll give you a quick tour. Shouldn't take very long since the school ain't very big. We have pretty much the same schedule, and I play football, too. I think that's why they asked me to show ya around," Ezra says, gesturing for Luka to follow him.

"Makes sense."

"Yeah. So, this is a super small school. Shouldn't take you long to learn your way around. Let's start with your locker," Ezra starts, walking down a hallway to the right, lined with trophy cases.

"You'll find that you will be in class with generally the same people all day, every day. It's based on test scores. They want to make sure kids are taking classes with other kids who are on their level, academically. The only classes that'll differ are general courses, like foreign languages and fine arts."

Luka nods along, listening to Ezra ramble about the school and pointing out various things, mostly understanding him, even with his heavy accent. They get to Luka's locker, where he successfully opens the combination lock, then they go on a quick tour. Luka is thankful that it seems class has already started, so he doesn't have to deal with the staring.

"Alright, time to go to our first class, I suppose," Ezra says with a chuckle, although Luka didn't find the statement all that funny. They walk into the choir classroom and a hush falls instantly, all of the students' eyes trained on them.

2

Harlan hits the snooze button on his alarm for the fifth time that morning, not wanting to go to school at all. He groans, looking at the clock. He doesn't have time to shower or anything before he has to catch the bus. *Fuck.* Why does school have to start so godsdamned early? He rubs his entire face in a weak attempt at waking himself up. He really should have gone to bed last night at a halfway decent time, but he was reading and didn't want to stop. Not like there is anyone to *make* him go to bed anyways.

He rolls out of bed and finds the nearest pair of black skinny jeans laying on the floor. He stumbles to his dresser, pulling out one of his many black band t-shirts. He doesn't even pay attention to which one it is as he pulls it over his mop of curls. He grabs all of his bracelets, putting them on one at a time, making sure they take up most of his forearms, covering his scars. Next, he puts on his necklaces, pulling them over his head so that they lay flat against his t-shirt. He slips each ring on, one by one, enjoying the feel of the cool metal against his skin.

He goes to the bathroom to brush his teeth, squinting at the harsh overhead light. He looks bad. Despite the fact that it's summer, his skin is pale, and there are dark rings around his eyes. He shrugs at his reflection. He isn't trying to impress anyone. No one will even notice him, like normal. He is just the weird kid. Most people at his school simply try to ignore his existence, or they are scared of him. They think he is a Satanist or something, going to cast a spell on them. He doesn't care. It gets them to leave him the fuck alone.

He finishes his minimal bathroom routine and goes down to the kitchen to grab an apple, not having time for actual breakfast. His mom has left him a note on the fridge, saying she is working both jobs today, so she won't be home until late. He sighs, mentally preparing himself for another lonely evening. Maybe he will find something to get into, but probably not.

He doesn't know if his mom actually loves him or just does the minimum to keep him alive because she has to. She is never around, but to be fair, she is a single mom. Just to put food on the table for him and his sister, she has had to work two jobs since his dad left when he was younger. Things have been easier on her since Emma moved out, but she still works a lot.

He eats his apple as he makes his way to the bus stop, his friend Cadeon greeting him with a huge smile. Harlan just rolls his eyes but allows his lips to curl into a soft smile. Cadeon is like an overexcited puppy, but he is Harlan's best friend. His only friend, really. Cadeon is one of those rare people who is liked by everyone and can fit in with any crowd. He is friends with everyone at school and fits into all the cliques easily. He sticks with Harlan the most though, and it's only because Harlan has told Cadeon all of his secrets. He is too nice to let Harlan always be alone.

"Hey, I didn't think you'd make it," Cadeon greets him, hugging his friend like he didn't just see him yesterday. Cadeon knows that Harlan hates hugs, but that doesn't stop him for a second.

"Yeah. I was up late last night," Harlan responds, shrugging his hunched-up shoulders.

"With a boy?" Cadeon asks with an exaggerated wink.

"Fuck off and keep that shit down. I am trying to not die on my first day of school," Harlan whispers, but Cadeon just rolls his eyes.

"Come on, you know I'd protect'cha."

"If you could keep your big fucking mouth shut, then I wouldn't need protection," Harlan hisses, but there is no bite in his tone. He loves Cadeon too much to actually be mad. Not that he actually gives a flying fuck what people think of him. His sexuality would be just one more thing to add to the list of 'weird' if they were to know. He just doesn't want to deal with that kind of crisis in his senior year. He would rather just move far away for college and become his own person; however, that's probably not even in the cards for him. He can't afford it. People like him don't get to go to college. It's as simple as that.

"So what classes are you in?" Cadeon asks, talking over the screeching of the bus' brakes as it pulls to a stop in front of them. They both get on, Cadeon heading straight to the back with Harlan hot on his heels. Cadeon greets everyone while Harlan tries not to make eye contact.

"Here," Harlan says, thrusting his schedule at Cadeon.

"Fuck yeah, we have all the same classes except for Art!" Cadeon exclaims, clearly happy about this turn of events.

"Awesome. Maybe I won't be terribly miserable," Harlan says, closing his eyes and resting his head on the seat in front of him. He just wants to go back to bed. Cadeon chats on and on about how he hopes the first day of school is going to go. Harlan doesn't even think Cadeon would realize it if he put his earbuds in to block out the noise, but he doesn't want to do that to his friend. He may be an ass, but he isn't that rude.

They get off the bus and walk to choir class together, stopping at Cadeon's new locker on the way. Harlan doesn't bother going to his. He didn't bring anything except his ancient cell phone, a pen, a notebook, and the brown, leather-bound journal he takes everywhere with him. Harlan is actually looking forward to this class and creative writing, but he doesn't voice this. He has had choir since the beginning of his high school career, even though he was only required to take it once. He enjoys music and singing. The ease of the class also provides a needed break from some of his harder ones, like Physics and Chemistry.

The room is set up with three rows of brown chairs all facing the front of the room. Harlan and Cadeon immediately go to the section where the baritones will be seated, familiar with the layout since they have both been in the class before. Mr. Tennant will probably make them test their vocal range again, since it can change with age, but both boys are pretty confident this is where they will end up. Cadeon keeps talking because he literally never shuts up. As more people begin to filter into the room, Cadeon greets each of them, starting a conversation. Seriously, how does he have the energy this early in the morning?

Harlan, for his part, just ignores everyone with his eyes trained firmly to the front of the room waiting for class to start, thinking about how boring this year is going to be. He contemplates, for the fourteenth time that morning, putting his ear buds in and drowning out everything with some rather loud music; however, class will start soon, and Mr. Tennant would just make him turn it off. Sure enough, a few moments later the last bell rings, signaling the beginning of class. Mr. Tennant takes roll, then starts bringing each student up one by one to test their vocal range, assigning them the appropriate section afterward.

When it's Harlan's turn, he walks to the front of the room, hating the feeling of all eyes on him. Thankfully, the other students are allowed to talk amongst themselves while their peers are being tested. It still doesn't ease his apprehension, though. Cadeon gives him a thumbs up, which kind of helps.

He pushes down the anxiety making its way up his throat and walks over to the piano. Mr. Tennant does an excellent job of making it painless because he understands that not everyone is a good singer, nor do they like being in front of people. Mr. Tennant, however, has told Harlan on multiple occasions that he is a great singer, and he would give him a solo if he just asked. Harlan ignores his comments, being perfectly happy to just be the weird kid in the corner.

"Baritone," Mr. Tennant starts with a smile, "but you can go as low as some bass notes. Well done."

"Thanks," Harlan mumbles, making his way back to his seat, feeling as though his cheeks are on fire at the compliment. Cadeon is called next, his results being a steady baritone. Before he knows it, everyone in the room is seated in their appropriate sections. Like normal, most of the girls are sopranos and a few are contraltos. Most of the boys are baritones, like him and Cadeon, with a few basses and tenors in the mix.

Mr. Tennant is in the front of the room beginning their lecture when the door opens. All eyes are immediately drawn to the pair entering the room. One guy Harlan recognizes as Ezra Carter. He is a jock and in his senior year as well. He has never explicitly made fun of Harlan, but he has also never really talked to him outside of the classroom. He has a good voice, though. His falsetto is killer.

The other guy, however, Harlan doesn't recognize, which is odd for a small town. He is quite attractive, even though he is preppy and clearly a jock. He is short with shapely legs, brown hair, lightly tanned skin, and freckles. His eyes, though. His eyes are a clear shade of blue, framed with ridiculously long eyelashes. Okay. He is cute. Very, very cute, but completely off limits. A guy like that would never even talk to Harlan, let alone actually date him. He is probably straight anyway, like everyone else in this godsforsaken town.

"Mr. Tennant," Ezra addresses his teacher, "Sorry I'm late, sir. I was showin' our new student around the school. This is Luka Thomas." Ezra then goes to take a seat beside Cadeon, knowing that Mr. Tennant probably wouldn't make him test his range.

"Hi, Luka. Nice to meet you. I'm glad you could join us this morning," Mr. Tennant smiles reassuringly. "Why don't you tell us a little bit about yourself, then we can test your vocal range."

Harlan watches a blush creep up Luka's freckled cheeks, turning them the prettiest shade of dark pink, to match his lips. Luka doesn't seem to want to do this, but he finally turns towards the class as a whole and gives them a tentative smile.

"Hi," he starts with a small wave. "As already established, my name's Luka. I hate doing these things. I'm an Army brat, so I've moved around a lot. My family just moved here last weekend. I guess I will be playing football." His voice is high and raspy, his accent very different from any Harlan has ever heard before, except on the television. He doesn't really have an accent, that's the thing. Everyone in this town sounds like a donkey eating an apple, but Luka is different.

"Very good. Come over here, and we can test your range to see where you will be seated," Mr. Tennant instructs. Luka does as he is asked and makes his way to the piano at the front of the room. When he starts to sing, Harlan is mesmerized by it. His voice is the most beautiful kind of oxymoron. It is light and raspy, but somehow bright with great projection. He sounds how silk feels, and it gives Harlan shivers.

"Don't see new kids very often 'round here," Cadeon's voice breaks into his subconscious, effectively taking his attention away from Luka and his voice.

"What? Oh, no. We don't. Seems like another jock, though, so he should fit right in," Harlan replies, bitterness seeping into his tone.

"Ya never know, he may be different," Cadeon observes, right as Mr. Tennant compliments Luka on his voice and seats him with the tenors of the class, on the other side of the room from the baritones.

3

So that wasn't the most terrible thing. Sure, he has never sung, but he didn't think it was that bad. It definitely could have been worse. The entire classroom could have laughed at him. He makes his way toward the tenor section of the room, looking for Ezra because, at this moment, he is the only familiar face. Ezra is seated with the baritones, therefore, on the other side of the classroom. Of fucking course.

Luka finally lets his gaze wander over the rest of the class. Some of the girls are looking at him and smiling. He smiles back, knowing that Matt is going to ask him about a girlfriend in a few weeks. It's the cycle. Ezra is sitting next to a loud guy with bleached blond hair and braces. He seems to be the life of the classroom, though, talking to everyone and making them laugh. Luka likes him already and hopes they have more classes together. Luka is known to be loud and a bit of a class clown once he gets used to his new school, so he could see them joking around together.

Finally, his gaze lands on the person hunched over in the chair beside the blond guy. His black skinny jeans make his legs look incredibly long. His arms are crossed over his black, t-shirt clad chest with rings on almost every one of his long fingers. His eyes are cast down, seemingly interested in the chair in front of him, so Luka can't make out their color. His hair is a dark mess of curls, making his skin look even paler, almost translucent. His red lips are shaped into a small pout and his brows are drawn, as if in concentration. He isn't speaking like everyone else in the class.

Luka suddenly wishes Ezra were beside him so he could ask about this guy. There is just something about him that has caught Luka's attention. Luka wants to get to know him but isn't sure how to go about it. Maybe they will have more classes together. As if he can feel Luka's gaze on him, Curly looks up, green eyes locking with his own.

It almost takes Luka's breath away, but then the guy glares. Luka briefly wonders if he did something wrong but doesn't drop his gaze. Curly, in a fluid motion, takes one long finger and flips Luka off. He doesn't even bother glancing to see if the teacher is watching. Luka can't believe the nerve of this guy, so he gives him a look as if to say 'Oh, yeah?' then flips him off with both hands. Curly rolls his eyes and looks away, crossing his long arms over his chest again.

Luka continues to watch the guy for the rest of class. He only sees him talk a few times, and it is always to the blond guy he is sitting next to. He never talks to anyone else, and they never pay any attention to him. Luka doesn't even know what his voice sounds like because he is too far away, which is a fucking travesty. He would bet money that his voice is as dark and dangerous as his looks. He wonders if he will have a thick southern drawl like everyone else. If that's the case, then the accent has suddenly become more appealing to Luka.

After class, Ezra comes up to him and asks to see his schedule. Luka gives it to him, already knowing that next they would be going to Chemistry. He watches as the rest of the class filters out, mostly keeping his eyes on the tall, curly-haired kid who flipped him off. Now that he is closer, Luka takes in a bit more of his appearance.

His jawline could cut glass. The black t-shirt he is wearing has a menacing logo of a band on it that Luka doesn't recognize. A few necklaces are hung around his long neck; one looks like some sort of star with a circle around it. The symbol looks familiar, but Luka can't place where he has seen it before. His skin is pale, the dark bracelets stacked on his thin wrist a stark contrast. He is beautiful in a haunting sort of way. A shiver runs down Luka's spine when their eyes meet one more time as he exits with his friend. His eyes are green, the color of a dark forest or a mysterious lake.

"Who is that kid?" Luka interrupts. He feels kind of bad because he hasn't been paying any attention to Ezra, but whatever. He is curious, and there is something magnetic about the boy.

"What kid?" Ezra asks, confused.

"The one with curly hair. Quiet. Wearing all black," Luka describes, trying not to get impatient. He just wants to know his name.

"Oh. Harlan. Harlan Sharp. He's a bit weird and a loner. He's friends with Cadeon, though, and Cadeon's cool," Ezra supplies, starting to exit the classroom.

"Harlan," Luka says letting the name roll off his tongue. He likes it. It fits. "Cadeon's the blond guy?"

"Oh, yeah. He's friends with everyone, so you'll definitely meet him at some point," Ezra answers. Luka lets this information roll over in his mind as they make their way to their next class. He is surprised to see Harlan in the room when they arrive, already seated in the back beside Cadeon.

4

Harlan notices as soon as Luka and Ezra walk through the door of his second class of the day. Fucking great. This is just shitting perfect. Luka is in Honors classes, so he will literally spend all day with him. He quickly averts his gaze when he notices that Luka is looking around the room, probably trying to find a seat. He glances up again, seeing Luka tap Ezra's shoulder then gesture for him to follow. Ezra does, seemingly confused when Luka starts moving toward Harlan and Cadeon.

What. The. Actual. Fuck. Luka won't. He couldn't. *Fuck*, he does. He sits right behind Harlan, while Ezra takes the seat next to him, behind Cadeon. No one ever sits behind Harlan. One would think he has the plague or something equally as devastating, so he is used to most people avoiding him. It's weird that Luka chose to sit behind him instead. He wants to scream. He shoots Cadeon a puzzled expression, but Cadeon just smiles.

"Hey, man. I'm Cadeon," he says by way of introduction, sticking his hand out for Luka to shake. Fucking Cadeon. Always having to be polite and friendly and shit.

"Nice to meet you," Luka responds politely, his clear voice ringing in Harlan's ears. He refuses to turn around, though, keeping his eyes trained on the chalkboard in front of him.

"This is my friend Harlan," he hears Cadeon say, and Harlan shoots him a death glare. He would have been perfectly content with Luka never even knowing his name.

"He doesn't talk much," Luka observes, but Harlan still refuses to look in his direction. He doesn't trust his intentions. Ever since middle school, he has been harassed by the popular kids. Sick jokes are always being played on him, some taking it too far. He will never forget those particular instances for as long as he lives. Quite frankly, he just doesn't trust a single one of them. Why should this Luka guy be any different? He is probably a sheep, just like the rest of them.

"Oh, he does. You just have to get him to open up," Cadeon assures, rolling his eyes when Harlan flips him off, still refusing to speak. Thank the gods that the teacher starts class, making Luka introduce himself again. He pretty much says the same thing, as if he has it memorized. Harlan briefly wonders just how often Luka changes schools since he is an Army brat, but quickly forgets the thought, not wanting to give him even that.

Mrs. Harris is notorious for never making her students do much, even in a more difficult course like Chemistry. She spends the first day of class briefly going over her lesson plans, then allows them all to 'talk and catch up from the summer break'. Harlan kind of hates her because Luka is behind him. He can feel Luka's gaze on the back of his head, but he still refuses to turn around.

Cadeon and Ezra are talking about something sports related, so Harlan opens his journal, intending to get some thoughts down. He sits there for several minutes, writing a new poem that he's been working on, occasionally chewing on his pen when he is stuck on a word, wanting it to rhyme. He can still feel eyes on the back of his head, and he thinks they are certainly blue.

"What are you doing?" A raspy voice asks the question from behind him, making his heart rate dramatically increase in mere seconds. Out of the corner of his eye, he can see Luka peeking over his shoulder. He quickly moves to cover the page from his prying eyes. Harlan glances up at the clock. Fuck. It's not quite time for the next bell to ring.

"Nothing," he responds, positioning his body over the journal and keeping his gaze down.

"Doesn't look like nothing," Luka observes, then he feels a warm hand on his shoulder, attempting to move his body. Harlan doesn't budge, though, and tries to ignore the spark of electricity that flashes down his spine from the touch. "Come on."

"Why are you even talking to me?" Harlan asks, shutting his journal and finally turning around, giving Luka what he hopes is a death glare. Luka's blue eyes are wide with shock, probably not expecting the question.

"Because I want to."

"No, you don't. I promise. I'm not interesting or popular. I don't have the hook up for drugs. I'm definitely not rich. You're smart, since you are in these classes, so I doubt I could do your homework better than you. There's no reason for you to be talking to me," Harlan rants, words falling from his lips quickly, even for him. He is just sick of this shit. He wants Luka to understand that he has nothing to offer him, and he should probably just leave him alone.

"Relax there, Curly. I don't want anything from you. Just wanna talk," Luka assures him, lifting two small hands up at chest level, blue eyes wide with his thin dark pink lips quirked into a small smile.

"No one ever *wants* to talk to me, and my name's not Curly," Harlan tells him, rolling his eyes and turning back around, crossing his arms in front of his chest.

"Well, I do," Luka insists, tapping him on the shoulder. This guy just won't stop. Ezra will probably inform him after class how uncool it is to talk to Harlan. "Look, we got off on the wrong foot back in Choir. I would like to properly introduce myself. I'm Luka."

"Yes. We have established that. I know who you are," Harlan says with an exasperated sigh, turning back around to face Luka. He's going to get whiplash if he keeps this up.

"Ah, but I don't know anything about you." Luka smiles, and, *fuck,* it's devastating. His teeth are straight and white, the smile making his blue eyes crinkle at the corners.

"You want to keep it that way, trust me. I'm a nobody. The weird kid that everyone thinks worships Satan or some shit. Talking to me on your first day will ruin your image," Harlan maintains, placing his palms on Luka's desk, trying to get him to understand.

"First, I don't give a fuck about my image. Well, not entirely. Second, do you? Worship Satan, I mean?"

"What?" Harlan asks, taken aback by this turn of events. Who the fuck is this Luka guy? The confusion must be apparent on his face because Luka just crosses his arms and narrows his eyes, waiting for Harlan to answer.

"Umm...no. I'd have to believe in God to believe in Satan. Can't worship something I don't think exists," Harlan finally answers, hoping his honesty would turn Luka away. He is probably a Christian like everyone else in the area. Yay for Bible Belt, U.S.A.

"So, you don't believe in God?" Luka looks shocked, yet slightly intrigued by the information. He is looking at Harlan as if he is a puzzle that he wants to solve, making Harlan feel uncomfortable. He shifts in his seat, not used to people taking an interest in him or asking him questions at all. His own mother barely asks him how school is going.

"No. Does that bother you?"

"I just don't understand how. Like, have you not read the Bible? Never gone to church?" Luka's blue eyes are narrowed, but he doesn't seem angry, just interested.

"Yes. I have read the Bible and gone to church. That's why I'm an atheist. Look, if you want to have a philosophical discussion about the Bible and Christianity, now is not the time or place to do it. You aren't going to convert me into a Christian, if that is what you are hoping for. I am a lost cause. Ask literally anyone in the school," Harlan says, already tired, and it's only the second class of the day.

"I may take you up on that philosophical discussion later," Luka says with an easy smile. *Later.* What the fuck does he mean by later? There will be no later. After class, Ezra will tell Luka that he shouldn't talk to Harlan because of his reputation, then he will never hear from him again. There will be no later. The bell rings then, stopping them from continuing their conversation and for this, Harlan is thankful.

Much to Harlan's surprise and displeasure, they spend the rest of the day like that. Luka sits behind or beside Harlan in almost every class since there is always an empty seat near him. He doesn't see Luka at lunch, thank the gods, so he just eats at his normal spot with Cadeon. The only class he and Luka do not have together is Spanish, and they must go somewhere different for their free period. The rest of their classes are quite busy, so he doesn't really have time to speak to Luka again; however, he could always feel his gaze on him. Harlan just doesn't understand why Luka is interested in him. He is sure that whatever his intent, it is malicious.

5

Harlan Sharp is Luka's new favorite thing to study. He is way more fascinating than classes, his family, and anyone else at school. Luka can't read him for the life of him, which is odd because Luka is fucking amazing at reading people. He considers it a gift, really. He has known Harlan for three weeks now, and he still can't seem to break through his walls.

Harlan has now taken to answering his questions with one word or putting his earbuds in during their free time in class and reading from a book, ignoring him completely. This is why Luka has decided to befriend Cadeon. Cadeon is the only one, it seems, that Harlan ever speaks to. So that must mean that Cadeon has superpowers or something. Maybe some kind of innate ability... like the Harlan Whisperer or some shit. Luka must find out his secrets.

"Luka! Time for breakfast!" his mom calls from downstairs. Luka rolls his eyes because he can fucking tell *time*. He is just so sick of his parents constantly controlling his every move. He joined the football team and the Bible Club as asked, yet he can't seem to get Harlan's words about religion out of his brain.

He has never really spoken to anyone that doesn't believe in God. Even though he moved around a lot, he was always gone to church and told to join Christian student organizations, so Harlan's atheism is new to him. He really wants to speak to Harlan about it, but the boy has been all but ignoring him since their first day, which just makes Luka want to try harder.

He goes downstairs and through the motions of saying grace, eating breakfast, and making small talk with his family, barely stopping himself from rolling his eyes a few times. He is almost out the door when the dreaded question comes from Matt. "So, Luka, do you have your eye on a girl yet?"

Fuck. He hates this question. He was expecting it, but that doesn't make it any easier. He has been putting off this whole girlfriend thing for as long as possible. He met a girl that he thinks would be the perfect candidate for his predicament. She is overly religious and a cheerleader; she won't expect sex, which is what he wants.

Luka holds a huge secret from his parents. They don't know that he's attracted to men. No one does. He, himself, will barely even acknowledge it because he knows it's wrong. He hates himself because of it. It's wrong. It says so in the Bible, but that doesn't stop his urges. It certainly hasn't stopped his attraction to Harlan. He will just beg forgiveness for his sins later and pray that maybe God will stop his urges.

"Yeah," he answers his stepdad, realizing that he has remained silent far too long, causing suspicion.

"That's my boy," Matt smiles, clapping him on the shoulder, almost causing Luka to stumble from the impact. Now he is going to have to ask this girl out, which kind of makes him sick. All he can think about is the curly-haired, green-eyed boy that seems to hate him. What will Harlan think? Would he really stop talking to him now? He doesn't even know if Harlan is into guys, and his inability to read him isn't helping.

"Umm...I may ask her out today. Her name is Leigh-Ann, and she is a junior," Luka supplies, thinking of the girl he met last week during football practice. She was certainly flirting with him in that sickening way popular high school girls do, laughing far too much and twirling her ridiculously long, blond hair that sounds as though it is actually crackling from all of the hairspray. He probably won't ask her out until next week, but maybe it will keep Matt off his back for now. He would just fake having a girlfriend, but his parents would *know*.

"Cheerleader?" Matt asks with a sickening wink.

"Yeah. Well, anyways, I better head to school. Don't wanna be late," Luka says with a tight smile because *eww*. He doesn't wait for a response before he is out the door, practically running to his car. Once he gets into his car, he bangs his head on the steering wheel a few times, trying to tell the contents of his stomach that they, in fact, do not want to make another appearance this morning.

He can do this. He has 'dated' a girl at every single school he has been to. This is just another day to him, but something about this time seems different. Perhaps it's because there is a guy he is actually interested in. Luka is no virgin, but he has only fucked around with guys who he knew would never tell his parents. Never an actual relationship or even feelings involved. He just needed to scratch an itch, that's all.

He sighs, starting his car. He makes his way towards Ezra's house to pick him up for school. Luka has become quite close with Ezra over the past couple of weeks. He would actually consider him a friend, even though he knows better than getting attached. Ezra is very serious, but he tends to balance out Luka's joking nature. He also doesn't seem to care about Luka's fascination with Harlan, unlike the rest of the football team, who have given him shit for it from the very beginning.

"Hey, man," Luka greets, watching as Ezra climbs into the passenger seat.

"Mornin'," Ezra responds, shooting Luka an easy smile.

"So…" Luka starts, not really sure how to ask his next question. He doesn't want Ezra to know the extent of his recent obsession. He has been doing a good job of not talking about it for the most part, but he needs to know more. He decides to just go for it. Ezra doesn't seem the type to judge, but he can't let him know *too* much, especially when it comes to his attraction. "What do you know about Harlan Sharp?"

Ezra shoots him a confused look, but answers, "Honestly? Not much. I know that he is super quiet and wears a lot of black clothes. The kids at school say he worships the devil or somethin', but I don't know if I believe it. Probably just gossipin'. I've seen him write in a diary of some sort, though, so that's kinda weird. He also likes to read. Umm...I think his family is super poor, and his parents are divorced. But I don't know for sure."

Luka considers this information. Most of it he already knew from his observations. It seems that not many people actually know a single bit of useful information about Harlan. Like real, solid information. Just theories. He is a mystery, and Luka loves a good mystery. He pauses before he asks his next question, not sure if it would seem like he is a bit *too* interested but plows ahead because he doesn't know another way to find out at this point. "Does he have a girlfriend?"

Ezra looks like he is considering this for a moment, tilting his head to the side in thought. Luka tries to pay attention to the road, as he waits. He doesn't want to look overly interested in the answer, but he holds his breath, awaiting a verdict. "Not that I know of. Come to think of it, I don't think he has ever had a girlfriend. Some kids say that he is gayer than a two-dollar bill, but I don't know 'bout all of that. Why?"

"Oh, no reason," Luka responds quickly, too quickly. His heart stopped when he heard Ezra use the word 'gay', but he doesn't really understand the phrase after that. A two-dollar bill? What the fuck? Do they even make those? And why on earth would they be gay? Some of these redneck phrases make absolutely no sense. "He just seems interesting is all."

"Mmm," Ezra says, and out of the corner of his eye, he can see the other boy studying him.

"Cadeon seems cool, too," Luka diverts, quickly changing the subject, kind of.

"Yeah. Cade is awesome. He's friends with everyone. Maybe we can all hang out after school, you know, after football practice. I think you'd like him."

Luka is unsure. On the one hand, it would be the perfect opportunity to get to know Cadeon and possibly even Harlan, if Cadeon convinces him to come. On the other hand, his parents probably won't let him. He is expected to come home as soon as practice is over. He could ask them if he can hang out with Ezra. They know Ezra. They met him and his family at church a few Sundays ago, so they may even trust him. "Let me ask my parents. They are super strict, so they may say no."

He decides to text his mom and ask once he parks at school. She is way more understanding than Matt. Matt is also working late today, so he won't even notice if Luka isn't home. Luka feels his phone vibrate in his pocket on their way to class.

"Awesome. She actually said yes. As long as I don't stay out past seven," Luka informs, surprised by his mom's answer.

"Great."

"Yeah. Maybe we can ask Cade here in a minute. I may be able to sneak over and sit with you all," Luka says with a laugh. He hates that he sits across the room from Ezra. He is surrounded by girls and every single one of them tries to flirt with him. He tries to ignore them, but he can't since he wants everyone to think he's into them. It's an issue. A really stupid, ridiculous fucking issue.

Once they walk through the doors of choir class, they take their assigned seats. Luka promises Ezra that he will come over when Mr. Tennant starts working with the sopranos on their part. He sits in his seat and waits patiently for Harlan to walk through the door, like he does every morning.

Luka's breath hitches in his chest when Harlan and Cadeon enter the classroom. Harlan is wearing his normal attire: black skinny jeans and a band t-shirt, but today is a bit different. Harlan's green eyes are outlined in coal black eyeliner, making the color pop. His long dark lashes add to the overall edginess of the look.

Luka can't seem to take his gaze off of him. He has never really been attracted to punk/goth people, but there is something about it that works for Harlan. It works well.

Harlan, like always, makes a point not to look anywhere near Luka's general direction. He sighs because he has to find a way to get Harlan to talk to him. There has to be something. He wonders who had hurt Harlan in the past to make him so suspicious of his fellow classmates. People don't become so distrusting for no reason.

He has a sudden urge to find whoever it is and hang them from a tree by their toenails. No one deserves to be made fun of, but he has a feeling that is exactly what happened to Harlan. Probably what continues to happen, and for some reason, this thought makes him incredibly sad and angry. With newfound determination, Luka makes his way towards Ezra and Cadeon.

"Hey, how are you all?" Luka greets both Cadeon and Harlan. Cadeon waves while Harlan just crosses his arms, rolls his green eyes, then looks away.

"We're just fine and dandy. Have a seat, man," Cadeon says, gesturing towards the empty chair in front of him and Ezra. What does fine and dandy even mean? Luka is going to have to start writing this shit down, maybe get a translator or something because sometimes it is as though they are speaking a different language. He has noticed, when he talks at least, that Harlan doesn't usually say phrases like that. His accent isn't as thick either, like he has worked on not speaking that way. It's still there, but more subtle. If he didn't know any better, he would have thought maybe Harlan had moved there from another state, but Ezra said otherwise.

Luka decides to get straight to the point, because that's what he does. "So, Ezra and I were gonna grab some food after practice today. You two wanna join us?" Ezra nods in agreement.

"Yeah," Cadeon starts, firmly hitting Harlan on the arm when the other boy scoffs. "We'd love to."

"Speak for yourself, Cade," Harlan says, glaring at Luka and Ezra. Luka is a bit taken aback by the clear disdain in Harlan's tone. He has never met anyone in his life who had been harder to crack than Harlan. It is frustrating.

"Come on, H. You never do anything after school," Cadeon pleads, looking over at his friend. Harlan's frown deepens.

"No," Harlan responds, tightening his arms that are crossed over his chest, making his biceps bulge. Luka wants to lick the crease where the muscle meets bone. He wonders if Harlan will taste as sinful as he looks. It suddenly dawns on him that Harlan is his forbidden fruit in the Garden of Eden. He understands Eve's perspective now because if that apple looked as good as Harlan, then it's no wonder she took a bite. He sure as fuck wants one. He shakes his head and tries to refocus on their conversation.

"Harlan, you're just bein' plain ornery," Cadeon huffs, clearly getting agitated with his friend's stubbornness. Luka is glad, even though he isn't exactly sure what the fuck 'ornery' means. From the context, though, he assumes it means stubborn. Maybe Cadeon can be on his side. Harlan, for his part, rolls his eyes. He slowly pulls out a pair of earbuds from his pockets. He doesn't spare them a glance as he plugs them into his phone. Luka can actually hear the moment Harlan starts the music because it's that loud. He can't make out the words or song, but it clearly has some pretty heavy guitar and drums. He sighs.

"Don't worry, y'all. I'll get him to come," Cadeon assures, rolling his eyes at Harlan.

"Why does he hate us?" Ezra asks curiously, glancing over at Harlan who has his eyes cast down. Ezra actually looks a bit hurt by Harlan's actions, which Luka appreciates. He is hurt as well.

"He doesn't. It's complicated," Cadeon tells them, clearly wanting to say more but not wanting to betray his friend's trust. While Luka understands that, it opens the door for more questions than answers. One way or another, he will figure Harlan Sharp out, even if it kills him.

6

"No, Cadeon," Harlan tells his friend during lunch, for what feels like the two-hundred and thirty seventh time.

"Come on, H, I'm not asking you to suck their dicks. It's just supper," Cadeon snaps, obviously becoming annoyed.

"No. I don't want to."

"Why the hell not?"

"Because."

"Come on. That doesn't make a lick of sense. Because why?"

"Because, Cade, I don't fit in with them," Harlan answers through gritted teeth, wishing Cadeon would just drop the godsdamned subject already. Cadeon knows how he feels about the popular kids because they have made Harlan's life a living hell ever since middle school, so why is it so hard for him to fucking accept that he doesn't want to be a part of their little group? He doesn't owe them shit, and he definitely doesn't want to be their friend, thank you very much.

"Oh, for Pete's sake, Harlan! Why the fuck does that matter? You certainly don't care about fittin' in here," Cadeon retorts, stabbing his Salisbury steak with his fork, shoving a bite of it in his mouth, and chewing angrily.

"You know I don't care about fitting in, Cade. That's not the point. The point is that they probably don't *really* want to hang out with me. They probably lost a bet or - or promised their other friends that they would find out if I'm a freak. Probably just trying to pretend to be my friend so that they can find something to use against me." The last line comes out bitterly, leaving a bad taste in his mouth. He takes a drink of his water in hopes that the liquid will wash it away.

"Seriously?" Cadeon asks, outraged. Harlan just nods in response. "Heavens to Betsy, this ain't no fucking teen romcom, H. Freddie Prinze, Jr. ain't gonna pop out of nowhere and confess his undying love to you. Did ya ever think that maybe, just maybe, they want to be our friends? Maybe they think you're interesting or cool. You don't get to decide what their motives are. I understand why you don't trust them - I do - but you can at least just have supper with 'em. You don't have to tell 'em anything you don't want them to know," Cadeon reasons, blue eyes going soft at Harlan's pointed look. Harlan hates the pity.

"Whatever. I can't go anyways. I don't have the money," Harlan admits, blushing at the confession. Cadeon knows he can't really do much because his mom couldn't afford to give him an allowance. He has put in applications all over town, but no one really wants to hire someone that looks like him.

"I'll buy," Cadeon offers, shooting down Harlan's last hope of getting out of this.

"Fine. I'll go, but don't expect this to become a *thing*. It's not. I will not be their friend," Harlan insists, pointing one long finger at Cadeon threateningly. He doesn't give his friend time to respond before he is stalking away, leaving his tray of mostly uneaten cafeteria food on the table. He normally wouldn't do that since he doesn't always know when he will get his next meal, but he is annoyed with Cadeon. At least he won't go hungry today because he will definitely be eating after school. Silver linings.

It's half an hour later, in Creative Writing, when Harlan feels a tap on his shoulder. He doesn't turn around because he knows it is Luka fucking Thomas. It is always Luka, it seems. He glances over at Cadeon, who just so happens to be looking at anyone but Harlan. They are supposed to be working quietly, outlining their upcoming assignment, but Harlan can't concentrate. He just keeps thinking about what was to come after school. What he stupidly agreed to.

The tapping on his shoulder continues, incessant this time, getting firmer with each new strike of the finger. Luka isn't going to be ignored today, it seems. Harlan sighs and turns around, facing him. Luka's blue eyes widen with surprise that he is actually able to get Harlan's attention. Good. He wants Luka to keep believing that he wants nothing to do with him because he doesn't. "What?" The word comes out low and menacing. It doesn't seem to faze the other boy, though. He just smirks. Fuck him.

"So, are you gonna hang out with us after practice?" Luka asks, propping his chin on one small hand, looking at Harlan curiously. Harlan hates when Luka looks at him like that. It makes the faded marks on his arm itch, like they want to come off his skin.

"Why are you asking? I am sure Cade already told you," Harlan responds, rolling his eyes.

"Nope," Luka tells him, clasping his dainty hands on the desk in front of him and popping the 'p', his thin lips pressing together to make the sound. The action shouldn't be obscene, but it is. He tilts his head to the side, as if he is studying Harlan. Harlan hates that. It makes him want to squirm, but he refuses to do so.

"Yes. I'm coming."

"Oh, I like the sound of that," Luka says with a small smile and a suggestive wink. Harlan's cheeks heat up at the innuendo that he didn't even realize he made.

"Not by choice," Harlan mutters, turning back around. He feels tapping again.

"Why do you hate me?" Luka asks when Harlan finally turns around to face him. Harlan is surprised. Luka looks genuinely curious and maybe a little hurt. He has his bottom lip pulled between his teeth, biting lightly.

"I don't hate you," Harlan admits. He should have just lied, maybe then he would be left alone.

"You act like you do, though."

"I don't know you. I can't hate someone that I don't know," Harlan reasons, watching Luka for any sign of amusement. He is almost waiting for Luka to laugh in his face and shout 'well I hate you because you're weird'. He doesn't.

"You can get to know me, you know. I don't bite. Unless you're into that kind of thing." Luka smirks again. Harlan can feel the blush on his cheeks getting worse. It almost seems like Luka is...flirting. With him. Like Luka is flirting with him. Harlan doesn't have a lot of experience with people flirting with him. He doesn't think anyone ever has, so he is probably reading the situation completely wrong.

"You don't want to get to know me," Harlan finally decides to say. Luka's expression falls, and he kind of hates himself for it. He just can't. He can't understand why Luka is talking to him. Why he keeps going on and on about getting to know him or whatever. He can't fathom this.

"I do. I promise, I do. How can I convince you?" Luka replies, tapping his nimble fingers on the desk as if in thought.

"I don't know," Harlan says honestly, and Luka looks somewhat crestfallen. Harlan finds himself adding, "You could start by telling me why you want to get to know me."

"That's easy. You're interesting. The most interesting person at this school if I'm being honest. You don't seem to give a fuck what people think of you, and I kind of admire that. You're you. Unabashedly you, and that's just amazing. Why wouldn't I want to get to know you? You're also impossible to read, and I love a good puzzle," Luka responds earnestly.

Harlan is taken aback by the honesty in his blue eyes. He *wants* to believe him. He wants to believe that someone would find him interesting or whatever, but it's just hard. He is just really surprised by Luka's answer. It's a lot, if it's true, that is. "What do you wanna know?"

"Whatever you want to tell me," Luka says with a shrug, prompting Harlan to just stare at him. Harlan doesn't just talk about himself. He never has. Everyone already knows him anyways. Well, at least they think they do, so what difference does it make?

"Well, I don't *want* to tell you anything."

"Shhh," Mrs. Moore hushes from the front of the room, giving both boys a stern look. Harlan quickly turns around, looking down at his paper, pretending to do actual work.

Not even a minute later, there is something nudging the back of his neck. He glances back to see Luka pressing a folded-up piece of paper towards him, the sharp edge poking him gently. Harlan rolls his eyes but accepts the note. He opens it to find Luka's handwriting, which he had never seen before. It is messy, but legible. He traces the words for a moment before he even reads it.

Luka: Start with your family.

Harlan: Just me and my mom. My older sister moved out as soon as she could.

Luka: That's cool. For me, it's my mom, stepdad, and 4 sisters.

This continues to happen for the rest of the class period. Harlan answers Luka's questions, even being brave enough to ask a few of his own. He discovers writing down his answers is much easier than voicing them, oftentimes finding himself divulging maybe a bit too much information.

Luka never makes fun of him for it, though, just continues to talk using a pen and paper. Most of the questions aren't overly invasive, just shallow queries. He finds himself starting to like

Luka. Even in his messy scrawl, Harlan can see his dry and sarcastic sense of humor. Harlan continues to get the feeling that Luka is flirting with him but brushes it off as a figment of his horny imagination.

Once the class ends, Harlan takes the note and rips it into small pieces, throwing it in the trash on his way out. He doesn't want Luka to keep it and perhaps use it against him later. It may be a bit pathetic and extremely paranoid, but he doesn't want to risk it. As Luka watches him do it, his eyes widen, but he doesn't say anything. He gives Harlan a small smile, then follows Ezra out of the classroom, chatting quietly. Harlan feels like he has stepped into an alternate universe. Nothing makes sense.

7

"There they are," Ezra says, pointing to Harlan and Cadeon, sitting on opposite sides in a booth. They are both dressed in the same clothes as they were wearing in school. Harlan's eyes are still outlined in black, the makeup smudged a bit, but still the same level of beautiful against his pale skin and green eyes. Ezra and Luka changed once they finished their showers after practice. Luka's hair is still somewhat damp. He runs his fingers through it self-consciously, not having had time to put any product in it.

He watches curiously as Harlan glances over, then slaps Cadeon's arm. Cadeon is wearing a confused expression while Harlan furiously whispers something to his friend, glancing over at Ezra and Luka every few seconds as they make their way toward the table. Even when they get closer, Luka can't hear what Harlan is saying, but he seems to have a pleading look on his face, dark brows drawn in worry, big hands pulling at the material of Cadeon's shirt. *Interesting.*

"Hey! Glad you could make it," Ezra greets, taking a seat in the booth next to Cadeon, leaving Luka- *thank fuck-* to sit next to Harlan. Luka barely stops himself from cheering and rubbing his hands together in delight. He will get to touch Harlan. Not in a creepy way, but he gets to be near him. He looks down at the other boy who has the most adorable pout on his face as he scoots as close to the wall as possible, giving Luka ample room. Luka shoots him a small smile as he slides into the booth, putting both hands on the table for support.

"Yeah. Thanks for inviting us," Cadeon says, shooting a pointed look at Harlan.

"Yeah. Thanks," Harlan mutters, not making eye contact with anyone at the table. Luka wants to reach out and hold his hand, but Harlan would just shake him off, maybe even run away from the restaurant altogether. He also doesn't want someone to possibly see. He is so afraid of getting caught. He should suppress his urges, but it's hard. With Harlan now beside him, looking like sin with black eyeliner and nail polish to match, it's downright fucking impossible. He figures he can just ask for God's forgiveness later. Scratching an itch. That's it.

"So, umm..., how was practice?" Cadeon asks, breaking some of the awkward tension that has settled over the booth. Luka likes Cadeon. Cadeon can stay. The three boys talk about football and how the season is going thus far as they order food and wait for it to come to the table. Harlan doesn't contribute to the conversation at all, probably not interested in sports. He keeps glancing over at Luka curiously, though, making Luka want to squirm. Harlan is intense when he looks at you. Like he is hanging off of your every word and boring into your soul. It is unsettling in some ways, but also makes Luka's dick twitch in interest.

"Food's here. Awesome. I'm fuckin' starving. I could eat the north end of a southbound mule," Cadeon announces, clapping his hands then rubbing them together, like he's warming up for a marathon. Where does Cadeon come up with this stuff? Luka seriously needs an 'English to Redneck' translation booklet, but despite the weird phrases, Luka finds himself smiling because he likes Cadeon. Not in an *I wanna fuck your brains out* kind of way, but more so *I think we could be friends.*

"Did you all get the Physics homework finished?" Ezra asks, looking at everyone at the table, including Harlan, obviously trying to involve the quiet boy in their conversation. Bless him.

"Way to ruin my supper, Ez," Cadeon answers, sighing dramatically and dropping his fry on his plate. He throws his hands up in the air, as if it is the worst thing to happen to him, making everyone laugh.

"I started it. What about you, Harland?" Luka addresses Harlan directly, putting emphasis on the 'd'. Harlan's eyes snap up from his plate when he hears the nickname, gaze landing on Luka, but he doesn't say anything about it. Luka gives him what he hopes is an encouraging gesture, and smiles.

"Me? Oh, I already finished it." Harlan shrugs, going back to his grilled chicken salad.

"What? That shit's hard." Luka tries to keep the conversation going, happy to have finally gotten a complete fucking sentence out of the other boy.

"Nah, I got it done two nights ago," Harlan says, taking a drink of his water, full lips wrapping obscenely around the straw and sucking the liquid into his big mouth. Luka has to physically shake himself. Fuck. What were they talking about? School? Oh yeah. Physics. That's right, Physics. He's sure there is some kind of equation in physics that could tell him at what force Harlan is able to suck using his mouth. Fuck. He's going down the rabbit hole, again. Right. Concentrate.

"Oh, Mr. Overachiever," Luka quips, clearing his throat. He hopes it comes out as a joke. When Harlan's lips quirk up into the tiniest smile Luka has ever seen, he takes that as a win.

"Not really. Just have a lot of free time at home, I guess." Harlan shrugs again, picking up his fork and stabbing at some lettuce. Harlan clearly doesn't like to talk much about his home life, so *obviously* Luka wants to know more. He just wants to know everything he can about Harlan.

"You know, I could help you with that free time thing," Luka murmurs, so only Harlan can hear. Luka can't really help him because his parents are ridiculous, but it seems like a good way to flirt. Cadeon and Ezra have begun talking about the paper due in Creative Writing, so he feels it is safe to try to engage Harlan in some kind of conversation.

"What?" Harlan asks, his head snapping up again, and Luka is slightly concerned for the long column of muscles and skin that make up his neck. It is bitable really, but that's neither here nor there. Harlan is almost looking as if he is trying to figure out if he actually heard Luka correctly.

"Free time. I could help you with it," Luka answers, winking.

"What do you mean?" Seriously, though, why is it so difficult for Harlan to understand that Luka is flirting with him. He knows he isn't being completely obvious, but he isn't being too subtle either. He is starting to think that Harlan has never been flirted with, which is a travesty of justice, really.

"Well, that's obvious, Curly. I am saying that I would like to hang out with you in your free time." Luka decides not to be flirtatious with this comment, not wanting to freak Harlan out. He only *thinks* he is into dudes; he doesn't know it for a fact.

"Why the fuck would you want that?" Harlan asks, and for once, Luka can kind of read his body language. Maybe he is getting better at it, or Harlan is letting his guard down. Either way, Harlan looks confused and somewhat defensive. His hand travels to his bracelets, scratching between the dark leather bands, something that Luka has noticed him subconsciously do when he is speaking to Luka.

"Harland, didn't we already establish this in class today? I think you're interesting, blah, blah, blah. Is it really that difficult to believe someone may want to actually spend time with you and get to know you?" Luka asks, feeling his temper rise. He is starting to get frustrated. He feels like he is having the same conversation with Harlan over and over again yet expecting a different result. Isn't that the definition of insanity or something? Is Harlan making him insane? Probably, but if Harlan Sharp is insanity, then sign Luka up for that shit.

"I still don't know if I believe you because I'm a nobody. Why would anyone want to get to know me? Like, really? I am boring and weird," Harlan starts, the slightest pout on his lips. Luka wants to kiss it off. "And stop calling me Harland. That's not my name. My name is Harlan."

"I know your name, Curly," Luka says, rolling his eyes and nudging Harlan's arm, his skin so fucking warm Luka wants to touch it some more. He refrains, though. Somehow. Put it down as a miracle at this point. "But to get back to the topic, please stop calling yourself weird and boring. You are neither. I..." Luka lets the sentence trail off, trying to think of what he wants to say. Finally, he decides to just go with it. "I like you."

"Yeah. Right." Harlan snorts. "You don't even know me."

"And whose fault is that, hmm?" Luka retaliates. Harlan doesn't seem to have an answer, so he just rolls his eyes. One point for Luka, not that he's keeping track. Honestly, if he were, Harlan would probably be winning, but he has definitely gained some ground today, so mental pat on the ass and all that. "Please believe me when I say I want to know you." Luka's eyes are wide with honesty. He tentatively reaches out and puts one hand on Harlan's knee, letting the natural heat the other boy produces seep into his hand. Harlan visibly stiffens at the gesture, not relaxing, but he doesn't remove Luka's hand either.

"Fine. I will try to believe you, but it's..." Harlan trails off, looking as if he is fighting an internal battle with himself. Finally, he sighs, looking somewhat defeated. "It's hard, okay? Like...I don't know if you have noticed, but nobody except Cade actually wants to talk to me. I don't mind since I prefer to keep to myself, but it's just odd."

Luka is shocked by Harlan's honesty. He thinks this is the most he has gotten him to open up since he started trying to talk to him. He is pleased with this turn of events and is going to do his best to keep it up. "Well, trust me, alright?"

Harlan just looks at him with wide green eyes but doesn't reply.

For a moment, it is as though they are suspended in time, teetering on the edge of something. The moment is pure and innocent, somehow. Their trance is broken when someone clears their throat nearby. He looks up, seeing Cadeon looking at them with a small smile while Ezra just looks confused and somewhat curious. *Shit.*

Luka had forgotten they were there. Fuck. Hopefully, Ezra didn't hear too much. Luka quickly and discreetly removes his hand from Harlan's warm knee, already missing the contact. He very much wanted to trace his fingers up the inside of Harlan's thigh. It probably would have taken days to get there, given Harlan's ridiculously long legs, but Luka would have dealt with the fatigue.

"Well, I have to be home by seven, so...umm...I should get going," Luka tells the group looking down at his phone to see it is half till.

"How would you like the checks?" The waitress asks, coming to the table and probably overhearing their conversations.

"Mine and his together," Cadeon chimes in, pointing to Harlan who has started to find his leftover food quite fascinating. Luka thinks there is more to Harlan Sharp than meets the eye, and he wants to peel back each layer to find out what is underneath.

8

Harlan is sitting on his bed, listening to music that is probably far too loud for the neighbors, but he doesn't actually care. He decided to try to get some of his feelings about Luka out on paper, so he has been writing for the better part of an hour. However, he doesn't like the way it flows quite yet. He sighs, shutting the journal and throwing it to the corner of the bed. He rolls over on his back and stares up at the ceiling, thinking about his predicament.

Could Luka really be that interested in him? He just doesn't see how. It has been a week since their dinner together, and he just can't get some of the things Luka said to him out of his head. His brain is trying to convince his heart that Luka hasn't been flirting with him and that he doesn't actually like him, even though he has said as much. He likes him? What does that even mean? Does he like him as a person? Does he like his style? Does he like him as more than just a friend? There are many ways to like a person, and all of these questions are making his head hurt.

Luka continues to pass him notes in class, and Harlan, against his better judgment, continues to answer them. He tries to be vague with the questions about his life, family, and past, but he answers shallow questions truthfully. He thought writing would help, but it didn't. He is just so confused about everything. No one in his life has ever shown him this much interest, or if they have, they've given up after Harlan gives them the cold shoulder. With the exception of one time, but Harlan refuses to let his mind wander there. He's not young and naive anymore. Luka is persistent, though, if nothing else.

With a sigh, he grabs his phone to text Cadeon, hoping a distraction may help his dark and muddled thoughts. He doesn't want to return to old habits, and he can already feel the panic rising in his throat, threatening to suffocate him. When he goes to open the messaging app on his phone, it starts vibrating in his hand. He doesn't recognize the number, but he answers it anyway.

"Umm...hHello." Okay, so it's probably not the best way to start a conversation, but it will have to do. Harlan hates talking on the phone. It always makes him feel awkward.

Mr. Sharp?

Harlan quickly turns the music down because this sounds important. "Yes, this is he," Harlan says, feeling like a complete and total loser. He has never been called Mr. Sharp before, but he supposes there is a first time for everything.

Good evening. This is Mac from Mac's Music. I saw you put in an application for a position we have available. If you're still interested in the job, I would like you to come in for an interview.

Harlan's heart skips a beat. Someone is actually calling him about a job. After all of the applications he filled out, maybe there's hope. He realizes then that he has been silent for far too long, so he swallows, his throat suddenly very dry. "Umm...Yes, I am still very much interested," Harlan stammers, hitting himself hard on the forehead in his frustration.

Okay, can you come in for an interview this weekend? Saturday around two o'clock?

"Sure thing," Harlan tells him quickly. He sounds eager, but he doesn't care because he is. The music store is one of the places he actually *wants* to work.

Okay. See you then.

The man hangs up, and Harlan stares at his phone for a few minutes, not actually able to believe what just happened. He has an interview. Fuck. He has an interview! He doesn't even think he has anything in his closet that is interview-worthy. What the fuck is he going to do? He can't go out and buy anything. He would actually need money for that, and his mom certainly won't be able to afford to buy him anything. He texts Cadeon his news and is a bit bummed when he doesn't get a quick reply. Cadeon is probably hanging out with one of his other friends.

Harlan makes his way downstairs, deciding it is time for a snack since he didn't really have anything for dinner. He opens the refrigerator to find it empty, like normal. He looks in the cabinets, seeing that they too are mostly empty. He can't even make anything with what little they do have because he is missing vital ingredients like milk or eggs. His good mood dissipates as he goes back to his room, deciding to just go to bed. It's the easiest way to deal with being hungry. If he gets this job, the first thing he will do with his paycheck is buy groceries.

9

Luka is tired and annoyed. He had a grueling football practice this afternoon, and now all he wants to do is go to bed; however, he has physics homework he needs to finish. He kind of wishes he had asked Harlan for help during class today instead of just passing a note talking about their favorite ice cream flavors. He can't say he regrets it, though; Harlan is finally, kind of, starting to open up to him. He is still super fucking vague about his family and home life, but Luka figures it will just take time. Luka looks up when he hears the door to his room open.

"Got a moment?" Matt asks by way of greeting, just barging in without even so much as knocking. Luka internally sighs and rubs his face. He knows what's coming. Fuck. He doesn't want to deal with Matt tonight. He just wants to finish this homework then lay in bed, have a nice jerk off session to images of Harlan, and pass out. Is that too fucking much to ask for? Seriously.

"Yeah," Luka lies, looking at his stepfather. Matt walks over and perches himself on the edge of Luka's bed. Luka hates when Matt comes into his room. He isn't sure why, but he finds the whole scenario really uncomfortable. His room is his space, where he is free to be who he is without judgment, but Matt judges. It is as though when he is there, he taints something private. Like a black fog rolling in on a lovely day. His presence is almost suffocating, like he is taking up the whole room, not leaving any free air or space for Luka to exist.

"Good. Wanted to talk to you for a minute," he starts, resting his elbows on his knees and clasping his large meaty hands in front of him. Luka turns his body towards him in his chair, doing his best to look interested in the conversation when, in reality, he would hop the first spaceship to fucking Uranus if it were an option. Uranus. Of course, that's the planet Luka would want to go to. He would be more interested if it were Harlan's anus, to be honest, but he doesn't say that out loud.

"Okay," Luka says, resisting the urge to roll his finger through the air, just wanting Matt to get on with it. He already knows what he is going to say, so what the fuck is the point in drawing out the process? He just wants him to fucking get to the goddamned point, so Luka can move on with his night in peace. He can already feel the headache building behind his eyes.

"Are you having girl issues, Son?" Matt asks, and Luka wants to vomit. He absolutely hates when Matt calls him Son. On one hand, Luka is grateful for everything the man has done for his mom and family, but on the other hand, Matt isn't his dad. His dad left him when he wasn't even a human yet. If he was really Matt's son, then Luka wouldn't feel the need to walk on eggshells around him. He wouldn't feel the need to hide, but it is what it is. Nothing he can do about it. The whole thing is hopeless really.

"Umm...not really," Luka answers. It's not a lie. He isn't having girl issues because he gives zero fucks about girls.

"Well, you mentioned that girl Leigh-Ann, but you haven't told us you were seeing her yet," Matt prompts, and oh right. He did tell him that. Fuck. Luka needs to think fast because he hasn't so much as spoken to the fake-ass cheerleader in a few weeks. He had completely forgotten about her in his desire to crack open Harlan's hard exterior. Honestly, the girl has never really been a blip on Luka's radar. She was just a means to an end, a way to satisfy his stepdad's insistence. Luka has to think fast, so he does what he always does in these situations, he lies through his goddamn teeth. He is quite good at it, having had years of practice thus far.

"Oh, yeah. Her. Yeah, she started dating this other guy. He had been talking to her for a while, apparently," Luka says, not realizing that with this lie, he is going to have to find a whole new girl to satisfy Matt's wishes. Fuck.

Oh well, he wasn't sure if he could handle Leigh-Ann anyways. What was that southern saying Cadeon used the other day? Oh, yeah. She certainly wasn't the brightest crayon in the box. If he had to give her a color, it would probably be like Sepia. Nothing particularly interesting or bright. Just kind of there and used as a filter on Instagram because it's so fake. She is shallow and vapid. She has no depth, and Luka doesn't know if he can handle a relationship like that, fake or not.

"Well, that's too bad, Son. Got your eye on any others?" Matt asks, studying him. It makes Luka want to squirm, but he doesn't. He refuses to give Matt that kind of satisfaction. He is lucky he wasn't shipped off to military school when he was younger.

"Not at the current moment. Been trying to focus on school and football, you know?" Luka hopes that his lie is convincing. Well, he hopes all of his lies concerning his parents are convincing, like any sane teenager.

"Oh," Matt says, and fuck, he doesn't sound all that convinced. He is still looking at him as if he is something to be studied. "I know that football and school is important to you, but girls should be too. You're a young man. You should go out and sow your wild oats if you know what I mean." Matt then winks at him, and Luka actually has to swallow the bile that has made its way up his throat. He wants to gag, but he can't. Maybe he can make a mad dash to the bathroom when all of this is over, although this conversation seems to be lasting forever and a fucking day at this point.

"Well. You and Mom don't make that exactly easy since I have the curfew of a third grader," Luka quips, suppressing his eye roll. He knows he shouldn't piss Matt off, but he is fucking tired. He hates this conversation, and he just wants his fucking room back. If pissing him off is the only way for him to get the fuck out, then Luka will take a grounding. Not like Matt can ground him from anything since he isn't allowed to do shit as it is.

"Watch that tone with me, boy." Matt points one stubby finger at him, and Luka swallows. "You're eighteen now, so I may start considering letting you do other things, as long as they are school-sponsored activities." Oh jeez, how sweet of Matt. What a fucking saint he is. Letting Luka do what normal kids his age are doing after he has been eighteen for several months. Luka barely suppresses another eye roll at his comment. Like Luka should be thankful to Matt for letting him out of his makeshift prison.

"Thank you, sir," Luka says quietly, looking down at the floor even though the words burn like acid on his tongue. He hates this submissive bullshit he has to put on for Matt.

"Good. Now set your eyes on another girl and bring her to dinner or something." Matt gets up from his place on the bed, groaning a bit when his knees make a loud popping noise. Luka can't help the small smile that crosses his face because it almost feels like karma. Karma is a thing, right? He should ask Harlan. Harlan seems to know about that kind of stuff. Harlan. Oh God, what is he going to think when Luka has a girlfriend? Will he hate him? Fuck.

Luka places his head in his hands, trying to bite back the panic as Matt finally leaves the room. Luka can breathe again, but at the same time he is he is suffocating. Suffocated by this life and who he has to be. Why is it so wrong to be attracted to someone? The Bible. That's why it's wrong. The Bible says so. Luka scrubs his hands over his face one last time before he dives back into his homework, doing everything in his power to take his mind off the mess that is his life.

10

"So, you and Lu have gotten all chummy in class lately. Like two peas in a pod," Cadeon says, laying back on Harlan's bed, throwing a clean pair of socks Harlan had laying there into the air and catching them.

"Cade, you are supposed to be helping me pick out clothes for this interview, not talking to me about a guy I have no interest in. And stop calling him Lu," Harlan responds, looking down at his friend, very unamused by the entire thing. Can't Cadeon see he is freaking out over this? He could really use the money, and he would very much like to help his mom out.

"We can do both," Cadeon replies with a shit-eating grin. If it wouldn't have been like kicking a puppy, Harlan would have done just that. Harlan sighs and rolls his eyes because that's all he can do. He was expecting this conversation, but that doesn't mean he actually wants to have it. He is nervous enough about his upcoming interview; he doesn't need to add discussing this Luka situation on top of that. A situation. That is really all it is.

"Why do we need to do one at all?" Harlan asks, trying to avoid the question as long as possible.

"Because you like him, and you need to come to terms with that," Cadeon tells him, a seriousness in his tone.

"No, I don't. He's a preppy jock. Why would I like someone like him? Or better yet, why would he like someone like me?" Harlan asks, still not answering the question. He doesn't like Luka. He doesn't. Luka just annoys the hell out of him until he gives in and talks to him. They never really have any deep conversations. Mostly just about random things that Luka asks him. He really doesn't know anything about Luka if he is being honest. He has a mom and a stepdad, as well as four sisters. He likes his banana splits to be 'traditional'. His favorite color is blue. Okay, well maybe he does know a decent amount about the other boy, but it certainly isn't by choice.

"You're bein' hypocritical," Cadeon says catching the socks and pointing an accusatory finger at Harlan before resuming his previous activity.

"How the fuck am I being hypocritical? Facts, Cade. I'm stating facts," Harlan defends, stretching both long arms out to the side, then letting them fall limply in exasperation.

"You constantly talk about how people are quick to judge you because of the clothes you wear or the fact that you wear eyeliner and paint your nails, but you sure as fuck are quick to judge someone when you deem their clothes preppy," he says as he lifts four fingers to place air quotes around the last word, then continues, "or even when they play sports. How is that any different than singing in choir? Why does his fucking polo shirt have to be any different than your band shirt? Yes, H, you're being hypocritical."

Fuck. Cadeon has a point. Harlan hates when Cadeon has a point. He never thought of himself as a hypocrite, but it seems he is being exactly that when it comes to Luka. He just, he doesn't know how to get past it. His entire life he has been used to people making fun of him for who he is and what he likes. It's hard to change years of behavior that has been ingrained. Luka may not be like everyone else, but it's hard to convince himself of that when he's had no one prove him wrong. Ever.

"That's not the point, Cade." Even if it really is the fucking point. "He probably isn't even gay."

"There you go again. Judging," Cadeon tsks, not taking his eyes off the socks he is still throwing. Harlan wants to bat them out of the air. He probably would, however he is athletically challenged, and that sounds like it would require actual hand-eye coordination. Instead, he just decides to glare at their movements, letting his heated gaze go up and down with them because glaring at fucking socks would solve all of his problems regarding a blue-eyed boy.

"No, I'm not. He probably isn't," Harlan insists, getting annoyed because Cadeon may or may not be correct about this, and he absolutely despises when his friend is correct.

"Just because he's a preppy jock means he isn't gay? That doesn't make a lick of sense. Jesus, Harlan, I thought you were progressive or whatever. Maybe he is just playin' a part to survive."

"We are still very different people." What if Luka really is playing a part? Harlan could understand that, but no. He is not going down that path. He believed that once, but all it got him was pain and misery, so he refuses to even entertain that thought. Sympathy would get him nowhere, he had to learn that the hard way.

"Opposites attract." Cadeon shrugs, hitting the light in Harlan's room with the socks, making the room dim for a split second before the item comes back to Cadeon's waiting grasp. "We learned that in science class when we were in 2nd grade. Remember?"

"That's magnets, Cade, not people," Harlan says, sitting down on the bed and nudging Cadeon's legs so he would move them. Cadeon grumbles a bit, but does as Harlan wants, not pausing his efforts with the stupid socks. Harlan watches because he doesn't really want to look Cadeon in the eye.

"Same difference," Cadeon replies. "If two people were exactly the same, they wouldn't fit together, like puzzle pieces or whatever. The point is, it's okay to be opposites. Sometimes that is the best thing because you have two different perspectives. Like you complete each other, ya know?"

"What are you? A fucking Hallmark card? Real life isn't like that, Cadeon. I know that better than anyone. One boy doesn't meet and fall in love with another boy in Bible Belt, USA and expect that boy to love him back. That's not how it works. You don't get to be yourself and love who you love at the end of the day." Harlan is breathing a bit heavy after his speech, breaths coming out as short bursts of air.

He can feel his anger and resentment rising because it's not fucking fair, but that is just how the world works. Sure, the LGBTQ + community has made strides in the past few years, but that doesn't change opinions overnight. It won't stop the judgment and the closeting and the homophobia. It certainly wouldn't allow two boys to fall in love in high school while they are still living in the Bible Belt.

"Why not, though? Like, why can't it be that way? You can bitch about it 'til the cows come home, but you can't expect the world to change unless you are willing to change it yourself, H."

"Great. Now you're a fucking fortune cookie," Harlan says, placing both hands on his knees to get up and pace the room, feeling the need to move around.

"You can divert all you'd like, H, but he flirts with you. A lot." The light reflects off Cadeon's braces as he tosses the socks in the air again.

"What is it with you and all of these big words? You never use words like 'divert' and 'hypocritical'," Harlan points out, deflecting again.

"Thank you for noticin'. Been studying for the SATs. Regardless, when you're in the room, it's like no one else exists to him. I don't know why you're bein' so stubborn about this. Luka isn't the people who teased you or a part of the group who hurt you. He shouldn't have to pay for their misdeeds," Cadeon says, finally catching the socks and not throwing them again, instead sitting up to meet Harlan's eyes. Cadeon's right. Fuck. Cadeon is right. Maybe Harlan is punishing Luka for things he never did or had a part in. That doesn't mean Harlan has to trust him, though.

"Cade, can we please drop it and discuss my interview. I really need this job," Harlan begs because he is really freaking out over this, and he desperately wants to change the subject. He has never had an interview, and he knows people are quick to judge him for his black clothes and overall aloofness.

"Alright," Cadeon concedes and thank the gods. Harlan sighs in relief. He just can't keep talking about Luka. He was fine before Luka ever came into the picture. Well, maybe not fine, but he was surviving. Sometimes he wishes Luka's family had never even moved to the area, so he could endure his senior year of high school in peace. Instead, Luka seems to be a wrench thrown into the cogs of his perfectly moving plans to get the fuck out of this place and find a job far, far away. It won't be a well-paying job, but he doesn't care as long as it's not here. "What do you have?"

"Erm. Band t-shirts and skinny jeans?" Harlan answers, even though it comes out like a question as he glances towards his sparse closet.

"Do you have anything with buttons besides jeans?" Cadeon tries, and Harlan has to think about it. Does he have anything with buttons? He places one long finger on his chin, tilting his head to the side in thought.

"Umm...I think I have a black button down that my mom made me wear to my grandma's funeral last year. It may be a bit tight, though," Harlan answers, glancing towards his closet and seeing the item of clothing. He pulls it out and holds it up to himself, looking at Cadeon.

Cadeon studies it for a moment, tilting his head to one side, then the other as if trying to decide something. "That should work with a pair of jeans. It's only a music store, not like you're interviewing to be the CEO of Samsung or something." Cadeon laughs like he just made the best joke on the planet. Harlan just smiles and shakes his head at his friend.

"What if they don't like me? I mean, I have no experience. I love music, but I don't know a ton about it. What could I offer?" Harlan asks, hanging the shirt back in the closet and going to sit back on the bed, placing his elbows on his knees and his head in his hands.

"Just be yourself, H. You'll be fine. You're smart, and you can be charismatic when you want to. They obviously aren't looking for someone with a degree in music. You're just going to be a sales guy, plus they can teach you about the instruments you're trying to sell." Harlan hears Cadeon say, then feels a sudden warmth when Cadeon pats him on the back.

"Okay. You're right," Harlan sighs, looking at his friend. Cadeon gives him a small smile, and Harlan returns it.

"Now, maybe you'll listen to me about other stuff," Cadeon smirks, and Harlan hits him with a pillow because really, what else is there to do at this point?

11

"Alright. Hit the showers," Coach Stanley says, clapping his meaty hands together. Luka takes a deep breath, glad to finally be done. Football practice was brutal today. It's nearing the end of the summer, but the heat is hanging on like a last goodbye. Luka has lived in warm, humid states before. Florida does exist after all, so he is somewhat used to it, but it doesn't mean it's easy to run in it for hours. The air around him is so humid that it is like he's trying to breathe water.

"Luka!" he hears someone yell from across the field. Luka turns around, finding Leigh-Ann smiling and waving him over. Luka barely stops himself from rolling his eyes. He begins walking in her direction, plastering on a fake smile.

She is wearing a cheerleading uniform, surrounded by other members of her squad. The school seems to think it will help the football players during practice if the cheerleaders are there to amp them up, so they all practice at the same time. It really does nothing for Luka, if he's honest, and it usually just serves as a distraction to the rest of his team.

"Hey, Leigh-Ann. How are you?" he asks, walking up to her. Luka tries not to look directly at her, so he scans his eyes over the nearby people, finding a redhead sitting on the bleachers. He doesn't think he has seen her before, or maybe he has. She is sitting on the bleachers, watching the scene in front of her. She doesn't seem to be paying attention to the football players like most girls do. No. Her eyes are fixated on one of the cheerleaders. She's blond and is currently doing a split. The redhead's mouth is open, her brown eyes gazing intensely.

"I was just talking to the girls here, and we have a question," she starts, her eyes lighting up with a flirtatious glint. Fuck. Luka is so happy he told Mark that Leigh-Ann was taken. He doesn't know why he even considered her as a potential 'girlfriend'. Everything about her annoys Luka.

"What's that?" Luka asks, looking around for anything to serve as a distraction. Harlan isn't here, unfortunately, and he is his favorite distraction. He does see Ezra, though, walking in their direction. Luka waves him over, thinking that maybe this conversation will be less painful if Ezra is there as a buffer.

"Oh my god. It was Tabby's idea. Tabby, you have to ask him," Leigh-Ann giggles, and Luka just really wants to leave. He's tired and hot. He wants to shower and go home. Do his homework and possibly jack off to images of his favorite person. Instead, he looks over to find that Tabby is the girl that was doing the split just moments ago.

"Hold on. Let me go get Will," Tabby says, and who the fuck is Will? Luka doesn't think there is a guy on the team by that name, but he could be wrong. He has never been good at names, and they typically go by last names or nicknames. Instead of running towards the rest of the football players on the field, Tabby jogs to the bleachers, the redhead's face lighting up when she approaches.

"Ugh. I don't know why she's friends with her. She's such a nerd. Like… big yikes," Leigh-Ann says to the small group, some of the girls giggling and nodding in response. Luka has to bite his tongue. What the fuck is wrong with being smart? Harlan is smart. He is a lovely fucking person, but they probably make fun of him, too. It's no wonder he doesn't trust these people because they talk about a person as soon as their back is turned.

"What was your question?" Luka asks, wanting to move on with the subject before he loses his shit on someone. Ezra has now joined the small group of people, smiling at them all in a friendly way.

"Leigh, you ask. You're the one that wanted to know," Tabby says, dragging the redhead behind her. He assumes her name is Will, but he's not sure what it's the shortened version of. Will comes to stand beside Luka, crossing her arms in front of her chest, almost defensively. Now that Luka is really looking at her, he thinks he has seen her here before. She is usually just watching from the bleachers. It's probably because she's friends with Tabby.

"No, you!" Leigh-Ann exclaims with a high-pitched giggle, and now Luka really does roll his eyes. Ezra looks unbothered, smiling at them. Will looks about as over it as Luka, though, as if she would literally rather be anywhere else than here.

"Ladies. Please," Luka butts in, trying to defuse the situation before it becomes a never-ending circle of giggles and 'no yous'. He is beginning to get a headache, and he doesn't know how much more he can handle. He misses the low cadence of Harlan's voice, the way he talks slow.

"Fine. I'll ask," Leigh-Ann relents, flipping her long blond hair over her shoulder as if she is a hero or something. Luka almost rolls his hand in the air, wanting to prompt her to say whatever it is faster. He refrains, though, not wanting to actually be rude. She giggles again, then finally says, "What do you look for in a girl?" Fuck.

"Umm..." Luka starts, then freezes. He is racking his brain for something to say, but he literally has no idea. He has never really been asked this question before. Sure, the guys in the locker room talk about it, but he usually just ignores them or provides the bare minimum in response.

"I like girls with dark hair," Ezra pipes in, and Luka feels like he is saved by God. Well, Ezra is definitely not God but close enough at this very moment in time. "I don't like it when they wear too much makeup; I prefer a girl's natural beauty. I also really like confident women."

Ezra is practically listing things off, and Luka cannot think of a single thing he wants in a woman. He really needs to figure it out because it may be a hitch in his whole 'marry a woman and have kids after he scratches his itch' plan. He can surely think of something he finds attractive about a woman, right? Boobs are nice. They look kind of comfortable, but he doesn't like...want to touch them or anything. That just sounds gross.

"What about you, Luka?" Leigh-Ann prompts, and fuck. She really isn't gonna let him get out of this, is she? Luka feels like he is a fish that has been pulled out of the water, and he is gasping on the air around him. He is racking his brain for anything to say to her. Anything to say to himself, other than the fact that he is clearly going to be very unhappy and dissatisfied when he does finally give his life to the Lord. He had hoped that maybe God would fix him before then.

"Someone who's smart and mysterious," Luka blurts out, his mind automatically going to Harlan. "Someone who's tall, too. Umm...I like green eyes and dark hair. Eyeliner is nice...and jewelry. Someone who has their own sense of style and isn't afraid of who they are." Luka realizes he is describing Harlan, but who can fucking blame him? Harlan is perfect in every fucking way.

"Oh," Leigh-Ann says, her face falling when she realizes that Luka hadn't described her at all. Really, the only person in the school that fit Luka's description is Harlan, but he hopes none of the people in the group will figure that out. Luka chances a glance at Ezra, who is looking at Luka as if he's a puzzle. Fuck. He hopes he didn't just fuck everything up. He wasn't even thinking.

"What about y'all? What do you like in a guy?" Ezra asks, giving Leigh-Ann his signature smile, brown eyes crinkling at the corners. Luka can admit that Ezra is an attractive guy. He has eyes, and he's seen the other man naked. It's hard not to look when he is surrounded by steam, wet bodies, and dicks, okay? Either way, Ezra is definitely not his type. Luka didn't realize he had a type until right now, but apparently, it's Harlan.

"Well, I really like blue eyes and freckles. I think they are so adorable. I also really love guys who are *fast*," Leigh-Ann responds, looking Luka up and down while emphasizing the last word of her sentence. Luka's fast, alright. He's going to be real fucking fast when he runs the fuck away from her while simultaneously gagging just from her tone of voice. Luka glances at Will, finding that she is rolling her eyes. He likes Will. She seems to be the only one that doesn't buy into all of this shit. She sort of reminds him of Harlan in that way.

"I'm sure Tabby agrees with me. Right, Tabs?" Leigh-Ann asks, looking over at her friend. She giggles, her blond hair falling in front of her face for a second before she brushes it away. Luka can feel Will stiffening beside him. Interesting. "Come on, Tabs, don't be shy. What do you look for in a guy? What gets you going?" Leigh-Ann has a playfulness to her voice as she winks at Luka. He barely suppresses a grimace, suddenly feeling dirty. He needs a shower, and it has nothing to do with the grueling football practice he just endured. He feels like Leigh-Ann's voice is clinging to his skin, tainting it somehow.

"Umm...well, it has to be a guy, obviously," Tabby starts, and Luka's ears perk up when Will scoffs from beside him, mumbling what sounds like 'not that important' under her breath before she covers the words with a cough. Luka has to hide his surprise at the comment. He doesn't think he was supposed to hear it, but... could she be? He could have easily misheard her, though, but it does make sense as to why she was staring at Tabby doing the splits like the girl was her last meal.

"What about you, Will?" Tabby asks, and fuck, Luka realizes he completely spaced out while she was describing her dream guy. It doesn't really matter, though. He is way more intrigued by Will's response, her posture going stiff again. She is definitely freezing, a lot like Luka had. Very interesting indeed.

"Umm...well...umm...I like blondes. Blue eyes are good. Someone who is funny and makes me laugh. Like my best friend or something," Will finally answers, looking at Tabby with an almost wistful expression. Holy fuck. Luka thinks...maybe? She shakes her head as if snapping herself out of her thoughts. "Tabs, we really need to go. My mom is expecting us for dinner."

"Oh, yeah. That's right. Well, it was nice talking to you guys," Tabitha says, waving as she walks away with her redheaded friend. Luka watches them go, hoping that the way they walk will tell him what he wants to know. It doesn't. Will is still a bit of a mystery to him, but he finds himself wanting to talk to her again.

12

"We really shouldn't be doing this," Harlan says, his low voice echoing off the walls in the dark back stairwell of the school, but he returns Luka's kiss despite his words. Luka breaks the kiss, the sucking sound bouncing off the walls in random directions. He quickly puts his mouth on Harlan's neck, the skin already beginning to bruise under his ministrations.

"Shut up," Luka mumbles, words muffled by Harlan's neck. Harlan's eyes roll back in his head with a particularly sharp bite, cock stirring in his too tight jeans. Harlan's vocal cords, of their own accord, release a low moan.

"What if someone sees us?" Harlan asks, voice needy and desperate. He is starting to get hard, and Luka grinding against him and sucking marks into his skin isn't helping him in the slightest. Then Luka removes his mouth to fucking smirk at him, and Harlan's knees almost give out, right then and there.

"That's what makes it fun," Luka responds, going back to his task of marking Harlan's neck. Harlan is now so unbelievably hard it is making him dizzy. He is just terrified of someone seeing them. Then they would know.

"We really shouldn't..." Harlan's reasoning is weak at best because his words and hands are in total disagreement. They have begun traveling down to grope Luka's round ass because they have a mind of their fucking own. Luka moans with the action, rubbing his own erection against Harlan's again. Harlan feels like he is going to die.

"I thought you were a bad boy who doesn't care. Don't you wanna fuck around at school?" Luka asks, his blue eyes glinting mischievously in the low light of the stairwell. Harlan can't breathe. It's a chal-

lenge. Harlan may be a virgin, but he wants to take this challenge.

"I don't care," Harlan responds, his voice strong despite the nervous anticipation flowing through his veins.

"Oh, yeah," Luka challenges, smirk returning in full force, blue eyes gleaming in the low light. "Prove it." Without thinking, Harlan hoists Luka up, the shorter boy bringing his legs to wrap around Harlan's hips instinctively.

Luka lets out an adorable little shriek before Harlan swallows it with his mouth. He slams Luka against the opposite wall, moving them further into the darkness underneath the stairwell. He knocks the breath out of Luka but takes it into himself, keeping one hand firmly on Luka's ass, the other coming up to cup his jaw, deepening their kiss.

"Fuck, Harlan," Luka whispers into his mouth, tightening his legs even more and grinding his hips down. Harlan reacts by pushing him that much harder against the wall, grinding back. Luka's hands are tangled in Harlan's curls as he continues to kiss him, their tongues battling for dominance.

Harlan really wants to taste Luka. He has to, but he has never done it before. However, Luka doesn't know that. Before he can second guess himself, he taps Luka's hip, a silent signal for Luka to drop to the ground. Luka obliges quickly, but doesn't remove his lips from Harlan's, using his grip in Harlan's hair to pull him down into the kiss.

"Wanna taste you," Harlan says between kisses, cheeks burning with the admission. Hopefully Luka can't see, their faces shadowed by the stairway above.

"Please," Luka begs, and Harlan's mouth waters with the thought of having Luka on his tongue. Without replying, Harlan drops to his knees in front of Luka, the cool tiles of the floor hard underneath them.

"Okay," Harlan whispers, looking up at Luka. Luka just nods, mouth open in surprise. Harlan gets to work popping the button on Luka's *jeans, then unzipping them slowly, the sound echoing in the darkness around them. He doesn't pull them down or off but reaches into the waistband of Luka's briefs and tugs them down a bit, allowing his cock to spring free. He tucks the elastic right under Luka's balls, trying to decide the best way to do this. He is overwhelmed, like he has a big task in front of him- pun intended- and he simply doesn't know where to start.*

"Fuck me, this is so hot," Luka says, voice high and raspy. Even in the semi-darkness, he can see Luka's cock twitching in interest. He takes a deep breath, trying to calm his racing heart and his own hard-on that is currently painful and throbbing. He decides to start by touching Luka, taking his hard length in his hand.

"Harlan." He hears Luka whisper his name into the quietness, almost as if he didn't mean to say it out loud. That gives Harlan the confidence he needs to poke out his tongue and lick the tip of Luka's cock, right over the slit, listening as Luka hisses out a breath. It must have been the right thing to do, judging by Luka's moan and the tightening of his fingers in Harlan's hair.

"Yeah. Fuck. That's perfect, babe," Luka rasps, squirming a bit when Harlan starts sinking down, taking him deeper into his mouth until he reaches his gag reflex. What he can't reach he takes in his hand. He pulls back up and swirls his tongue around the head to get another taste before he sinks back down, repeating the motion again and again. He can feel his confidence growing with every moan, groan, and growl he pulls from Luka, as if he is actually doing a halfway decent job.

"Oh my God, Harlan. Feels so good." Harlan would make a comment about God if he didn't have a cock shoved in his mouth, so he is just going to let it slide. Literally. He is now sliding Luka's shaft in and out of his mouth, sucking hard with each withdrawal. Luka seems to not be able to stay still, his legs squirming around, his fingers gripping tightly to Harlan's hair, his hips thrusting subtly. He is acting like Harlan is driving him mad with need, which makes Harlan want to work that much harder. He wants Luka to come. He needs it.

"Fuck. Shit," Luka chokes out when Harlan grazes Luka's tight balls with one long finger while simultaneously tightening his lips and sucking hard. Luka's hips buck, almost of their own accord, when Harlan sinks down again. Harlan's eyes water, but he keeps going, not minding the feeling of being gagged just a bit. Not when what he is being gagged by tastes like heaven and feels close to perfect on his tongue. Harlan freezes with Luka's cock deep in his throat when they hear the door to the stairwell open loudly.

Neither of them makes a sound or even breathe as they listen, hoping that they don't get caught. Harlan's cock gets impossibly harder in his jeans at just the idea of getting caught, though, and he thinks Luka is having the same thoughts because he can feel his cock twitch in his throat. Harlan almost wants to be mean and start sucking again, but decides the risk is far too great.

They hear it when the person starts climbing the stairs, the footsteps loud above them, almost deafening. It's the only sound Harlan can hear over his own beating heart and the blood, not currently in his cock, rushing to his ears. Harlan doesn't think he has taken in a microgram of air since the mystery person entered the stairwell.

Neither boy has moved an inch since the intruder came in. Luka's cock is still in Harlan's mouth, his fingers still tangled in his dark hair. Harlan can feel how tense he is, his body more motionless than Harlan has ever seen it. Luka is always moving. Harlan's own body is tense, his shoulders stiff, his fingers gripping onto Luka's hips, stuck midmotion.

The intruder is slow to go up the stairs, each footstep measured, almost as if they want to piss Harlan off. Harlan just wants to pull off Luka's cock and tell them to hurry the fuck up so he can get back to sucking Luka off.

Both boys visibly relax, and Luka lets out a sigh of relief when they hear the door to the second floor close, leaving them alone again. Harlan looks up at Luka with wide eyes, asking him if he wants to continue. He probably looks ridiculous with Luka's still impossibly hard cock in his mouth, but at the same time he doesn't want to release *it just yet. He likes the way it feels. Likes his lips wrapped around it while it twitches on his tongue.*

"Keep going. 'M close." *Luka answers the unspoken question, his hand reaching down to cup Harlan's jaw, moving his head up and down on his shaft until Harlan registers what he said and takes over the movement with his own muscles.*

Luka is close. Harlan has Luka close to orgasming. He did that. Holy shit. He doesn't know how he hasn't come in his pants yet, because that thought has him teetering on the edge of oblivion, but he wants Luka to finish. Needs him to, so he goes back to doing exactly what he had been before they were so rudely interrupted.

"You liked that, didn't you? The idea of being caught," *Luka whispers, surprising Harlan a bit with both the sound of his voice and his words. He was not expecting Luka to talk. Harlan looks up at Luka and nods.*

Despite the low light, Harlan can make out Luka's fucked out expression. His eyes are hooded, his obscenely long eyelashes casting a dark shadow on his sharp, freckled cheekbones. His rouge-colored lips are parted as his breath comes out in short huffs. Fuck. Harlan is seconds away from coming. Even if he weren't close before, seeing Luka look like this would send anyone over the edge.

"Fuck. Knew you would. You would love to be caught with my dick down your throat. Then they would all know. Know who you belong to." *Holy shit. Harlan has never heard anything so dirty in his life, but he has certainly read it. He has been reading gay fanfiction since he was fourteen, always preferring Drarry over almost anything else. He just doesn't think he would ever have the courage to voice his thoughts; however, when Luka does it, it's hot as fuck. He kind of wants to cry, but instead he whines around Luka's cock, unsure of how else to express how unbelievably turned on he truly is.*

"Fuck. Harlan. I'm close. Shit. Pull off. Pull off," *Luka says, grabbing Harlan's jaw, but Harlan stiffens his neck and doesn't pause his sucking as he looks up at Luka, shaking his head.* "Fuck. Love, are you *sure?" Luka gets out, clearly trying to stave off his orgasm for just a few more seconds. Harlan nods, then takes Luka deep, swallowing around the head and that must be what does it.*

A moment later, Harlan feels it when Luka orgasms, his entire body tensing around him and his cock twitching as he releases into Harlan's waiting mouth. Harlan moans at the taste coating his mouth, not even thinking about it as he swallows quickly, telling himself not to fucking come because he doesn't have a change of clothes.

Luka pulls his hair; the prickles of the strands being tugged taking over Harlan's senses. It is probably because he is becoming over sensitive, but Harlan just doesn't want to release his new favorite thing. Luka is addictive. So, with one final wet pop, Harlan allows Luka to pull his mouth away. He grabs Luka's outstretched hands, allowing him to pull him off the floor. To his surprise, Luka sinks down on his own knees.

Luka is silent as he undoes Harlan's belt, button, and zipper. He glances down at his watch then looks back up at Harlan. "Class is letting out in five minutes, then this stairway will definitely have people in it. Think you can come in less than five minutes?" He asks, looking up at Harlan through his long eyelashes. Suddenly his blue eyes morph into brown. The light dusting of freckles on his cheeks disappears, giving way to clear skin. His brown hair lightens, sandy blond strands gleaming in the lowlight. It's the face of Harlan's nightmares.

"What's the matter, Sugar?"

Harlan wakes up with a start, his chest heaving with each breath. It takes him a few long moments to realize that he's not in the back stairwell with Luka who turned into...fuck. No. He's home, in his bed. It was a dream. What the fuck? Harlan shakes his head, trying to get the image of Luka looking up at him out of his mind, then Luka's beautiful features morphing into ones that make his stomach churn.

He shakes his head, trying to get himself to concentrate. He can still taste Luka's orgasm on his tongue, even though Harlan has no idea what come actually tastes like. He tries not to focus on who Luka turned into and what that means.

Harlan looks at the clock. Fuck. He needs to get ready for his interview. He doesn't have time for this, but his cock is hard and heavy between his legs. Apparently seeing the face of his nightmares does nothing to quelch his desire for Luka. It's not going to go away. He can get himself off pretty quickly, right? So, what if it will be to images of a boy he will never have. He doesn't have to tell anyone.

Harlan allows himself to fall back onto his bed, letting his hand travel down his naked torso. He pushes it into the waistband of his underwear, grabbing his cock a moment later. He hisses out a breath, closing his eyes and allowing his mind to go back into his dream, making himself avoid the horrific end.

He loses himself in it. Watching the dream unfold again in his mind's eye. Luka's firm lips. Luka's long eyelashes. Luka's perfect high cheekbones. The way his raspy voice would sound when he's telling Harlan to come. Three minutes later, he is coming all over himself, shouting Luka's name. Fuck.

13

Harlan looks at his reflection in the storefront windows of Mac's Music. He looks kind of disheveled, having gotten dressed quickly after waking up from his dream and having the best orgasm of his life. He still hasn't been able to shake it off. He knows a part of it is attributed to the overactive imagination of a horny teenager, but it's the whole morphing thing that is giving him pause. He hates admitting it, but it's clear what it meant. He's afraid Luka will become the person who hurt him. He is afraid Luka will hurt him.

He just...he can't let that happen again. He can't let a stupid crush do that again. He doesn't know if he will survive it another time. So yes, he really needs to stop this bullshit. He needs to get control of his mind and stop dreaming about giving head to a blue-eyed boy under the back stairwell at school, no matter how hot it was. His cock twitches again at the thought. Jesus Christ. Harlan could jack off for weeks just from the images from his dream alone, but no. No. He needs to stop.

He takes another deep breath, telling his half-boner to go the fuck away. He is pretty sure that going into an interview with a semi is simply unprofessional. He really needs this job. He looks at his reflection again. He supposes he looks okay. He's dressed in all black, as always. The only shitty thing about black clothing is that the late summer sun heats up the material like a brownie in an Easy-Bake oven. Maybe that isn't the best metaphor, since he has never had an Easy-Bake oven, so he wouldn't know.

He runs his fingers through his curls, making sure they aren't overly sweaty, considering he walked to his destination. He smooths his hands over his almost too tight shirt and nods his head one last time. He pushes any remaining thoughts of Luka and his dream from his mind and opens the door with a sweaty palm. The cool air from the shop hits him in the face, cooling him down a tiny bit.

He peers around the store hoping to find Mac, but instead of a man, a young girl sitting behind the counter. She doesn't even look up as the door closes, the bell above it ringing loudly. She is too engrossed in whatever book she is reading.

Harlan wants to know which book it is because he loves reading, and he is always looking for good recommendations. He doesn't want to disturb her because he knows how much he hates it when people interrupt his reading, but he also doesn't want to be late for his interview. He takes a quiet, deep breath and slowly walks up to the counter.

"Um...hi," he starts awkwardly. He clears his throat right as her head snaps up, large brown eyes studying him. "I'm Harlan Sharp, and I'm here for an interview."

"Oh, yeah. I think Mac mentioned something about you. Hold on," she says as she places what looks to be a receipt between the pages of her book, using it as a bookmark. She uses one hand to push her red shoulder-length hair out of her face before she hops off the stool and disappears into the back room.

She returns a moment later, her thin lips pulled into a bright smile. Harlan recognizes her from school, but he doesn't think he has ever spoken to her. He thinks she is a grade behind him, but he can't be positive. She always seemed cool and laid-back, not really hanging out with any of the popular kids that liked to make his life hell.

"Mac said he will be out in a minute," she tells him, placing both hands on the counter to hoist her short frame back onto the stool. Harlan bites his lip nervously, barely suppressing the urge to gnaw on his fingers like he tends to do when he gets nervous.

He looks down at his feet, seeing they are turned in and consciously straightens their position.

A few seconds later, a tall man with a graying ponytail emerges from the back room. He is wearing a Metallica t-shirt that looks older than Harlan himself, a pair of dark jeans, and heavy black boots. He has a sleeve of tattoos on one arm and a few random ones on the other, which look more like the 'classic' tattoos with flames, skulls, and the like. Harlan is jealous because he has been wanting a tattoo for years.

"Hi, Harlan. I'm Mac," the man greets him, his voice lacking the normal southern drawl of the area. He holds out a large hand for Harlan to take. Harlan shakes his hand, hoping his palms aren't too sweaty, as they tend to be when he is nervous. He silently curses himself for not wiping it on his jeans beforehand.

"Nice to meet you," Harlan replies politely, because he may be a bit of a dick to the people at school, but he does have some semblance of manners.

"Alright, come back to my office, and we'll get started." Mac gestures, leading Harlan through the back room and into a very small office. The walls are a dull gray, the space just big enough for a desk. The computer on the desk looks dated and the area is a disorganized chaos, papers littering every open surface making the space seem even more cramped and small.

There are posters and pictures all over the wall, most of the old bands Harlan recognizes and enjoys listening to daily. Some even look like they were taken by Mac himself. Harlan could see this man as being someone he would like to talk to about his experiences, and it immediately puts him at ease. Mac sits behind the messy desk, then gestures for Harlan to take the chair opposite. Harlan quickly obliges, sitting down with nervous anticipation.

"So, Harlan, tell me a little bit about yourself," Mac starts, clasping his long bony fingers together and setting them on top of the paperwork that is on the desk. Harlan thinks for a moment, panicking about the question a bit. He never really likes talking about himself, and it seems that is all he's been asked to do lately.

"Well...um...I'm eighteen and a senior, so I go to school full time throughout the day. But my schedule is mostly open on weekends and afternoons. I'm not really involved in any after-school activities other than the occasional choir performance," Harlan says, feeling like he is rambling a bit because the man probably doesn't actually care that Harlan is in choir.

"Interesting. Why did you apply to work here?" Mac asks next, nodding his head along with Harlan's words. It's a lie. Nothing about himself or his life is interesting, but he powers through to the next question.

"Well, I wanted to get a job to help my Mom with bills and groceries and stuff. She is a single parent, so I thought it would be nice to take some of the burden off of her, you know?" Harlan has no idea why he is telling Mac this. The only person that knows this specific information is Cadeon, and Harlan isn't one to share his personal issues with anyone, let alone total strangers or future employers.

He pauses for a moment, swallowing, and continues, "I also have always had a passion for music. I love listening to it, singing. I'd like to learn how to play the guitar and know a decent amount about it. Unfortunately, I don't really know much about any other instruments."

"Thank you for your honesty, Harlan. I really appreciate that. Knowledge of instruments can be taught, but passion can't be. So, you have never been employed anywhere else before?"

"No, sir," Harlan answers, searching Mac's expression for disappointment. He finds none.

"Are you good with people?" Mac asks, prompting Harlan to panic again. It's not that he isn't good with people, he just doesn't really care about them. Okay, that may not be completely true. He just doesn't care what they think which leads him to not care in general.

"I can talk to anyone," Harlan answers, and it's not a lie. He can carry on a conversation with a variety of people, from the old lady that owns the bakery to Luka, who is very different from him. He may not technically speak to Luka, since most of their conversation happens on paper, nor does he actually want to speak to Luka, but they still communicate.

"Good. This next question is very important," Mac says, a serious expression marring his face. Harlan freezes scared to death he is going to be asked to promise his firstborn child or his soul or something equally terrifying.

"What are your favorite bands?" Mac asks, smiling widely, and Harlan instantly relaxes. For the next hour, they discuss music. Mac tells Harlan about all of the concerts that he has been to over the years and his background in stage setup. Harlan tells him about the concerts he wants to go to when he has extra money. They discuss British vs. American rock bands, Harlan preferring the former.

"Well, Harlan, I'd like it if you could start on Wednesday. Maybe just come in after school. The shop is closed on Mondays, and I mostly need someone to work evenings and weekends. Willow is my other employee. It's a small business, so you may be working alone at sometimes or just with her." Harlan nods, barely breathing because he actually got the job. He is employed. Fuck. He can help buy groceries, pay bills, maybe even finally save up enough for a tattoo.

"Yeah. That would be perfect. Thank you," Harlan says, quickly thrusting out his hand to shake Mac's one more time. He knows he is smiling wide, both dimples popping as he bids Mac and Willow farewell and walks out the door, the gross September heat enveloping him on all sides like a warm blanket straight out of the dryer. He shoots a quick text to Cadeon as he begins walking down the sidewalk, feeling like he is on a cloud. He starts to get out his headphones as he is walking past a park and glances up just in time to see very familiar blue eyes looking back at him. He quickly turns, praying to whoever is listening that he wasn't recognized.

"Hazza!" comes a raspy voice from behind him and fuck, why always him? No. He can't deal with this. Not after the dream he just managed to fucking forget. His day was just starting to turn around, too. He just got a job. Minus the whole dream thing, it was a good day, until he heard that all too familiar raspy voice calls out a version of his name. Seriously, what is it with Luka and nicknames? Harlan isn't even that difficult to say. Harlan tries to ignore him, quickly popping his headphones in.

"Hey, Haz!" He hears him again, closer this time. Fuck. How fast is Luka? Harlan doesn't know what position he plays in football, but there is some type of running position, isn't there? He doesn't mull over it too long because a small finger is tapping him on the shoulder, much like it does in class. Harlan sighs, closing his eyes for a moment before he turns around and opening them to find a crinkly-eyed smile from Luka. It's Harlan's favorite type of Luka smile, but he is going to pretend he doesn't have a favorite Luka anything.

"Hey," Harlan says, popping out his earbuds and shoving them in his tight pocket. He makes it a point not to return Luka's smile, but Cadeon's words from the other day ring in his ear. Fucking Cadeon.

"You look good. Where have you been?" Luka asks, eyes raking down Harlan's body then back up, a small pink tongue coming out to lick his firm lips. He puts a hand up to his mouth, swipes it, then shakes his head as if coming out of a thought. Harlan's brain short circuits, images from his dream overflowing it. Something about the way Luka looked at him reminded him of his dream, and fuck. Luka asked him a question. He needs to concentrate.

"Oh um...thanks. I had an interview," Harlan answers, then mentally scolds himself because he actually gave Luka a real answer and not something vague. What the fuck has gotten into him? The dream. He is being thrown off his game by that fucking dream. He needs to forget it. It won't ever happen in his real life, but it's so hard when the person the dream was about is standing right in front of him.

"Oh, that's cool. Did you get the job?" Luka asks, actually looking interested in what Harlan has to say, a direct contrast to their peers. The subject is helping Harlan not think about the thing he refuses to think about. This subject is safe; it can stay.

"Yeah. I start Wednesday." Harlan can't help the smile that has bloomed on his face because he is so happy to have gotten the job.

"Congrats, Haz. I'm proud of you." Luka's warm hand claps him on the shoulder. It is the most Luka has really touched him in a while. Harlan can feel himself blushing from the compliment and hopes Luka will think it's just the sun. "Where at?"

"Oh...um...Mac's Music," Harlan supplies awkwardly, pointing in the direction of the shop. Luka nods, so Harlan continues, "Won't be a bad walk from my place."

"You don't have a car?" Luka asks, looking surprised. Fuck. Harlan is torn between telling Luka the truth or being an asshole about the whole thing. He decides to go with a little from column A and a little from column B.

"Not everyone can afford a car," He says with no real venom. He does roll his eyes for good measure.

"Oh. Of course..." Luka's sentence is cut off by a small voice.

"Lulu. Who's that?" Harlan is surprised by the voice and looks down, finding two identical little girls hiding behind Luka's shapely legs. Both have blonde hair and blue eyes, but one is wearing a purple shirt while the other is in yellow. They must be Luka's sisters.

Harlan glances around to find two other girls. They both look much younger than Luka, though they have the same hair color as him. They stare at Harlan with curious blue eyes, coming to stand next to their brother. Fuck. Harlan is trying not to panic. This can't actually be happening. He can't be meeting Luka's family. Fuck.

"This is Harlan. He's a friend from school," Luka introduces him, easily catching the small brown football one of the older sisters tosses him. "Harlan, these are my sisters. That's Elizabeth - aka Lizzie or Liz - and Mary, but we call her Marz." He points at the two older girls. Suddenly, Luka deciding that Harlan's name needs to end in a 'z' makes perfect sense. He shortens other names to have a 'z'.

The oldest girl waves while the other is still looking at him curiously. It's the same expression Luka has on his face when he looks at Harlan, as if she is studying him. Harlan hates it because it is startlingly similar to how her brother looks at him. "This is Gabby and Becca." Gabby is wearing the yellow shirt. Harlan tries to remember, but this is a lot of information that he wasn't expecting.

"Nice to meet you," Lizzie says, smiling shyly.

"Yeah. Lu hasn't said much about you, though," Mary adds, eyes squinting in the bright sun.

"Why don't you go and get us some water? There is a vending machine over there," Luka tells them through gritted teeth. Mary accepts the cash he gives her, and Lizzie rolls her eyes, a gesture so very much like Luka, both making their way over to the vending machine.

"Are you gonna pway wif us?" Gabby asks once her sisters are gone, more of her body emerging from behind Luka's legs. Harlan doesn't know much about small children - well, he doesn't really know anything about them - but he thinks that means she is getting more comfortable with him. He isn't exactly sure what the small human asked, so he looks at Luka for help.

"She asked if you're gonna play with us?" Luka translates with a small, fond smile, glancing down at his sister and running his fingers through her soft blonde hair.

"Oh. Play what?" Harlan asks, confused by the question, really. Why would they want him to play with them? He is a complete stranger.

"Football, silly," the other little girl pipes in, pointing to Luka's hands. Harlan understands that.

"Nope, I don't do sports balling," Harlan answers, putting one hand up in the air, dismissing the idea because fuck no. He is uncoordinated and doesn't know the first thing about any sport. He doesn't even think he could name more than one position or a single NFL player.

"Sports balling? Really? That's what you call it?" Luka asks, a bemused smile on his face. "Come on, Haz. It's just football, not balls balls." With that comment, Luka glances down at his sisters, who decided that holding hands and spinning in a circle is way more fun than paying attention to their brother and his friend.

"Balls of any kind," Harlan specifies, and that's a fucking lie.

"I bet I could find some balls that you would play with." With that statement, Luka winks. Jesus, is he trying to kill Harlan? Does he want him to die? Harlan is beginning to think so because it isn't the first time Luka has made a comment like that, and he has a sneaking suspicion that it certainly won't be the last. Thoughts of the dream are back in full force again. Fuck, Harlan was actually starting to forget. Luka won't let that happen, and he doesn't even fucking know about it.

"They will be blue before that happens. Any sports played with blue balls?" Harlan asks with his own wide smile. Two can play at this game.

"Nope. Just sports players. I'm sure you could help out there, though. You don't need to know much, and I could guide you through the process." Fuck. Abort! Harlan can't play. He doesn't even know enough innuendos to be on the same level as Luka, much less in the same game. Guide him through the process? Did Luka just hint at showing him how to give a handjob or maybe a blowjob? Holy fuck. Harlan's cock twitches in his overly tight jeans at the very thought.

"Um..." Harlan audibly swallows, mouth suddenly feeling incredibly dry.

"Come on, Hazzy. Pway wif us!" Harlan's attention snaps to Becca as she runs over and grabs his hand, Gabby coming over to do the same with his other hand. Harlan doesn't know if he has ever touched a small child until that very moment, other than when he was a small child himself. His heart feels warm when they start pulling on his arms, jumping up and down with excitement.

"I don't have anything to wear," Harlan excuses, not having it in him to say no outright to the little girls. His heart breaks a bit when a pout forms on Becca's lip, reminding him very much of Luka when Harlan refused to eat out with them.

"I have some extra gym clothes in my bag in the car. They're clean and should fit you, maybe a little tight, but most of your clothes are anyway," Luka supplies, giving Harlan's body another once over.

"So, you can pway!" Gabby exclaims, both girls beginning to jump up and down again. Harlan glances at Luka, pleadingly. Luka just smiles as if he knows Harlan won't say no to these two adorable little girls. Luka is right. Harlan didn't think he liked children, but here he is, getting ready to agree to spend time with Luka outside of school because of them.

"Um-...okay, but I don't know how," Harlan says, looking down and smiling when both girls cheer, high fiving each other.

"I already told you, Haz. Don't worry about it; I'll teach you." Luka winks, and Harlan is confident he stops breathing for a full minute trying to process the information. He is almost positive Luka is flirting with him. He doesn't know shit about flirting, but it is the only plausible explanation for Luka's behavior. "Alright girls, go find Marz and Liz while I get Harlan here some clothes." Luka watches with another fond smile as the twin girls run up to his other sisters, excitedly telling them the news. He gestures for Harlan to follow him.

"You just made their day," he tells Harlan as they walk the short distance to what he assumes is Luka's car. "They don't get to hang out with anyone outside of the family except when they're in school. Our parents are pretty strict." Luka uses his key fob to pop the trunk, quickly locating a gym bag and rummaging through it. He pulls out a pair of athletic shorts and a t-shirt, a victorious expression on his face. Harlan takes the proffered items, wondering why Luka just told him that information, feeling as though it was a bit personal for the other boy.

"Thanks," Harlan says, following the direction Luka is pointing to the public restrooms. In the far too small stall, he pulls off his skinny jeans and button up, folding them neatly and laying them on the closed toilet. He only bangs his elbow on the side of the stall once and only trips twice, thank you very much. He slips Luka's too short shorts over his hips, the material clinging to his thighs. He leaves his bracelets on, knowing they would look ridiculous but not wanting to deal with the alternative. He then takes Luka's shirt in both hands. It is a simple, light gray t-shirt with navy blocked lettering across the front. At least it's gray and not like, light blue, or something. Gray isn't too far off from black.

He sighs, wondering for the one hundred and twenty third time that hour what exactly he has gotten himself into. When he pulls the material over his head, all he can smell is Luka. Fuck.

His cock instantly gets hard in his shorts just from Luka's smell. He briefly considers jerking off in the dirty bathroom stall of a public park but decides to think of way more disgusting things like pop music, the Republican Party, and kissing Cadeon. Kissing Cadeon. That did it.

He opens the stall door and shuffles outside, squinting against the harsh sunlight. He supposes it will be okay to run around in his old, black Converse shoes that are beat to hell. "You didn't run away," Luka yells, jogging up to him and wearing another devastating, crinkly-eyed grin. He looks Harlan up and down, his eyes dark with what almost looks like desire. The sun must be fucking with Harlan's head.

"I did not," Harlan confirms because it really is a fucking miracle. What will Luka's friends think if they see him outside of class with Harlan? Ezra doesn't seem that bothered by it, but he is sure that the other jocks would feel differently.

"You gonna take your bracelets off?" Luka asks, pointing to Harlan's arm. Harlan's hand automatically goes to wrap around them tightly, feeling as if they are burning his skin.

"Um...no. I like to wear them," Harlan excuses lamely and is relieved when Luka just nods his head, not pushing the matter.

"Come on." Luka pats his arm, sending sparks of electricity through him.

"I...um...I told you I don't know how to play," Harlan admits, looking down and suddenly feeling awkward, holding his clothes in his hands.

"We can teach you. If Gabby and Becca can grasp the rules, I am sure a smart guy like yourself will be just fine." Luka smiles, probably trying to put him at ease, and it works. Harlan can feel his body relaxing just a bit at the words. He is also very nervous, for some reason wanting to impress Luka and not wanting to embarrass himself. He got through his one year of PE, and that was it. He doesn't mind physical activity, but he hates sports.

He doesn't understand them, and he just isn't competitive. Winning or losing at a sporting event isn't going to change the world.

"Okay, now that we have Hazza here, we have even teams," Luka starts, clapping his hands together when they have made their way over to his sisters. Becca and Gabby cheer at the mention of Harlan's name, well, his nickname. Again, what is it with Luka and nicknames anyways? So far, he has given Harlan four, if he counts Curly. Harlan thinks for a moment, and he can't recall one other person who has been given four nicknames by Luka. Interesting.

"Haz, you're gonna be on a team with Marz and Becca. Me, Lizzie, and Gabby will be on the other team. This is two-hand touch football. The rules are easy. Your goal is down there next to Harlan's clothes, and ours is on the other side, next to the water bottle." Luka points to the locations, and Harlan thinks he is following so far; however, he keeps getting distracted by the way Luka's firm lips form around words, the cute look of concentration he gets in his eyes while he gives them instructions, and the way he gesticulates as he speaks. Right, Luka is telling him the rules. He should probably pay attention.

"You are not allowed to touch the quarterback unless they start running with the ball. You are not allowed to tackle, and if you have the ball and get touched with two hands, not just one, Mary..." Luka looks pointedly at his sister with the statement who just smiles back at him. Quarterback. Harlan thinks he knows what the quarterback is. He may have watched a movie about sports once. The quarterback is the one that throws the ball, right? Fuck, he hopes so, or he is going to really embarrass himself. "If you have the ball and get touched with two hands, the play is over. No kicking the ball or tackling. Each touchdown is worth a point. First to five wins."

Fuck, that is a lot of information, and Harlan got distracted again by the way the sunlight was reflecting off of Luka's brown hair, making some strands look caramel, and the way his blue eyes sparkle with it. Harlan thinks he was counting the freckles on Luka's tan cheeks when he was talking about a touchdown. Isn't that what they call scoring in football? Fuck, this is hopeless. Harlan is screwed. At least it won't require touching Luka much. Maybe just two hands. Hopefully, he doesn't pop a boner just from that.

"Any questions?" Luka asks, looking at Harlan in particular. Yes, Harlan has a lot of questions, none of which pertain to the game of two-hand touch that they will be playing. Harlan shakes his head, licking his suddenly very dry lips. "Okay. Lizzie and Marz are the quarterbacks."

"What? That's not fair, Lu! You're too fast!" Mary exclaims, crossing her arms.

"I don't make the rules," Luka says, smug smile on his face.

"You literally just made the rules," Mary shoots back, looking like she really wants to slap her brother. Harlan can't blame her. He already knows Luka is fast with his curvy legs and ass. They are going to lose terribly.

"Alright, ready?" Luka asks, ignoring her and throwing the ball from one hand to the other, eyes following the movement. He winks at Harlan before they get into their individual team huddles. Harlan doesn't know what to do or say. He is still trying to figure out how this is all happening. He is almost positive he has somehow landed in the Twilight Zone or he's dreaming again, but he quickly realizes it's not either scenario when they start playing.

Luka's team scores the first point easily, Mary being correct when saying that Luka is fast. Really fucking fast. Harlan's eyes can barely keep up with him as he runs across the grass down their makeshift goal line. He is just a blur of green and brown. Jesus. Harlan looks like fucking Bambi when he runs, unable to get his legs to work properly, both seeming to move independently from the other.

The first time Harlan is passed the ball and actually catches it, he thinks he may faint. He briefly hears Mary yell 'GO!', as she starts to try to hold off Luka, and he just runs. He can feel the wind sweeping back his curls. He glances back to see Luka hot on his heels, so he doubles his efforts, pumping his free arm through the air.

He doesn't feel two hands on him until after he has passed their goal, meaning he actually scored a touchdown. Holy fucking shit. He turns around in disbelief, dropping the football to the ground. Mary and Becca run up to him and hug him, which is odd. He doesn't like being hugged, but he doesn't mind it when it is in congratulations.

"Well, well. Looks like young Harland can do stuff with balls after all," Luka murmurs, once the girls pull away. Harlan can feel his ears becoming hotter with his blush and hopes that it looks like he is just getting sunburnt. It's just...the way Luka murmured that one sentence reminds Harlan of the way he murmured his name in the dream. He suddenly feels like the dream is written all over his face, and Luka has somehow figured it out.

"I'm only a few months younger than you," Harlan points out. He tells himself that the only reason he even bothered to remember Luka's birthday is because it is the day before Christmas.

"But still so much to learn," Luka tsks, picking up the dropped football and beginning to walk towards his sisters.

"Who's gonna teach me? Seeing as I just scored against you, it certainly can't be you. You don't seem to be very good with balls," Harlan quips. Luka turns around, eyes narrowed at Harlan. Harlan just smiles, and what the fuck? What has gotten into him? Harlan doesn't smile, and is he flirting? No, he can't be. Harlan doesn't know how to flirt.

"You're gonna pay for that comment," Luka threatens, pointing at Harlan, winking, and running toward his sister. Harlan shakes his head and follows, completely unsure of what just happened. He is almost positive he is hallucinating at this point. This is all just fabricated. Maybe he and Cadeon are in his bedroom and got their hands on some really good weed. Either way, it can't be real.

The next hour is spent sweating, running, and mostly laughing. Harlan watches with a fond smile when Luka acts like he can't catch Becca, allowing the small girl to score. She giggles and taunts him, Luka pretending he is wounded by her words. Mary and Harlan do the same, allowing Gabby to score, acting as if she is just too quick to catch. She eats it up, smiling broadly as if she has just won an Olympic gold medal instead of scoring in a game of two-hand touch football with her siblings.

They are tied, four points each, and Harlan's team has the ball. Mary passes it to Harlan, and he immediately begins running down their makeshift field. What feels like two seconds later, a body collides against his, tackling him to the ground roughly. A thrill shoots up Harlan's spine when he opens his eyes to find that Luka is now on top of him, arms still wrapped around his waist, looking at him with blue eyes and a smirk.

This exact position happened in his dream; except they were standing. Harlan can still feel Luka's light body in his arms, the way his legs wrapped around his waist. He can hear his moans and taste his lips. Jesus fucking Christ. Bad. This is bad. He is gonna get hard, but he can't stop thinking about it. He can't stop remembering something that was so fucking vivid.

"Thought you said there was no tackling allowed?" Harlan asks, feeling his cock twitch in his shorts. From their position, he can feel Luka's soft dick against his own through the material of their shorts, and he wants to groan. Fuck. He can't get hard now. This is the worst possible time when he has a gorgeous, probably straight boy practically straddling him in the park with his sisters most likely running toward them. The fucking dream.

"I tripped." Luka shrugs, smiling down at him. He unwraps his arms and sits up, looking around for a second. Harlan takes a few deep breaths, willing his semi-erection to go away. He cannot be hard in the middle of a park with children present, even if Luka is what wet dreams are made of. Literally. He had that fucking wet dream just hours ago. "The fact that I *accidentally* ended up straddling you after the fall was not my fault at all. Can't be blamed on me. It just may be the best way to fall, though."

Harlan knows his mouth is hanging open in shock at the comment, and he stares dumbly as Luka braces one hand on the side of his head, blows him a kiss with the other, and hoists himself into a standing position. He reaches a hand down, grabbing Harlan's, and pulls him up soon after. Harlan tries to ignore the spark in his spine from their hands touching and prays that his still somewhat hard cock is hidden by the shorts. Fuck.

He barely listens when Luka and Mary start arguing over the foul, Luka maintaining that he tripped. They soon get back into position to run another play, with Harlan's team still having the ball since it is decided that it was, in fact, a foul. Harlan really isn't paying attention when Mary runs the ball, getting them the winning point. He snaps back to reality when he has his arms full of two younger girls, jumping up and down against him. "We never beat Lu!" Mary exclaims, smiling brightly, looking so much like Luka in that moment it is eerie.

"Yay! Hazzy! We did it!" Becca adds, jumping up on Harlan. Harlan thankfully catches her, the little girl quickly wrapping her tiny legs around his waist in a side hug, squeezing tightly.

"We did," Harlan confirms, still feeling as if his senses are in overload from everything - Luka's comment, Luka straddling him, and now being hugged - when he isn't used to any of it.

"Good job, guys," Luka smiles, coming up to them. Harlan allows Becca to slide down his body, much to her displeasure, given the pout marring her little features.

"Yeah. You should come hang out more often," Lizzie says, coming up to them with Gabby's hand in her own. "It's nice having an even number."

"I agree. Harlan should hang out with me more often," Luka concedes, and Harlan doesn't miss the smug smile on his face. "Well, I had better get you girls home, or Matt is going to have my head." Luka grabs both of his youngest sisters' hands, holding them firmly.

"Yeah. Thanks for...umm...inviting me," Harlan replies awkwardly, running his fingers through his sweaty curls. He makes a mental note to bring a headband next time, his curls becoming far too long to do this without one. Next time? What the fuck? There isn't going to be a next time.

"You're always invited, love," Luka whispers the last word so low, Harlan isn't sure he even heard it correctly. He called him 'love' in his dream, and now that it's a reality, Harlan just isn't sure what to do with that information. "I have never seen you smile so much. I like it. The dimples look good on you. Would love to see you wearing nothing else." Harlan doesn't miss the innuendo in the statement. He stares dumbly at Luka, as he and his sisters turn toward the car.

"What about your clothes?" Harlan asks, coming back to his senses.

"Just bring 'em to school," Luka shouts from his car as he and Lizzie buckle the younger girls into their booster seats.

"Okay," Harlan agrees, grabbing his clothes and waving one last time before walking in the direction of his home. Harlan thinks this has been the strangest day, but he feels like he has had a lot of those lately since meeting Luka Thomas. He still can't seem to wipe the smile off his face the entire way home, debating about texting Cadeon to tell him how his afternoon was spent. He ultimately decides against it, not really wanting to have that conversation again.

14

Luka has been searching the school for a potential fake girl-friend for three days, but the very idea of kissing a girl, fake relationship or not, makes bile rise in his throat. Maybe he should have taken Leigh-Ann up on her very clear advances. He just couldn't. He wants to vomit every time he speaks to her for more than seven seconds. He should probably get used to it, though, because he will probably end up married to a woman and living a life he hates. He pushes that unpleasant thought away, committing himself to just living in the now and not really considering a future that consists of church, a wife, and children.

Speaking of church, he is on his way to the monthly Bible Club that meets during lunch period. This will be the first time he has gone to the Bible Club meetings at this school. He just fuck-ing hates them all. They are all the same. He would skip, like he did the first meeting last month, but he is paranoid that Matt would somehow find out, and that would lead him to find out other facts about his stepson. Luka shudders at the thought as he opens the door to the library where Bible Club is held.

When the subject was brought up in a note with Harlan, the other boy had said that it is ironic that a Bible Club would be held in a place known for learning and knowledge. Luka doesn't really understand what he meant by that, though. The Bible is full of knowledge and a moral code. He learns from the Bible, doesn't he? He sits down, not really paying attention to any-one around him. They open today's meeting with a prayer. Luka bows his head, and for the first time in his life, he feels almost silly. He pushes that thought away and imagines he is talking to an all-loving father figure in the clouds.

"Alright. I see some new faces. My name is Jeremiah, and I'm a youth pastor. Today during Bible Club, we are going to be breaking into groups of two," Jeremiah says softly, standing in front of the small assembly of students. His checkered button-up shirt is tucked into his light khakis, mousy brown hair parted to the side. Something about the boy annoys Luka, and he isn't sure what. Maybe it's his holier-than-thou attitude or because he probably has a sign in his closet that says 'God Hates Fags'. Either way, Luka really doesn't like him. "When you find your partner, I will pass out a piece of paper. We will be playing Bible Hangman."

What the fuck? What are they, like, eight? Luka is sure he watched his five-year-old sisters play Hangman just this weekend. In fact, if it weren't for his younger siblings, Luka probably would have forgotten the game even existed. This is a game for children, not teenagers. He is snapped out of his musings by a female voice. "Wanna be my partner?"

"Huh?" Luka asks, brain not really registering what the girl beside him just said. He looks over, finding Will, the same girl from practice a few weeks ago, sitting there. How did he not notice her before? She definitely wasn't there when he had sat down. He feels horrible for not having greeted her before. He was just so lost in his own thoughts, but she doesn't seem angry. She is smiling at him, her small button nose wrinkling on the sides.

"I asked if you want to be my partner in this game?" She repeats, her voice low and somewhat soothing. He didn't notice that before, but then again, she barely talked when he first met her. It doesn't grate on his brain like most girls' voices tend to. She flashes him a small smile, one side of her thin lips crooked up to the side. She's cute in a 'wanna be my fag hag' sort of way.

"Oh. Why me?" Luka asks, slightly confused as to why she would choose him out of everyone in the room. He isn't complaining though. She seems cool, and he wanted to learn more about her, especially after the comment he thinks he heard her say that day after practice. He has replayed her words over and over in his head, but he always hears 'not that important'.

"Because you look like you think this is as fucking ridiculous as I do," she responds, smirking when Luka looks a bit shocked at her use of language. Most people in this shit club won't go near what they deem to be a 'dirty word' because, again, they are children. "You also look like you don't wanna be here, so we could not want to be here together, at least."

Luka laughs at that, relaxing a bit in his seat, uncrossing his arms. He likes her already. Again, she reminds him of Harlan for some reason, but he can't for the life of him figure out why. "Yeah, that's true. Why are you here?" Luka isn't really listening as Jeremiah explains the rules because he knows how to fucking play hangman, thank you very much.

"Parents," she responds, sighing and sitting back in her seat, taking the sheets of paper being handed out. There is nothing flirtatious in her tone, her body language is open to him, but her legs are crossed in the opposite direction, telling Luka she really has no interest in him. He almost wants to sigh in relief. "You?"

"Same," Luka answers, clicking his pen a few times, needing something to do with his hands. "I know we kinda talked that one day, but I don't think I've ever introduced myself. My name's Luka. I don't think we have any classes together, do we? You're Will, right?"

"Yeah. It's short for Willow, but I don't mind if you call me Will. Everyone else does. I'm in junior, so that's why we don't have any classes together," she explains, and that makes sense. He just assumed she was his age because she acts so mature. She is definitely different than most of the other girls her age. Luka likes her.

"Well, it's nice to actually meet you, Willow, you know, away from all of the cheerleaders and all that," Luka says, smiling and sitting up in his chair, giving her a handshake. She returns his smile, and they get to work playing the stupid game. They mostly laugh their way through it, their chosen words and phrases getting more and more satirical as the game progresses.

After Willow chose the word 'Jezebel', Luka knew she would be fine with his phrase choice of 'seven wives of David'. Willow laughed loudly at that, causing their stick-up-the-ass club peers to glare at them. He almost flips them off but decides it's not worth his time. Plus, being banned from Bible Club would surely get him beaten by Matt.

Luka bites his lip as he decides to go out on a limb with his next choice of words, hoping it will go over the way he wants. He just keeps hearing her phrase 'not that important' over and over in his head. He keeps seeing the way she was practically salivating while watching Tabby in a promiscuous position. With shaky lines, he draws the hanging post and sixteen dashes, with the appropriate spaces between each of the three words.

"Hmm," she hums curiously as she studies the blank spaces with squinted brown eyes, placing her index finger and thumb on her jaw in thought. She only has the legs left to guess before she loses. She has managed to guess some correct letters, including 'a', 'r', and 'm'. "O," she guesses.

"Yes," Luka tells her, filling in the four o's in the phrase. Her eyes light up when she sees where they are placed, probably figuring it out.

"Sodom and Gomorrah!" She shouts triumphantly, prompting Drag-emiah to shush them and give them a dirty look that he probably hopes sends them straight to hell for their insolence. Luka giggles when she rolls her eyes.

"Correct!" He exclaims just as loudly because fuck these assholes. Well, not literally, he doesn't think he would actually fuck a single one of them. The only person he currently wants to fuck is Harlan, and that doesn't seems to be happening anytime soon.

"What a crock of shit," she says, looking down at the words on the paper. Luka doesn't miss it when she quickly glances across the room at a girl who is laughing at something her partner said. Wait... it's Tabby. Luka hadn't even realized Tabby was in this club as well. He wonders why Willow didn't sit beside her instead since they are obviously friends. Interesting.

"I agree. It's bullshit, really," he responds, trying to get a feel for her thoughts on homosexuality. He doesn't even know his own thoughts on it, but he needs to know hers.

"Yeah. I don't see what's wrong with being attracted to the same sex," she replies, this time more quietly, glancing at Tabby again. Okay... Luka is definitely starting to think that Willow may like girls. Statistically speaking, there should be more than one gay student at their school. Has Luka found another one?

He would count Harlan, but Harlan is impossible to read; therefore, he is completely unsure about his sexuality. He thinks he may have felt a hard-on in Harlan's shorts on Saturday, but he can't be sure. It was probably a figment of his overactive and very horny imagination. Straddling a very cute boy with chocolate-colored curls probably did weird things to his mind. Luka shakes his head, realizing his thoughts about Harlan have run away with him again. Tends to happen a lot if he's honest.

"I couldn't agree more," Luka says with a smile, just as Jeremiah makes his way to the front of the room, clapping his hands loudly.

"Thank you all for coming today. We will close the club in prayer. Please bow your heads," he instructs. For the first time in his life, Luka doesn't bow his head in prayer. Instead, he silently thinks about his observation regarding Willow. He decides he needs to get to know her a bit better, but he may have a plan. After the prayer is over, he gathers his things and smiles when he notices that Tabby is walking in their direction.

"Hey, Will! Why didn't you come sit beside me? I saved you a seat!" she exclaims, smiling broadly. Willow's cheeks suddenly become the same shade as her hair as she looks down, not making eye contact with the other girl. Interesting.

"Hi, Tabitha. Yeah. I'm sorry. I came in kind of late and didn't want to disrupt Jermiah, so I sat in the first empty chair I found," Willow explains, her voice at a higher pitch that Luka had become accustomed too. It's just a hair away from a full-on squeak, as if she is nervous and wasn't expecting Tabitha to ask her about her seating choice. When the silence stretches to an uncomfortable length, making the whole thing feel awkward. Willow finally looks up, smiling at Tabitha. Well, it's more of a grimace if Luka is perfectly honest, but at least she tried.

"I was wondering how you think you did on the math test?" Tabitha inquires after another few moments of pregnant silence. Luka is learning so much just from the three sentences that have been said between them, the silence speaking more than the words ever could.

"Oh, umm...I... umm... I think I d-did okay," Willow stutters out, playing with her fingers in a way that reminds Luka very much of Harlan when Luka flirts with him.

"Awesome. Me too..." Tabitha's sentence trails off, her blue eyes finally landing on Luka.

"Luka? Right?" She asks, eyes narrowing. Her question almost seems...jealous. Fuck. This keeps getting better and better.

"Yup, and you're Tabitha. We've talked once, but Willow has told me so much about you," he lies, shooting Willow a knowing smile. Willow glances down quickly, her face becoming redder with each passing moment. He hopes his comment has smoothed things over with Tabitha.

"Oh. Um...that's cool. Well, anyways, I have to go. I'll be late if I

don't. See you in class, Will, and it was nice meeting you, Luka."
She waves, then disappears out the door. Willow visibly deflates
when she is out of sight, a deep sigh coming from her chest. They
walk out of the library together in silence. She waves once before they part ways, each heading in a different direction. Luka's
head is spinning with the new information, starting to think up
a plan. He wants to watch her a bit more first.

15

"Didn't see you at lunch," Harlan says by way of greeting when Luka sits down behind him in Creative Writing. Fuck. He told himself he would never initiate conversation with Luka, but here he is, letting his inquisitive nature get the best of him. He is just so used to Luka always being around, that's all. He noticed that he was nowhere to be found during lunch. He saw him in the lunch line, then eating with Ezra for a few minutes, and then he just disappeared…and Harlan is curious. Just curious. That's all.

"Miss me, Curly?" Luka asks, smirking at Harlan, who just rolls his eyes in response. It's his own fault, really. He should never have said anything.

"No," Harlan insists, even though it's kind of a lie. He didn't really miss him; he just noticed that he wasn't there. When Luka smirks at him again, all Harlan can see is the same smirking face that was straddling him on Saturday. The sun that had been shining from behind him had almost made his hair look like a halo. Harlan doesn't believe in angels, but Luka is probably the closest he will ever come to one.

"I was in Bible Club, if you must know," Luka tells him, and of course that's where Luka had disappeared to. Harlan didn't even think of that because he doesn't care when the Bible Club meets, or if there is even a club for it. He was invited once. It was quite hilarious seeing the look on the dude's face when Harlan told him that he worships at the Church of the Flying Spaghetti Monster. He hopes he Googled it later, since education is important.

"Do you just all sit in a cross formation and read from the Bible for an hour?" Harlan asks, and much to his surprise, Luka lets out a loud laugh and covers his mouth with a small hand, eyes shining in the fluorescent lights. Harlan thought he would be offended by the joke, not actually laugh.

"May as well have been. We played Bible Hangman," Luka tells him, getting out his notebook and a pencil, setting the items on his desk. His notebook is mangled, with doodles all over the cover. Harlan can make out a paper airplane, a stick figure skateboarding, and a spider web. Harlan smiles down at the small doodles, having a few of his own in his journal.

"Bible Hangman? What are you, fucking five?" Harlan asks, brows drawn in confusion because Luka can't be serious. The Bible Club surely doesn't expect teenagers to play a game made for children.

"Eight, actually, but those were my thoughts exactly," Luka responds, glancing up as Ms. Moore tells them to work in groups on their newest assignment. Harlan turns to Luka, as if they are actually going to discuss the assignment. He glances over at Cadeon, who seems to have distracted Ezra, debating with a debate about the pros and cons of first person. Harlan agrees with Cadeon; writing in first person is terrible.

"Well, children also have imaginary friends, so it's not that different, I suppose," Harlan points out with a shrug, watching Luka's expression as he understands exactly what Harlan was inferring with the statement.

"What's that supposed to mean?" Luka asks with the most endearing look on his face, a mixture of intrigue and offense.

"I am simply pointing out that believing there is a man in the sky who grants your wishes if you do good deeds is the equivalent to a child having an imaginary friend." Harlan then stands up, straddles his chair so the back of it is pressed against his chest and interlocks his fingers, placing them on Luka's desk, giving the other boy his full attention. This is rare for Harlan, but he has been talking to Luka for longer than he wants to admit, so maybe this won't be a terrible mistake.

Luka's blue eyes squint as if trying to think of a reply. "That is hardly the same thing," is what he comes up with, and he doesn't even look like he believes what he is saying.

"I think it is. I mean, think about it, Lu." Harlan pauses when the nickname slips from his mouth but quickly recovers, not wanting to draw attention to his mistake. "Both religious people and children with imaginary friends wholeheartedly believe that such a being exists with no physical evidence. They talk with that being, ask it for favors, and even make up backstories about its existence. Tell me, how is it any different?"

He watches as Luka considers his question, clearly getting frustrated when he doesn't seem to have a real answer. "It's not the same because God exists."

"Do you have proof?"

"I have faith."

"That doesn't count, Luka. Faith isn't proof. Having a feeling in your heart doesn't make it true. Facts and evidence are what make something real." Harlan is giving calm, calculated answers. The same answers he gave himself when he was first starting to come to the conclusion that religion is bullshit after everything that had happened to him.

"So you don't have faith in anything?" Luka asks, clearly diverting from the current discussion. Harlan thinks about the question for a moment because he hasn't really been asked that in a long time.

"I have faith in science, evidence, and nature," Harlan answers finally, watching as Luka puckers his lips a little, mulling Harlan's words over in his head. He looks like an angry hedgehog, and if it wasn't for the seriousness of their conversation, Harlan would have kind of wanted to kiss him.

"The Bible is proof," Luka says, pointing triumphantly, his eyes lighting up as if he got one on Harlan. Harlan shakes his head, though, and Luka looks at him curiously.

"No, it's not."

"How so?" Luka asks, curiosity marring his features.

"The Bible was written by men. It wasn't written by some divine hand," Harlan answers, and he can already predict what Luka is going to say. He just lets the other boy walk into the trap.

"It was written by God through man," Luka corrects, and there it is. The answer Harlan knew was coming.

"Do you seriously believe that, though? If someone in this day and age were to say 'God spoke to me, and I wrote it down in a book. Here it is, so worship his word,' we would put them in a mental hospital because they are clearly psychotic. Don't even get me started on all of the books from that time period that the Catholic Church deemed less than desirable, so they say it's not canon." Harlan thinks it's a great point. Luka cannot possibly deny it.

Luka looks like he is having an internal battle with himself and that he may cry at any moment. Harlan kind of wants to hug him and tell him that it will be okay. That a world without God is okay because it is the same world it was before. He doesn't, though, just lets him find out for himself. If he wants to actually talk about it, though, Harlan knows he will be there to listen. He has no idea why, but he will be.

"What do you mean, 'other books'?" Luka asks finally, his voice barely above a whisper. He is looking down at his desk, but it seems more like he is looking through it, lost in thought.

"There are loads of other books and gospels written by supposed prophets. Bet they didn't teach you that in church. There is the Book of Enoch, which was found with the Dead Sea Scrolls.

You know what those are, right?" Harlan asks, a small smile on his face.

"Yes. I know what those are," Luka answers, gaze finally landing on Harlan. He looks paler for some reason, his eyes searching Harlan for answers Harlan isn't sure he has.

"Well, the Book of Enoch was found among those. It is a lot and an interesting read. It is only canon in the Ethiopian Bible. Most Christian sects do not accept it as canon, and by canon, I mean books that aren't accepted by the Catholic Church and therefore are not allowed in the Bible. The Gospel of Matthew is canon, for example, while the Book of Enoch is not," Harlan explains, thinking back to his late-night research a few years ago.

"But if it was found with the scrolls, then why isn't it canon?" Luka asks.

"That's a good question. You will have to ask your church that. Churches do love to cherry pick, though. Maybe it didn't fit in with their narrative. I'm not sure."

"Is that the only one?" Luka asks, and Harlan thinks it is kind of funny that an atheist seems to be teaching Luka more about his own religion than years of church and Bible study.

"Nope," Harlan answers, popping the 'p'. "Like I said, there are more. Um..." He pauses, thinking about another book he has read about. "There is the Gospel of Thomas. That one is super interesting, but it's not shocking why it wasn't included in the canonical text." Harlan hopes his words are tempting, and when Luka looks even more intrigued, he knows he's won.

"Why? What happens in it?"

"Are you sure you wanna know?" Harlan asks, giving Luka a chance to stay in his lovely little bubble. When Luka nods, Harlan smiles, feeling proud for some unfathomable reason. "Well, it insinuates that Jesus actually had a twin brother. The Infancy Gospel of Thomas writes about Jesus as a small child, which is interesting, considering the canon text is missing 30-some-odd years. Canonically, his birth is discussed, then it pretty much skips to his death, but the Gospels of Thomas discusses his childhood. At one point, another child bumped into him on the street, and it angered him, so he killed the child. When the people around them see the dead child and become fearful, he makes them all go blind. There are a lot of other stories. You can find them online if you're curious."

"If you're an atheist, then why do you know so much about religion?" Luka asks, his question genuine.

Harlan thinks about it for a moment, wanting to give Luka a truthful answer for once, but not too truthful. There are many reasons why he has so much knowledge about religion, especially since he began really examining it after the worst day of his life, but his main reason is simple. "Know your enemy."

Luka looks like he has seen a ghost. His face is pale, and his hands have the slightest tremor. Harlan barely stops himself from reaching out and holding them, since they are mere inches away from his own. Luka swallows dryly, his throat bobbing with the action and licks his lips. He looks almost spaced out, as if he is so lost in his thoughts, he may never resurface. A silence settles over them for a few minutes, Luka staring off into the distance, barely breathing. Harlan is getting worried about him, so he takes pity on him, glancing around the room to make sure nobody is really watching them.

"Look, Lu, it's fine if you don't believe me or if you wanna see for yourself. I am just stating facts. I just find it fascinating what the canonical text of the Bible doesn't include, yet…" he pauses, unsure if he wants to continue his thought. He takes a deep breath and plows on, "yet they are more than happy to keep terrible text from the Old Testament about stoning women for being promiscuous or that homosexuality is an abomination." The bell signaling the end of the period rings with Harlan's last statement, seeming to snap Luka out of his trance. Luka mutters a goodbye and shoots Harlan a small, almost pained smile. Harlan exhales through his mouth, unsure of what the fuck just happened.

16

Luka has been trying not to dwell too much on the conversation he had with Harlan a few days ago. That night, he lay awake, lost in thought about what Harlan had said. He found his laptop, turning it on and dimming the screen, not wanting his parents to know what he was doing. It was like he was getting ready to search for porn and not for the information Harlan had provided earlier that day. He Googled the books Harlan had mentioned and had no trouble finding them. He spent the next two hours poring over the information, brain spinning with it all. Harlan didn't lie at all. Those texts are real; he was even honest about where the Book of Enoch was found.

At nearly 2 am, Luka shut his computer and scrubbed at his eyes, trying to erase the conversation from his mind, but it wouldn't budge. His discussion with Harlan left more questions than answers, and he hadn't been expecting that at all. He thought when they discussed religion, he would know more than Harlan, being that he was the one that believed in God, but that wasn't the case. In fact, he learned more in his half hour conversation with Harlan than he had in his years of church and Bible study. He went to bed, dreaming of prophets and angels, but he wasn't sure he believed any of it.

He didn't tell Harlan of his thoughts, though. Instead, they went back to quietly passing notes, Luka occasionally flirting with the other boy. He is starting to be able to read him just a bit more. For example, Luka has found the tip of his ears turn pink when he is being flirted with; however, his ears are mostly covered by his longish curls, so he rarely gets to see it. Harlan also scrunches up his nose just the tiniest bit when he is lying, or perhaps not telling the entire truth. He wipes the tip of his nose when he doesn't want to answer a question and coughs when he is uncomfortable. Luka needs to start writing this shit down, almost as if it is a code to how to crack Harlan Sharp.

He has also been watching Willow from afar in the hallways and during lunch. They even talk occasionally between classes, her sense of humor much like his own, but there is something about her that reminds him of Harlan. Luka just can't figure out exactly what it is, but he is sure he will put his finger on it sooner or later. He is currently nervous because he is going to ask her something after class is over, and it could either work out in his favor or go very, very wrong. He hopes it is the former. He is running out of time and options.

He sighs, then takes a deep breath, trying to calm his racing heart and looking around for something or someone to distract him. Harlan. Harlan is sitting beside him at one of the long black tables, with Ezra and Cadeon on Luka's other side. Originally Cadeon had sat next to Harlan, but Luka stole his spot enough times for Cadeon to get the hint. Harlan is looking down at his work, effectively ignoring him, and that just won't do. He pokes him on his cheek, right where his dimple would be if he were smiling. Luka may or may not have memorized the location the first time he caught a peek of it.

"What?" comes Harlan's deep voice, glancing up from his work to meet Luka's eyes.

"I don't know. I'm bored," Luka says, shrugging. He isn't. He needs to be distracted for the last fifteen minutes of class, and Harlan is his favorite type of distraction.

"Okay," Harlan responds, going back to his work. Luka sighs again, hoping to annoy him. When that doesn't work, he glances around to make sure nobody is watching and places a finger on Harlan's knee, working it up his thigh before Harlan jumps and pulls away.

He grins when Harlan glares at him, lifting up both arms in a stretch. Luka can hear the bones cracking with it. The bracelets fall down his arm just a tiny bit, touching the rolled-up sleeve of his flannel, and Luka notices something. "Fuck. Is that a tattoo?" Luka asks, pointing to the black padlock on the top of Harlan's wrist peeking out between the bracelets. He could have sworn it wasn't there earlier that day, but he could be wrong since the jewelry always covers it.

"No. It's just Sharpie," Harlan answers, glancing down at it, then back up to Luka. He moves his hand quickly, repositioning the bracelets so that they cover the drawing.

"Oh," Luka says, relieved. "That's good. I don't really like tattoos." He scrunches up his nose at the thought.

"Why? 'Cause they're against the Bible?" Harlan asks, leaning his body more towards Luka, so he could hear his low voice. Luka leans in a bit further because, well, he wants to be closer so sue him. When their elbows touch on the table, Harlan's eyes widen a bit, but he doesn't pull away. The touch gives Luka butterflies for whatever reason.

"Yeah, and I don't know. I think they look kind of trashy or something," Luka answers, honestly. He has had that thought about tattoos for a long time, never quite understanding the appeal of marking your body in such a permanent way.

"I want a tattoo," Harlan tells him, and oh.

"Don't," Luka says, even though now his mind is very much wanting to know what Harlan would look like with a tattoo.

"Not your body." Harlan rolls his eyes, clearly getting annoyed with Luka's attitude.

"You have such pretty skin and a lovely body. It would be a shame to mark it up like that." Luka allows his gaze to sweep over Harlan's long, pale limbs. He has imagined those limbs arranged in a variety of different positions, including but not limited to caging him in, under him, and his personal favorite, holding him against a wall.

"Would you rather mark it in different ways?" Harlan asks, and fuck, he was not expecting Harlan to say that in his deep, deep voice with his sinful mouth. Luka's dick twitches at the thought of sucking a red bruise into Harlan's long neck, even though he has never seen the appeal of being marked or marking someone else. Doesn't help that his mind is already in the gutter.

"Yeah. Actually, I would," he answers, smiling when he realizes Harlan's pupils are dilated. He looks down, spotting a black Sharpie poking out of the tight pocket of Harlan's skinny jeans. Before Luka can second guess his actions, he uses two fingers to slide it out. Harlan looks surprised and confused by the move. Luka glances around again, making sure nobody is watching. He takes Harlan's hand, and Jesus, it's huge. Luka allows himself to imagine, for a brief moment, what it would look like wrapped around his dick. He shakes the thought away, going back to what he originally had planned.

He can feel Harlan's curious green eyes on him as Luka turns his hand palm up. He skims his fingers over the soft skin of Harlan's palm, wanting to memorize every line in case he never lets him do this again. He glances up at Harlan one more time, smirking as he opens the marker, then writes an 'L' in the dead center of Harlan's ridiculously wide palm. He admires the letter for a minute, then looks up to find Harlan staring at it. After a few moments, Harlan looks up, meeting his gaze. Luka can't tell what is going through Harlan's mind, like normal, but he doesn't look angry. In fact, his pupils are still blown, and his lips are red, as if he had been biting them recently.

The final bell of the day rings, effectively ending their moment. Harlan looks around, moving the hand with Luka's initial below the table out of Luka's view, but Luka thinks he may be adjusting himself. Luka is in the same boat, so he doesn't say anything as he discreetly does the exact same thing.

Harlan bolts out the door before he gets a chance to say good-bye. Luka tries to push the thought of Harlan's soft skin covered in tattoos out of his mind as he looks for Willow in the hallway. He finds her at her locker and is suddenly feeling really nervous again, so he wipes his clammy hands on his jeans and strides towards her. She smiles when she sees him and waves a silent hello.

"Hey. Umm...do you got a minute to talk?" he asks, glancing around the crowded hallway, "Privately," he adds for good measure.

"Yeah, sure. Everything alright?" She asks, curious expression on her face.

"Yeah, fine," Luka answers, looking around and spotting an empty classroom. He pulls her inside, shutting the door firmly behind them. His breaths are coming out in short pants, and he tries to calm his heart rate. He goes to hop on the teacher's desk, swinging his legs as his Vans repeatedly hit the metal frame.

"No offense, but you're kind of scaring me, Luka. What's this about?" Willow's red eyebrows are drawn into a frown, brown eyes wide with concern as she stares at him suspiciously.

Luka sighs and decides to just jump straight to the point. He would laugh at his double meaning of the word straight, but he is too fucking nervous. "Look. I know you're in love with Tabitha."

"What? No...no, I'm not," she stutters out, backing away from him a bit. She looks frightened, like she may run at any moment, so Luka needs to act fast. Her breaths are coming out short and quick, and she is glancing around the room as if looking for something that could help her out of this.

"It's okay. I promise I won't tell anyone," Luka starts, holding both hands up at his chest in a non-threatening gesture.

"Tell anyone what?" She asks, narrowing her dark eyes at him.

"That you're gay. That you're in love with Tabitha," Luka answers easily, not wanting to pretend for a second that he doesn't know.

"I never said that." She almost whispers the statement, avoiding Luka's eyes as she looks at the window, the rain beating down on the glass.

He jumps off the desk, deciding he can't stay still in this moment, the nervous energy in his veins needing an outlet. "Will, you didn't have to. It is written all over your face, but it's fine. I was kind of hoping we could come to an agreement," Luka says, and he knows immediately it came out wrong.

"Are you blackmailing me?" She asks, anger in her tone, eyes finally snapping to his. Luka immediately backs up because she is kind of scary when she's angry. He didn't mean to upset her. This whole conversation isn't going like he had planned in his head.

"No! God, no! Not at all. I just...I need your help. Regardless of your answer, I promise I will keep your secret and hope we can still be friends. Please, just listen to me, though," Luka pleads, hoping to convey how important this is with his eyes.

"Go on," she replies, visibly relaxing in front of him, but her posture is still closed off, arms folded over her chest protectively.

Luka releases a breath he didn't know he was holding as he steps forward, getting closer to her because he doesn't want to say this next part too loudly, even though they are in a closed off classroom away from the ears of their fellow classmates. He takes a deep breath because this will be the first time, he says it out loud too, but he thinks of kissing a girl again. He thinks of Harlan and hopes this will be worth it. He prays this doesn't backfire.

"I'm..." he starts but pauses, not sure if he can actually say the words out loud. Saying them out loud means acknowledging them. He clears his throat, deciding to go with a different choice of words, because he just can't. "I'm just like you." He bites his lip, hoping she will understand his meaning without making him actually say the words out loud. He just, he doesn't know if he can. Not yet. It's one thing to give in to his urges when he is less than sober with total strangers, but it's a completely different thing to say out loud.

"Okay, but that still doesn't tell me what you want," She crosses her arms, but her features soften, almost as if she is relieved to know she isn't the only gay student in school.

"Okay. I don't wanna bore you with the details, so here's the gist. My stepdad Matt is a total dick, and my entire family is religious, which I'm sure you understand," he pauses his statement, watching as she nods her head because she clearly understands. "Well, anyways, my stepdad has been on my ass about getting a girlfriend since I started at this school. I normally just find some overly Christian bimbo who won't expect sex and pretend, but I... I just don't think I can this time. The mere thought of kissing someone who isn't-" he almost finishes the sentence with 'Harlan', but stops himself, swallowing the name back, "-of kissing a girl makes me want to puke."

"Funny, I have the opposite problem," she cracks with a smile, prompting Luka to laugh about the absurdity of the situation. Just like that, the tension in the room is broken. Luka can breathe again, as if a weight has been lifted off his chest. He didn't realize how much not telling anyone was weighing on him, but now that his secret is somewhat out, it is as though he is breathing for the first time. "So, let me guess where you are going with this. You want me to pretend to be your girlfriend to keep your stepdad off your back?"

"Yes, but I thought it could also help you. You said your parents are religious. They have to be wondering why you don't have a boyfriend," he ventures, and when she releases her arms to her side and sighs, he knows he is correct in his assumption.

"So, you want to fake date?" She clarifies again.

"Yes. Nothing major. Maybe holding hands around school, coming to my house for dinner with my parents, hanging out with each other's friends. You're the coolest girl I know, and I just...I can't stomach the thought of fake dating another girl when she thinks it is real dating. I just...fuck, I can't."

"Okay. I'll do it. It's not like Tabby will actually care, and it will get my parents off my case, too," she says after a few moments of thought, the first part coming out almost bitterly. Luka sighs in relief that this whole thing didn't backfire on him, but he feels just a stab of guilt over the whole Tabitha situation. He pushes it away because he knows this is what is best for both of them.

"What's your number? We can come up with a story over the weekend of how we met and shit," Luka tells her, pulling out his phone and handing it to her.

"Yeah, that's fine," she replies, typing in her number and shooting a quick text to herself so she has his.

"Thank you. Fuck, thank you so much for doing this; you have no idea," Luka tells her, giving her a meaningful look. He almost hugs her, but they aren't to that level of friendship yet; however, he hopes they can be. He starts making his way to the door, not wanting to be anymore late for football practice.

"One more thing, Lu." He freezes when her voice carries over the sound of his relief. He turns around to face her, uncertain about her next statement. "Who are *you* in love with?"

"What?" Luka sputters because he was not expecting that question at all.

"Who are you in love with?" She asks again, words measured and slow.

"I'm not..." Luka begins, placing a hand over his heart. He feels like a deer caught in the headlights, like he can't move under her gaze and that she is seeing into his very soul.

"I can see it in your eyes. If you're not in love, you definitely have a crush. It's okay, you don't have to tell me right now. I just...I wanna help." She gives him a small smile and runs a hand down his arm in a comforting gesture. "You know my crush, so it only seems fair." She smiles one last time and is gone, the door shutting quietly behind her. Luka is still standing rooted to the spot, unsure of what just happened. He thinks he could cry with relief, though, because he doesn't really have to pretend to be someone, he isn't with her.

17

"Come on, H, it's our senior year. You have to go to Homecoming game," Cadeon begs him over their lunch of shitty fucking pizza.

"No. It's stupid. Picking a single week of school where people dress up like fools, depending on the day, to lead up to a football game where we are forced to show school spirit is the dumbest fucking concept, we as a society have ever come up with, save religion in general. Why does it fucking matter if we win a football game? Will it impact the world in any way?"

"Yeah, yeah, I've heard it all before. You should at least go to the dance, though." Cadeon rolls his eyes at what was the beginning of another rant about religion and football from Harlan.

"Oh, an even better idea. Of course, I'd want to go to some antiquated sexist dance where everyone's aim is to spike the punch and lose their virginity. Since I have more than three brain cells, that doesn't sound like my idea of a good time, Cade," Harlan responds.

School dances are fucking stupid. He hates being around his classmates on a normal day, so why on earth would he choose to be around them when he doesn't have to be? It is just another excuse to show who is the most popular and who has the most money. The ridiculous amount of time and energy people put into things that don't matter is unfathomable to Harlan.

"Stop the fucking rant, H. I get it. You're an asshole," Cadeon waves away, rolling his eyes at his stubborn friend. "Luka would probably love it if you went to the game, though."

"What does Luka have to do with this?" Harlan asks, wondering how he was even brought into the conversation, but Cadeon always finds a way, it seems.

"He likes you, and he's the running back of the team, Haz," Cadeon answers, looking at Harlan like he has two heads for not knowing the position Luka plays. Harlan rolls his eyes at the nickname, Cadeon having picked it up from Luka a few weeks prior. At first, Harlan acted like it annoyed him that Cadeon used the nickname, but Cadeon ignored him. He's gotten used to it now, deciding only Luka and Cadeon are allowed to call him that.

"I figured he played something that had to do with running. He's incredibly fast," Harlan says mostly to himself, pointedly ignoring the first part of the sentence while he takes a bite of the cardboard his school calls pizza, but hey, beggars can't be choosers.

It's not like he has any food waiting for him at home when he gets out of school. He has to eat what is available, even though it is cardboard with shitty bits of imitation pepperoni on top and something that is passable as cheese. It is exactly three point seven seconds later when he realizes he fucked up with the comment. He holds his breath to see if Cadeon will pick up on what he had just said.

"Yeah. He's a running back," Cadeon agrees, then drops his pizza slice on his tray and fixes Harlan with quizzical blue eyes. Harlan swallows dryly, waiting for the question that is coming. "Wait, I smell somethin' fishy. How do you know he's fast? When have you seen him run? I know for a fact you've never seen him play in any of his football games."

"Umm..." Harlan briefly considers lying, but Cadeon will see right through him. He is a terrible liar, and Cadeon knows all of his tells. He decides to go with his usual approach, giving as little information as possible. "I saw him at the park this weekend after my interview."

"Is that why you didn't text me back for hours after your interview? You were with him?" Cadeon accuses loudly, pointing a finger at Harlan.

"Shh, Cade. Fuck," Harlan says, puckering his lips and placing a finger up to them, trying to get his very loud friend to shut the fuck up. He doesn't need the entire fucking school to know he hung out with Luka over the weekend.

"Harlan, you've been keeping shit from me, which hurts because I am *supposed* to be your best friend," Cadeon responds, and he really does look hurt. Harlan can't handle that. He may be a heartless bastard, but not even a serial killer could handle the look Cadeon is giving him. Fuck.

"I just ran into him at the park when I had finished my interview. He was with his sisters. They asked me to play two-hand touch with them. That's all. End of story," Harlan explains, sighing afterwards.

"So, you played two-hand touch, as in football, in your inter-view outfit?" Cadeon asks disbelievingly, and yes when it is said that way, it does sound unbelievable. Harlan barely believes it happened himself. He would think it was a dream if it weren't for Luka's clothes sitting neatly folded on his bed, waiting to be returned to him. Harlan kept forgetting them. He almost hated when he washed them because then they no longer smelled like the other boy.

"Um...no... not really. Luka had some extra clothes that he let me borrow," Harlan mumbles, looking down at his food, not wanting to meet Cadeon's eyes. He is embarrassed, like a child who has been caught with their hand in the cookie jar.

"This shit just keeps getting better and better," Cadeon says with a shit-eating grin. He claps his hands together, rubbing them back and forth as if it is Christmas morning, and Santa brought him an Xbox.

"It's not like that. His little sisters begged me, and I couldn't turn them down." It is a lame excuse, even to Harlan's ears.

Cadeon's smile doesn't even falter with it. In fact, it gets bigger.

"So, already meeting the family, I see. What else happened? Give me details." Cadeon's eyes are sparkling with amusement, his lunch forgotten. When Cadeon forgets about food, Harlan knows he is interested in the conversation because Cadeon never neglects food.

"Nothing," Harlan insists; however, he can feel a blush rising on his cheeks when he remembers 'the straddling incident', as he has been referring to it in his head, and Luka's words while it was happening. His cock twitches in his overly tight jeans. Fuck.

"Bullshit. You're blushing. Something else had to have happened. You never blush unless it involves Luka Thomas." Cadeon points an accusatory finger at him. Harlan sighs, knowing he will probably give in soon.

"Fine. There may have been an accidental straddling incident," Harlan replies, not making eye contact with his friend. He is fidgeting, his toes turned inward under the table. He really doesn't want to admit it out loud, and his face feels hot. It sounds so much worse when it's said out loud, and he was really trying not to think about it. He has already stopped himself from jacking off to the memory more times than he can count.

"How do you 'accidentally' straddle someone, Haz? You can accidentally lose your keys or accidentally trip over your own feet, but you don't accidently straddle someone." Cadeon looks unconvinced, but remembers he has food and takes a large bite of his pizza.

"It was an accident," Harlan maintains, finally meeting Cadeon's gaze. "He tackled me, and we kind of just sort of ended up that way."

"But you said it was two-hand touch. Why would he have tackled you?" Cadeon argues, letting his pizza fall to the tray again and fixing Harlan with a hard stare, practically daring him to lie.

"Um...he said he tripped," Harlan says, shrugging because he really did say he tripped.

"Yeah, and I am the Easter Bunny," Cadeon responds, rolling his eyes.

"Anyways, I am not going to Homecoming," Harlan says, changing the subject because he doesn't think his poor neglected cock can even handle any more discussion of the straddling incident.

"You have that night off. You already told me as much. Think about it, please? It will be fun, and it will get you out of the house," Cadeon begs.

"Fine. I will think about it, but no promises," Harlan tells him, finishing off his pizza and standing up to take his tray to the trash.

"Alright. I'll see you in class. I need to go catch Jacob to see if he needs any help on his math homework," Cadeon says, getting up and taking his tray in the opposite direction. Harlan waves, dumping what is left on his tray in the trash can, then placing it in its designated spot.

He turns around, surprised to see Luka talking to Ezra, but Luka isn't just with Ezra. He is with Willow, and his arm is wrapped around her waist, his small hand absentmindedly stroking her hip. What the fuck? Why is Luka holding her that way? Why... why is he holding her with his hand on her fucking hip? Luka can't. He can't be holding her that way. Not after everything that has transpired between them. Not after the fucking straddling incident.

Harlan was beginning to actually believe that Luka liked him as more than just a friend. He can't go through this again. Not again. This can't be happening again. Bile rises in his throat as the pizza turns over in his stomach. How could he have been so stupid? His eyes come back up to Luka's face, making eye contact for a brief second.

Luka's expression is unreadable from this distance, but Harlan just *knows* there is probably a smug smirk there, taunting him. This has probably been his plan all along. Torment the weird kid. How could he have been so stupid as to believe that this was anything other than that?

Harlan quickly turns around and walks away, not giving Luka a chance to react, *to lie* again. He decides to leave the school grounds completely. He can't deal with any more of Luka's lies. He was just starting to believe him and now this? Luka and Willow are obviously dating. You don't just stand like that, holding someone so intimately in the hallway with a hand on their hip if you're not dating.

He needs to get the fuck away. His heart is in his throat, beating erratically, and his limbs start to shake. He absentmindedly scratches at the skin under his bracelets, feeling the raised scars from so long ago under his fingernails, taunting him and serving as a reminder of the past. He just wants to get as far away from the school and as far away from Luka as possible. Not like his mom will actually do anything if he skips school. The school officials probably won't even notice he isn't there. Words from his past float through his mind like dark clouds in the sky.

I hope you enjoy your time in hell, you fag.

His eyes are stinging with unshed tears as he walks home, begging himself not to cry over Luka. He just can't fathom it. Luka has a girlfriend. It's the only possible conclusion to their close proximity to one another in the hallway. Luka is dating Willow. Willow, the person he works with. He should have known better than to believe Luka had actually been *flirting* with him. Why would a guy like Luka ever be interested in someone as low on the social scale as Harlan? Harlan is nothing. Barely a blip on the radar of their high school. He feels so fucking naive to have ever let himself be convinced that Luka was actually *interested* in him. He has now made the same mistake twice. Harlan runs his fingers through his dark curls, pulling hard while silently belittling himself with words like 'stupid', 'naive', and 'idiotic'.

Why on Earth would anyone ever be interested in a freak like you?

When he finally gets home, he goes straight to his bedroom, pulling off all of his clothes and jewelry. Sitt neatly folded on his bed are Luka's clothes. He breaks at the sight. He grabs them and throws them across the room, so angry at the reminder of his own stupidity. That day at the park was one of the best days he has had in a long time. He actually felt happy, and he thought...he thought Luka was really flirting with him that day. With the jokes about balls and straddling him and all of that. He was, wasn't he? He watches as the clothes fall to the floor of his bedroom in a small heap, reminding him of when he first put them on. The smell of Luka that had taken over his senses. Fuck.

Maybe this will teach you to fix your wicked ways.

He is shaking when he sits down on the bed, fat tears streaming down his face and landing on his chest, just staring at the stupid fucking clothes. A painful reminder of his own stupidity. Memories from middle school flash through his mind, the faces being replaced by Luka's. He can't breathe, as if something heavy is sitting on his chest. It hurts as he struggles to take in air; his breath is coming out in short puffs. He glances down at the scars littering his forearm, then looks around frantically for a few moments, needing the one thing that could make him feel better, that could take his mind off of the shitshow that is his life. He opens his nightstand and tries to find the only item that will take the pain away. He just needs a physical manifestation of how he is feeling.

God hates you. He hates your kind. You're not worth the dirt you walk on.

After a few moments of rummaging around, his large hand finally lands on his pocketknife, and he pulls it out of his nightstand drawer, using shaking fingers to open the blade. He lets it glint in the natural sunlight of the room, briefly looking at his reflection in the shiny surface. His hair is disheveled, and his eyes are rimmed red. He quickly shuts them, not wanting to see himself or the shame written all over his features. He doesn't even open them or second guess his hasty decision as he brings the blade down to his own alabaster skin, making a fist as he slices a clean and shallow horizontal line onto his forearm. It burns, but it takes his mind away from the pain he is feeling in his chest, which is exactly what he intended.

You're nothing but a filthy fag, an abomination.

He finally opens his eyes to watch the blood pool to the surface, a stark contrast to the paleness of the broken skin around the cut. He lets his tears mingle with the red liquid, the salt making the area burn even more. They mix with the thickness of his blood, thinning it out so it runs down his arm, towards his elbow. As more memories from that night in middle school flash through his mind, he cuts more lesions into his skin, marking the area permanently. He barely feels it, but it is far better than the alternative, which is reliving the worst night of his life. After a few more cuts, he looks down at what he has done, horrified that he let it come to this again. He let someone get to him. He hates himself so fucking much. He deserves this, deserves the pain he's causing himself. It's a punishment for being so fucking stupid, so naive. He made a promise to himself that he would never let anyone get to him again. Never let anyone bring him to this, but here he is, cutting himself again. He's so fucking pathetic.

Someone needs to teach you what's right and wrong.

Suddenly feeling ashamed of his actions, he throws the knife across the room and curls up on his bed in the fetal position under the covers, trying to make himself as small as possible. He covers his ears, attempting to block out the voices in his head. He can't. All he can see are the memories and Luka's small hand wrapped around Willow's waist, fingers stroking her fucking hip. The very same fingers that were tracing his palm just the other day. Fat tears are streaming down his face onto his pillow as his breaths start to come out short and sharp. He presses into the marks on his arm, trying to distract himself, but the action doesn't work.

You're disgusting. You're so fucking stupid for thinking any of this was real.

He can feel himself sinking deeper and deeper, but he doesn't know if he wants to pull himself out of it. He doesn't know if he can. His chest hurts, and he can't breathe. His whole body begins to shake with his sobs, and his vision is starting to get blurry around the edges from lack of air. He is pretty sure he's dying, even though he has been through this before. He closes his eyes as more words are said viciously in his mind, being repeated over and over again like some kind of sick prayer. This time the voice has morphed into a familiar rasp, sounding like silk feels.

*You're a **freak**, a nobody. No one would miss you, you know? I don't know why you don't just do the world a favor and kill yourself, you sick fuck.*

18

"Luka! If you don't get down here right this second, we will be late for the Church Homecoming!" his mom yells up the stairs. Luka sighs, rolling his eyes. He pulls his phone out for the five hundred and seventy-seventh time that day, checking to see if Cadeon has texted him back. He is disappointed to see that he has no new notifications.

Luka didn't miss the pain that passed across Harlan's features when he saw him touching Willow so intimately during lunch on Friday. Harlan disappeared after that. He wasn't in class for the rest of the day, and nobody knew where he had gone. Cadeon had even seemed lost, saying that he had just seen him at lunch, and he seemed fine. Luka couldn't shake the feeling that he had something to do with Harlan's disappearance. He felt sick just thinking about it, desperately wanting to explain everything to him.

He had texted Cadeon a few times, but he hadn't really texted him back. The only thing he had said the first time was that he would check on Harlan, but that was it. Luka is beginning to fear the worst about the whole situation. He really should have talked to Harlan about it first, but he didn't think he would react badly. Harlan always seemed like he didn't care about anyone or anything, so why would he care about this? Luka sighs, rubbing his face. This whole thing is fucked up, and he definitely doesn't want to sit through church service and the church's Homecoming celebration.

"Coming!" Luka finally replies, glancing in the mirror. He looks weary and tired, older than his mere eighteen years. He told his mom and Matt about Willow. They were both very pleased with the news and told him to invite her to dinner next week. Luka didn't really want to think about it, but he is glad Willow knows everything. At least he doesn't have to do more than touch her waist and occasionally hold her hand.

He walks down the stairs, already dreading the coming hours. He's thankful that Ezra will be there to keep him company. When he gets to the bottom of the stairs, he smiles at his sisters, who are dressed in their Sunday best. This church service is going to be a bit different than usual. It is being held later in the afternoon because they are all celebrating with a communal dinner afterwards to commemorate the opening of the church twenty-six years ago. Southern people are so strange.

"Ready to go? Got your Bible?" Matt asks, coming to stand in front of him. Luka nods in response, not really in the mood to talk. They all make a single file line as they head to his parents' van and pile in, Luka and Lizzie strapping Becca and Gabby into their booster seats.

The car is loud, like everything else in Luka's life. It is exhausting constantly being surrounded by people. He rests his head against the window, trying to tune out the noise as he silently wishes he could be alone in his room. It suddenly dawns on him that he has never once in his entire life been truly alone. His parents have never ever left him alone in the house; he is always with them or surrounded by his family. At this moment, Luka wants nothing more than silence.

They arrive at the church quickly. There are an absurd amount of churches in the area for how small the town actually is. There is a church across the street from another church which is beside another church. What is the point in that? They are different denominations, but don't they all believe in and worship the same God? Why does there have to be so many denominations in the same religion? If they are all correct in their beliefs of the same God, then why all of the differences? He wants to ask

Harlan these questions, but he doesn't even know if Harlan is currently speaking to him. He doesn't have Harlan's phone number, so he can't text him. Luka is feeling a level of frustration that he has never felt before.

He gets out of the van, the rest of his siblings following behind him in their dresses, careful not to show anything inappropriate. The fact that his sisters have to wear dresses while he gets to wear actual pants is kind of bullshit to him. Why are women treated so differently in church? He shakes the thought away, eyes going to the marquee located next to the entrance of the red brick building. They change the message out every week, and this time it reads 'Some books are written for our information. The Bible was written for our transformation.' What the fuck does that even mean? They need to fire whichever old lady it is that scours the internet to find these things because that one is terrible.

Luka walks through the doors of the small church, shaking hands with everyone he sees and smiling politely. His smile is genuine when his eyes meet with Ezra's who is sitting next to his mom. They exchange friendly waves then Luka takes his normal seat in the fifth pew back, sitting on the end beside Gabby. He and Lizzie sandwich the two younger girls between them, helping to keep them quiet during the service.

He doesn't blame them. Five-year-olds must be bored out of their skull during something that they don't understand. His mom didn't start going to church until after she met Matt, and then he was forced to go along as well. He was around six at that point. He just remembers constantly being told to sit still and listen to the preacher. It was hard for him. He was always an active child who struggled with sitting in one place. It is still hard for him now, and he is an adult.

Luka sits quietly as the preacher opens the service with a prayer, bowing his head at the appropriate moment and kind of praying along. He usually enjoys church, listening to the songs and singing along. He always likes hearing what the preacher has to say and learning from him, but today he would rather be anywhere but here. Harlan's words and his own research float through his brain as members get up to sing religious songs off key, like *I'll Fly Away* and *Victory in Jesus,* with no music. He sings along, mostly because he knows the songs by heart.

Next, people get up one at a time to sing a song of their choosing, some good singers, others in desperate need of a lesson from Mr. Tennant. After this, one of the preachers in attendance rises from his seat and asks if there are any prayer requests, and so the seemingly unending segment of 'Please pray for my son, he hasn't found God yet, blah blah blah' begins. Great, another fucking prayer. He bows his head again, trying to count how many there are in a single church service. He still isn't sure when the last 'Amen' is said and he is allowed to look up again.

Finally, the first preacher comes up to the altar, starting off with a story about his grandchild seeing a gay couple on television. Fucking great. Luka knows exactly where this is going. In a matter of minutes, the preacher is practically screaming at them. His face resembles the American flag, white skin, lips blue from lack of oxygen, and red blotches all over. Fitting now that Luka thinks about it. His old worn Bible is held in the air above his head as he paces the stage, taking in huge gulps of air every few words or so.

Luka can barely understand what he is saying and wonders if anyone else does as they nod their heads. Occasionally, someone holds up their hand, shouting 'Amen' in agreement. He can pick out yelled words here and there like 'hellfire', 'abomination', 'damnation', and 'Lord', but nothing of substance. It is like he is watching the church service with new eyes. It all seems so strange now that he really considers it.

"So, if you know," the out-of-shape man starts, winding down and breathing heavily with the exertion of screaming. His face is now the color of a tomato, spit on his chin and lips, and breaths coming out in short puffs. It is seriously grossing Luka out and makes him want to hurl. He briefly wonders if the man is going to go into cardiac arrest, then surprises himself when he realizes he may not want to actually call an ambulance for him.

"So, if you know someone who is suffering from the disease that is homosexuality, bring them in and let the Lord's saving grace heal them. May He lay His healing hands on their skin and repair their mind to His ways. Through Him, they will see light and salvation. So, pray for them. Pray that they see the flaw in their filthy ways and seek out the Lord for deliverance." Luka barely suppresses an eye roll when he hears several people say 'Amen', Matt raising his hand to the ceiling when the word leaves his lips.

"That's all the preaching that we will have today, seein' as we still need to celebrate Homecoming. Women, you are excused to go and serve the food. The rest of you, please come up and sing while we pass around the collection plate; any money given is a donation to God and His word." Luka watches the women, including his mother and sisters, file out of the church to do as they are told. Luka thinks it is completely unfair that the women are dismissed to serve the food. Why do he and Matt get to sit here and listen to the rest of the sermon while his mom and sisters have to go and set up the table for them to eat? It seems like sexist bullshit to him.

Some of the remaining members of the congregation walk up to the altar and begin singing even more old church hymns as the preacher stands in front of the pulpit yelling, yet again, about being saved and giving your heart to the Lord. A gold collection plate is being passed around and filled with money. Matt drops a fifty-dollar bill in it when it gets into his hands.

Luka thinks of all the better ways Matt could spend that fifty dollars, all of the meals he could buy for starving children. In-stead, it is going into the pocket of some preacher to keep the lights on in one of the many churches located in the area. Luka sighs in relief when he bows his head for the last prayer, thanking the heavens that it is almost over. Yes, he realizes the irony in that sentiment, but it is what it is.

"Hey, how are ya?" Ezra asks when everyone gets up from their seats and begins exiting the sanctuary to walk to the adjacent building where the food is being served.

"I'm okay, I suppose," Luka answers, not wanting to tell him that he now has a migraine from the stupid shit the preacher was spouting. He is pretty sure that wouldn't go over too well with Ezra and all of the nosey people crowded around them. He thinks that a plastic surgeon would make a killing in this town, seeing as everyone has big noses that they place firmly in everyone else's business. Then again, he would probably starve to death from lack of work since none of them seemingly want to change. They can easily see what they deem the error of the general population's ways but could never see their own sins. It is ridiculous, really. He follows Ezra as they make their way into the auxiliary building, the smell of home-cooked food hitting Luka's nostrils and making his stomach growl.

"Delbert will be here to bless the food in just a moment," a woman tells them when Luka reaches for a plate. Oh yes, he forgot. He can't fucking eat without God's blessing. Please forgive him. Finally, the preacher from earlier, Delbert, arrives and says grace, Luka bowing his head simply because he doesn't want Matt to notice if he doesn't. He and Ezra talk about football as they make their way through the line, piling their plates high with food. If nothing else, at least these people can cook.

They find a seat at a table by themselves, but it doesn't stay that way for long. A group of five old women sit at the long table with them, discussing the most recent sermon. Luka knows them all. One of them is Delbert's wife and the others are married to various men of power at the church. Luka tunes them out while he eats, answering Ezra's questions on the made-up story about how he met Willow. Well, it's not really made-up, but he skillfully eliminated the details of their deal.

"You know who I think needs Jesus? That Harlan Sharp boy," one of the old ladies says, moving her fork around in the air with the statement. Luka's ears prick up Harlan's name is on the lady's lips. He glances over at Ezra, who also seems to be listening intently to their conversation.

"Oh. That boy who wears them there tight pants and black clothes? He's kind of funny, ain't he? Not right, I tell ya," Ruth replies, beady eyes watching as all the women nod in agreement. What the fuck does that even mean? He's kind of funny? As in, he has a good sense of humor? Luka doesn't think that's what they are referring to in this case, though.

He thinks it's some weird Southern phrase that he will need to add to his fucking list, since he has never heard that term before. He's beginning to think his definition of funny is very different from theirs because there is malice in Ruth's voice when she says it, her tone dripping with disdain. Almost as though she believes she's too good to say the actual word she wants to use. As if the word itself will taint her blessed soul.

"I think that boy's queerer than a football bat, mark my words on that 'un. He's got the devil in him," Esther agrees, nodding her head while she puts a fork full of green beans in her mouth, chewing slowly. She probably doesn't want her dentures to fall out. So that's what the phrase 'kind of funny' means. It means she thinks Harlan is gay. Queerer than a football bat? Who comes up with this shit? Luka can feel the anger rising in his chest, gripping his throat like a vice. How dare these women talk about Harlan when he can't even defend himself. So, what if he wears tight pants and black clothes? That doesn't make him bad in any way. Or necessarily gay, for that matter.

"I'd have a hissy fit if he were my son. I would make him straighten up. Doesn't make a lick of sense why his momma would let him act that way," Thelma adds, the other women making sounds of approval. Is a 'hissy fit' the equivalent to a tantrum? Luka wants to scream at every single one of these despicable excuses for good Christian women. He bites his tongue to hold the words in, the metallic taste of blood filling his mouth. He chances a glance at Ezra, who looks just as angry, a fire behind his dark eyes.

"I agree. He is gayer than a two-dollar bill. He is going straight to hell in a handbasket if he don't change his wicked ways, though." Glady's decrepit and blotched hands are shaking as she scoops up some chicken and dumplings with her fork, bringing the food to her wrinkled lips. She shakes her head, and Luka wonders if her fake hairpiece is going to go flying off and land in her food. Why on earth would anyone go to hell in a handbasket? What the fuck does that even mean? He can feel his cheeks heating up with his anger. He just wants to yell at them to mind their own fucking business, but he can't. Matt would ground him for a month if he even so much as utters a single word to defend someone like Harlan. Someone like himself.

"It's 'cause he's from a broken home. He don't have a father to beat him like a red-headed stepchild for acting that way," Flossie says around a mouth full of food, spitting the contents all over her plate and the table in front of her. Luka barely suppresses a grimace. Beat him for being himself? What the fuck does a ginger child who was adopted have to do with this? Was it really necessary to bring Harlan's family into this? Why do these people have to be so hypocritical? He is sure their hands aren't clean. They aren't perfect and sin-free. The more Luka thinks about it, the angrier he gets.

"All we can do is pray for his wicked soul. Pray that the Holy Father helps him see the error in his ways and brings him into the church. Bless his heart," Esther says, bowing her head and shaking it, as if it is the most despicable thing she had ever heard. How dare they talk about Harlan like that. They don't know him. They wouldn't even want to get to know him. He just dresses in dark clothes and wears tight jeans. Neither of those things make him gay. Even if he is gay, why does it matter? There are way worse things that a person could be. He could be a pedophile, or he could torture puppies in his free time. Gay isn't bad. Is it?

"I think I need some air," Luka mumbles to Ezra, getting up from the table, leaving his half-eaten food behind. He goes outside, breathing in the humid air, trying to calm his racing mind and tamp down the anger. He is physically shaking from his rage, wanting to strangle those old women, as terrible as that sounds. It's just that...they had no right to talk about Harlan like that. They don't even know him. Why does he have to go to hell for being different? Is he doing anything wrong? Is Luka doing anything wrong? Is there something inherently evil about loving a person of the same sex? Luka used to think so, but now he isn't so sure.

If there is one thing Harlan has taught him, it's that religion is flawed. Luka closes his eyes against the questions racing through his mind. He can feel his eyes stinging with unshed tears, frustrating him even further. He is helpless and confused. He hits the brick wall of the church in anger and cries out when pain shoots through his hand and up his arm.

At least it's a fucking distraction from his thoughts: Harlan, the church, fucking everything. He blinks away tears of pain and anger, willing himself not to cry. His mom or Matt could come out looking for him at any second, and he has no idea what he would say to them. He certainly can't tell them the truth. 'Sorry, Mom and Matt. I came out here because those old bitches were talking badly about a guy that I am completely falling for. The whole thing is incredibly frustrating because I can't tell how he feels about me. Oh yeah, by the way, I am going to hell for liking men. Apparently in a handbasket, whatever the fuck that means.' He could never ever say that. He doesn't even know if he can admit half of it to himself yet.

"You alright, man?" Luka hears Ezra's voice behind him. Luka takes a deep breath and puts his now bleeding and shaking hand down to his side. Fuck, what has his life become? Before they came to this godforsaken town, he thought he knew everything. He knew that God was real and would love him after he apologized for his sins of being with men. He was supposed to find a good Christian wife to settle down with, have their 2.5 perfect children, and live the fucking American dream. Now everything has changed. His whole world is tilted on its axis, and he is so fucking dizzy.

He should hate Harlan. He should blame him for all of this, but he can't because Luka asked the fucking questions. Harlan even warned him and made sure he truly wanted to know. He said he did and what an overconfident idiot he was. He thought nothing Harlan could say would change his mind because he had faith.

Faith in a church that hates him. Faith in a God that would send him to hell for love. He had faith, and he thought that with faith, nothing could shake him. He can't blame Harlan for telling him the fucking truth. He tightens his good hand into a fist, frustrated with everything. He thought he had faith in his heart, but now he isn't so sure. He isn't sure of anything, and he wants to scream. He blinks a few times before he turns to his friend, pasting on what he hopes to be a reassuring smile.

"Yeah. I'm fine. I just needed some air, I think," Luka tells him. It's not a lie. He did need air; he just hopes it is convincing enough. He can tell by the look on Ezra's face that he failed. It is not. Fuck.

"Look, man." Ezra's dark eyebrows draw together in worry, eyes looking at him tenderly. Luka takes a deep breath, completely unsure of where this conversation is going to go. "I heard what they were saying about Harlan. I know he's your friend, kind of. I'm sorry they were being like that."

"It's fine. Not your fault. Plus, Harlan is barely my friend. Sure, we talk occasionally, but that's about it," Luka lies because what else is he supposed to do? He isn't embarrassed by Harlan, but he also doesn't know if he trusts Ezra enough to not tell his parents. He is terrified of his parents, Matt more specifically.

"Lu, I know you talk more than occasionally. You constantly pass notes in class. You're the only person he doesn't openly ignore besides Cadeon," Ezra says, a small knowing smile on his lips. Fuck. He didn't know he was being that obvious. If Ezra noticed, then how many people at school did? How long would it be before it got back to his family?

That Luka was friends with a guy some of the people in the church think is...what were the terms? 'Kind of funny', 'queerer than a football bat', and his favorite 'gayer than a two-dollar bill'. Maybe they won't hear or believe the old women. His parents are the type to prefer living in blissful ignorance than cold hard truth. They would probably convince themselves that he was a fine young man, despite the clothes. They may not have even heard the old ladies talking. He may be panicking for nothing.

"I'm sorry. It just pissed me off. Like, they don't even know him, Ez, and they were talking about him when he wasn't even there to defend himself!" Luka can feel the anger rising in his throat, gripping at his heart for a second time. He tightens his hands into fists again, wincing at the pain in his right hand.

"It made me angry, too. I get it. In fact, after you left, I might have told them that it wasn't very Christianly to gossip about teenage boys. They were appalled, but I don't care." Ezra shrugs, and for the first time in his shitty fucking day, Luka smiles. He is so happy he could kiss him, if Ezra were his type that is, but it seems his only type is green eyes, curly hair, intellect, and dark clothes. Go figure.

"Thank you, Ez. Fuck, thank you," Luka says, beaming at his friend now. Ezra's features break into a smile of his own.

"You're welcome. Maybe Harlan won't hate me if he finds out." Ezra laughs. Luka doesn't think Harlan hates Ezra. He just doesn't trust him. Luka is pretty sure that Harlan currently hates him, though, which hurts him more than he thinks he can admit.

"He probably likes you better than he likes me," Luka mumbles, looking down.

"Look, I don't know what happened on Friday, but I could tell you were worried about him. I'm sure he doesn't hate you, though. I meant what I said. You're the only person in school he doesn't glare at for so much as looking in his direction besides Cadeon. That's gotta count for something, right?" Ezra reassures him, smiling when Luka finally looks up.

"I hope so," Luka responds, not entirely convinced by Ezra's words, but at least his friend tried.

"Come on. Let's go in and get that hand of yours cleaned up, then go back in there and eat so our parents don't notice," Ezra says, looking down at Luka's now throbbing hand. He has blood dripping down his fingers, hitting the gravel beside his feet. He didn't mind the pain at the time; it was a good distraction. Now it just hurts, but it is still serving as a distraction to his inner turmoil. He just nods and follows Ezra inside.

19

Harlan feels sick as he walks to work on Sunday. He will be seeing Willow since he is relieving her for the afternoon. She has evening church service with her family, of fucking course. That's probably why Luka likes her. She is a perfect little church girl. Three things that he can't be. Three things that make him the total opposite of her.

They probably met in the Bible Club. She's probably a virgin and clings to the old, rugged cross with her purity ring perfectly intact on her finger. Probably the type that doesn't say the word 'shit' because it's dirty, and the 's' stands for Satan or something equally ridiculous. She most likely cries in Biology class when evolution is discussed and firmly believes both Darwin and Obama are the Antichrist. Fuck. She probably makes a cake on Christmas because she believes it to be Jesus' birthday, which it isn't.

It isn't logical to blame her. She isn't a bad person. He has talked to her a few times since starting at the shop, but they haven't really worked together yet. She seems cool, which makes Harlan somehow angrier. He doesn't think she is overly popular, not the type to date a jock, but still, she is dating a jock. His jock. Fuck. No. Luka isn't his. He never was, it seems. Harlan is a fucking moron for ever believing differently. Again. He did it again.

At least this time he didn't get physically hurt. Well, no more than what he inflicted on himself. He glances down, making sure the sleeves of his shirt are covering the new marks. They are. Thankfully, it is getting cooler now, so he will be able to wear long sleeves more often. He pulls himself from his dark thoughts as he swings the door to the shop open. It is usually pretty slow on Sundays, given that it's 'God's day' and all, but Mac doesn't seem to care about that. Thank the gods.

"Hey, Harlan. Good to see you." Willow smiles at him, looking unsure of her words. She must have noticed him on Friday. Fuck. That means Luka must have noticed, too. Great. That's all he fucking needs. Thankfully, Luka doesn't have his cell number, and he threatened Cadeon by life and limb if he so much as even considered giving it to him. Cadeon is a good friend. He keeps texting him, but Harlan keeps ignoring it, ashamed that he went back to his old habits.

Cadeon is the only person in the world that knows about it. Well, his mom kind of knows, but she doesn't know the extent of it. Cadeon even went as far as coming over to his house yesterday, but he pretended not to be home. Instead, he laid in his bed and ignored the constant knocking for twenty minutes until Cadeon gave up. He is being cruel to his friend, but he just can't deal. He just can't. He doesn't want to think about it, and he sure as shit doesn't want to see the disappointment written all over Cadeon's face. The pity. Harlan hates pity.

"Is it true?" Harlan blurts out, not knowing what else to say to his coworker. It is the question that has been on his mind for the past few days. The only thing he can think of, besides the words to belittle himself and old memories he is trying to suppress.

He spent the rest of Friday and all of Saturday mostly in bed or writing in his journal, attempting to get his feelings on paper. He barely got up to eat, but that is mostly because they didn't have any food in the house. His mom was home for a few hours on Saturday. He was surprised when she asked him if he was okay since she usually ignores his very existence. He lied. Of course, he lied. She didn't need the added burden of a fucked-up son. She already had that once.

"Is what true?" Willow stutters out.

"You know what I'm talking about. Don't play dumb with me. Is it true that you're dating Luka fucking Thomas?" He asks, his anger rising and threatening to suffocate him. He knows she isn't dumb, and he doesn't appreciate people avoiding his questions. He is the only person allowed to avoid questions, thank you very much. His hands are clenched into fists as she stutters again, looking down at them and looking back up at him, brown eyes large with fear.

"Harlan. I... I think that is s-something you need to ask Luka," she responds, quickly grabbing her jacket and running for the door. "Um...I'll see you at school tomorrow. I'm sorry. Talk to Luka and let him explain. Bye." Before Harlan can utter another sentence, she is gone. What the fuck? He doesn't need to talk to Luka. In fact, he would be perfectly content never seeing the bastard's face ever again. What does she mean by 'explain'? What the fuck would Luka have to explain? Harlan feels sick just thinking about it, more questions than answers floating around in his mind.

He sighs, looking around the now empty shop. He is just so fucking tired. He hasn't slept in the last two days, insomnia kicking in full force. He doesn't even know how he is still standing and breathing. More importantly, he doesn't know *why* he is. He feels absent, like he is living his life from outside his own body, simply going through the motions.

He doesn't really feel anything anymore, closing himself off from the outside world, from people like Luka. Mostly he feels like he is watching his life being played out in a movie, not really living it. It is welcome. This way he doesn't have to think, just watch himself go through the motions of his own existence. A pathetic existence at that.

At first, he felt betrayed and stupid, victim to a blinding anger that almost consumed him. Now, he is simply numb. Numb to the pain and the hurt. Numb to the reality that he was stupid enough to put himself in this position again. He made a promise to himself that he would never let anything like this happen to him again, and yet, he had fallen for the new kid. With his bright blue eyes, his wide, perfect smile, and his endless fucking questions that Harlan had been unable to ignore.

It is he who bears the scars of that choice, of the decision to put his faith and trust in Luka. Faith. There is that stupid fucking word again. Faith is for people who actually want to believe in something. Faith is for sheep, and Harlan will not be a fucking sheep. Harlan should never have had faith in anyone or anything except truth, facts, science, and himself. Luka fucking Thomas does not fit into any of those categories.

It is unfathomable that he actually began to allow himself to believe that Luka really was different from all the others. That he saw the real him. The Harlan that he hid away from the world. The part of himself that so desperately wanted to be set free but never could be. He let himself believe that Luka genuinely saw that in him, saw past the brick walls he'd so carefully erected all those years ago.

Luka had put a crack in one of those walls, letting sunlight through for the first time in years, and now Harlan's heart and mind are in tatters. Harlan deserves this. He deserves what he got because he is stupid. He deserves to pay for his misplaced faith and trust. He should know better. So yes, Harlan deserves this. He deserves the pain, the cuts, and the scars. The marks that will serve as punishment and a reminder of his own stupidity. He thought he had enough of those, but it seems he didn't learn his lesson the first time.

Slipping on the mask again is easy. He never should have let his guard down in the first place. Should never have let someone in. How could he be foolish enough to let someone see him without his mask firmly in place, even though it was mere moments in time? Luka still saw it, though. He still saw Harlan smile and laugh. He still had knowledge of the intimate details of Harlan's existence. It still happened. He just hopes that Luka won't use it against him now. It was stupid on his part. Pure fucking stupidity. He doesn't know if he has ever hated himself more.

The first time was a mistake of his own naivete. This time, though, he has no excuse. What is the old saying? Oh yeah: Fool him once, shame on them. Fool him twice, shame on him. Fuck. He just wants to sleep because it is the only time that he is free from the thoughts swirling around in his mind, but that won't be happening any time soon. His brain won't shut off, so after his shift he will probably go home and just stare at the walls for hours, trying not to think of blue eyes, freckled cheeks, or a bright, crinkly-eyed smile.

20

Harlan skipped school on both Monday and Tuesday. It is now Wednesday, and Luka is biting on his fingers anxiously, waiting to see if Harlan will walk through the door. When he asked Cadeon where Harlan had been, the other boy just said he was sick and left it at that. Something about that excuse doesn't sit right with Luka, though.

His stomach churns in knots at the idea of Harlan being upset because of him, *with* him. Fuck. This whole fucking situation is a mess. He rubs his hands up and down his face, feeling the bandage on his right-hand scratch at his skin as if it's trying to rub away the remnants of this hellish week, starting with last Friday. It doesn't work. No matter how hard he tries, he can't shake the feeling that something is wrong with Harlan. He feels sick thinking about it. Fuck.

His head snaps up when the door opens, eyes landing on Harlan's tall frame. He is wearing a long-sleeved, plain gray t-shirt, a pair of skinny jeans, and black boots. His hair is a tangled mess, as if he tossed and turned in his sleep, black beanie perched on top of his curls, covering most of them. His skin is pale, and his face looks gaunt, like he hasn't eaten or slept in days. His eyes, though. His eyes send a painful pang through Luka's heart. They are hollow, almost as if he has pulled away from the world itself, and bloodshot, the green contrasting with the red, with deep bags under them. His lips are still red, so fucking red, Luka just wants to kiss them.

Luka tries to get Harlan's attention as he walks through the door, but Harlan ignores him completely, taking a seat beside

Cadeon with his head down, headphones firmly in place. Luka's heart drops when he realizes he may be back to square one with Harlan. All of the time and effort he put into trying to break through Harlan's walls has gone to waste. Harlan has sealed up any cracks Luka managed to make with fucking concrete, closing himself off once again.

Harlan obviously hates him, this time with good reason. Luka wants to scream or cry or hit something...or maybe all three. Anything to relieve the tightness in his chest. Fuck. He doesn't even know if he can get Harlan to speak to him. The other boy isn't even talking to Cadeon. Luka forces away tears and tries to ignore the knot in his stomach as Mr. Tennent starts speaking.

Luka spends the rest of the day being completely ignored by Harlan, the other boy even going as far as to change his seat in all of their shared classes, preferring to sit with the nerdy kids over Luka, Cadeon, and Ezra. Luka is so upset by the end of the day, he's sure his heart may stop beating at any minute, and his stomach feels like it was left in the lunchroom on Friday when this shitstorm began.

He never meant to hurt Harlan, and he hates himself for doing so. He had just gotten him to smile around him, too. He thought he was making strides in their friendship, leading to possibly more, but Matt had to go and fuck that up. Matt is destined to fuck Luka's entire life up at the rate he is going. Just as Luka is finishing football practice, he sees Willow and runs to meet her, waving to her as he approaches.

"Any luck?" She asks, her brown eyes large and hopeful. She told him about her conversation with Harlan at the music store on Sunday. She figured out that Harlan was the one Luka had a crush on from there. Luka is just shocked that Harlan asked her about it. That should have been his clue that Harlan had been upset about the whole situation, but he ignorantly believed that Harlan would actually allow Luka to speak to him.

Luka desperately wants to clear this up and tell Harlan the

reason why he is dating Willow, but he can't. Harlan won't even so much as look at him, and telling Harlan means telling another person that he is attracted to men. He doesn't know if he can. As of now, the only person in his life that knows is Willow. Can he really tell someone else the secret he has been hiding for so long? He only suspects that Harlan is just like him, but he doesn't *know*.

"No," Luka sighs, blinking back tears for the one hundred and sixty third time that day. How did everything get so fucked up? It was going so well.

"He'll come around eventually. You just need to get him to talk to you," Willow reassures, placing a comforting hand on his bicep.

"Even if I did, what the fuck would I say?" Luka asks, closing his eyes and wishing to go back in time. To talk to Harlan before all of this happened. Why the fuck was he so stupid?

"The truth?" Willow says with a questioning tone.

"What if...what if he isn't like me?" Luka finally asks the question that has been plaguing him since this morning. This is the first chance he has gotten to voice it, being alone outside with the one person in the world that knows his secret.

"Do you really think he would be acting this way if he didn't have some sort of feelings for you? He couldn't mask the hurt in his eyes when he asked me about it on Sunday," Willow reasons, trying to get Luka to look her in the eyes.

"No. I can't think of another reason for him to be so upset with me. I literally did nothing wrong. Maybe I did, and I didn't even realize it. Maybe I have missed the mark completely, and he isn't mad at me for dating someone," he responds, searching Willow's brown eyes for answers he can only find in green ones. He feels so confused about the whole fucked-up situation. He racks his brain for anything that could have happened before lunch on Friday. Anything at all, but he comes up short. He literally can't think of anything else that could be bothering Harlan.

"I don't think you've missed the mark, Lu. I really don't," Willow says earnestly, like she really believes her words. Luka wishes he could, but he just doesn't know.

"What if it has nothing to do with me, and he is just having family issues or something? Like, what if I'm jumping to conclusions, and I'm totally wrong, then I tell him about how I feel?" Luka is rambling, coming up with the most outrageous scenarios, but he can't help it.

He doesn't know if he can actually tell Harlan. He has no idea why he decided to pursue the other boy in the first place. It's not like him to do so. All of the previous times he has been with men, it was in a dark room with a practical stranger, the thumping music from the party outside drowning out any thoughts of sin. They would drunkenly grope each other, eventually leading to some kind of sexual experience. Luka would leave without so much as giving his name. He never saw them again, and he preferred it that way. They were never more than that. Sex. A means to scratch an itch he had.

Harlan is different, though. Luka has been actively pursuing him. Harlan knows his name. Harlan knows his face and where he lives. Fuck. Harlan even knows his family. He never thought much about the day he would actually have to tell someone. Maybe he believed that Harlan would be the first to come out with it, literally, but that was a false hope. Getting Harlan to tell him his name was like pulling teeth, so why was Luka delusional enough to believe Harlan would have told him first?

"What if I was totally wrong all along, and he finds out and tells the whole fucking school? What if he tells my parents?" He asks, eyes stinging with tears, frustrated by everything.

"That's just a chance you have to be willing to take. Is he worth the risk?" Willow asks, and that is a good fucking question.

Is Harlan Sharp worth the risk? His brain is screaming 'no'. His heart, though, has been in physical pain all day from this, each thought of Harlan sending another stab right where it hurts. His fucking heart says 'yes.' Just picturing Harlan smiling again makes it float like a bubble on the breeze but the moment he thinks of the opposite, the bubble bursts.

"Maybe I should just let him be upset and forget about him. I never thought of what would actually come of this. That I would have to tell him, and I don't know if I can. I just don't. Maybe this is the perfect opportunity to put it all behind me with my secret perfectly intact."

He just feels like such an idiot, like he should have actually thought about it before he even considered flirting with Harlan. What the hell had he been thinking? He wasn't, and that is the problem. He is so fucking stupid. His head hurts with the endless questions, and his heart hurts from the whole fucking situation. He just wants to go home and sleep, but he can't.

"Are you really going to let your own fear make the decision for you?" Willow asks, her tone stern, like this is something she is passionate about.

Luka almost throws Tabitha in her face. Willow certainly won't tell Tabitha about her feelings, but Luka would never do that. Willow and Tabitha are in a completely different situation, and it would be unfair to compare them. Plus, Willow is just trying to help. She is the only person he can talk to and be honest with, and he fears pissing her off because she knows enough to bury him. Literally, since Matt would probably kill him if he ever found out.

"I don't know," he says finally, biting his lip. He takes a deep breath in through his nose, as if the fresh air will make his heart stop aching. It doesn't. Nothing seems to help. He has even tried praying about it, which sounds stupid in hindsight because he is praying over a man that he has feelings for, and God would never answer a prayer that could lead to sin.

Maybe this is all happening because God is trying to teach him a lesson. God wants him to know that he shouldn't be questioning his faith, and he shouldn't be lusting after a man. He knows it's wrong, so maybe this is his punishment. Maybe he deserves this pain and heartache for being attracted to someone of the same sex. This could be a sign from God telling him he should stop. The idea makes him want to cry.

The very thought takes him back to church on Sunday when those hypocritical old women were saying those awful things about Harlan. He was angry for Harlan at the time, but also for himself. They may as well have been talking about him, but he can't help but wonder if this is God's way of telling him that he shouldn't be with Harlan. Harlan acting this way and ignoring him is a sign that he should never have been attracted to him in the first place.

The pain in his chest and gut serve as a harsh reminder that his desire is an abomination against God, a direct violation of His holy word. Everything in the universe kind of points to it right now, doesn't it? The church service about homosexuality, Luka questioning his faith, and now Harlan being upset with him all adds up to God being angry. He may not approve of their union together, but Luka wants them to be together. Why aren't they allowed to be together like couples of the opposite sex? Why can't they be the same?

"Just...just think about it," she tells him, snapping Luka out of his turbulent thoughts.

She looks him in the eye, gives him a small smile, then pulls him in for a hug. This is the most they have touched, but fuck, he needs it. He is so lost, and even worse, he is alone. He would normally talk to Harlan when he is questioning his faith, but Harlan won't speak to him. Bringing him back again, full-fucking-circle, to his previous conclusion. God doesn't want them to be together.

"Thanks, Will," Luka says, returning her hug, sinking into her warmth. He pulls away slowly, leaving his hand on her arms. "Ready to go to my house for dinner? Meet the parents?" He freezes after he says the last words, eyes trained behind Willow.

Harlan is already quickly walking away from them, down the street. He doesn't have his headphones in, and Luka is almost sure Harlan heard the question. Panic is gripping his throat. What if he heard the entire fucking conversation? What if he now knows Luka's secret? Oh, God. Luka is going to be sick. He barely ate lunch, and now it is most certainly going to come back up at any moment. Fuck.

"What?" Willow asks, feeling Luka change in posture and demeanor. She looks around, spotting Harlan's quickly retreating form. "Oh, shit."

"Oh, shit indeed," Luka says, debating about running after his...well, he isn't sure what Harlan is to him anymore. He isn't sure if they were ever really friends. He decides not to run after him because Harlan obviously doesn't want to speak to him, and his parents are already going to be angry at him for being late, since his conversation with Willow put them five minutes behind. With a sigh, he starts walking towards his car, Willow following silently behind him. Luka takes the few minutes they have during the car ride home to prepare Willow for what is to come, which also takes his mind off the Harlan situation for the first time today.

21

"Mom, Matt! We're here," Luka yells, announcing their presence as soon as they walk through the door. He offers Willow an encouraging smile before he turns back towards the noise of someone entering the area.

"Luka. I told you not to call me that, especially not in front of guests. You are to call me Dad or Father," Matt warns, and Luka barely suppresses an eyeroll. He hates calling Matt either of those titles because he simply doesn't deserve it, in Luka's eyes.

He has been trying to change Luka since the very moment he married his mother. He wants to mold Luka into his ideal son, which is something Luka doesn't think he is capable of being. He will never be the perfect son in Matt's eyes, and honestly, he is getting tired of trying. It is difficult being a constant disappointment to the only man who has ever resembled a father figure to him. He is too short, his voice too high-pitched, his actions too feminine. Luka is honestly surprised he hasn't ended up in military school to 'toughen him up', like Matt has threatened in the past. He has a suspicion that his mom has something to do with him still being in public school.

It has only been recently that Luka began referring to him by his actual name in conversation, which has just served to piss Matt off even more. Luka may or may not do it for that reason, though. Anything to help him feel like he has control over his own life, even something as small as calling Matt by his given name and not a title he doesn't deserve.

He would much rather refer to Matt with a title like 'asshole', 'shitprick', or his personal favorite, 'fuckstick', since those are titles Matt deserves. He would be murdered if he so much as even muttered those words anywhere near Matt, since they are curse words, and he isn't allowed to swear. Matt does it, but he is a fucking hypocrite. He is a 'do as I say and not as I do' kind of 'leader', so Luka doesn't even want to consider what Matt would do to him if he called him any of those names.

"I'm sorry," Luka mumbles, looking down at the floor. He decides to toe off his shoes, so it doesn't seem like he is avoiding Matt's gaze, even though that is definitely what he is doing.

"You must be Willow. Luka has told us so much about you," Josie greets, coming to stand beside Matt, smiling at Willow warmly and shaking her hand. Luka's mom really is amazing and caring. He has no idea why she chose to marry someone like Matt. Financial security. That has to be it.

"Yup. That's me," Willow responds, smiling nervously, then moving to shake Matt's hand. "Thank you for having me, Mr. and Mrs. Thomas."

"Please, call me Josie," she waves off.

"You may refer to me as Mr. Thomas," Matt replies, standing so tensely, that stick lodged so firmly up his ass that it will never ever have the chance to come out and see the light of day. That poor fucking stick. What a terrible existence. Being in a dark place, gripped tightly, with no light for the rest of its life. Luka kind of feels its pain, though, since most days he leads a similar existence.

Luka glances over at Willow, watching as she barely conceals a grimace at Matt's comment. Maybe Harlan can teach her how to better hide her facial expressions, if Harlan ever talks to either one of them again, that is. Fuck, at this point, he will be lucky if Willow doesn't call this whole shitshow off within the hour.

"Well. Dinner is ready," Josie says, somewhat breaking the tension that has built in the room.

"Yes. Hopefully, it is not cold, since Luka seems to have taken his time getting you two here." Just like that, the tension is back tenfold. Matt turns towards the dining room without another comment. Luka tries to offer Willow a reassuring smile as they follow Matt and Josie into the dining room.

"Lu! You're here!" Gabby exclaims from the table, causing the rest of his sisters to look at them.

"Yup, love. We just got here." Luka smiles at his sisters. They always put him in a better mood.

"Who's that?" Becca asks, pointing at Willow.

"It's not nice to point, Rebecca," Matt reprimands, and Luka very much wants to punch him. She is a child. It is normal to be curious, but heaven forbid she actually asks a question. Literally, it seems as though heaven actually forbids questions.

"This is Willow, my girlfriend," Luka introduces, smiling at his sister, deciding to ignore Matt's comment completely.

"Oh. What about Harlan?" Becca asks, her blue eyes wide, expression innocent. Luka freezes, though. Fuck. Maybe his parents didn't hear the question. At least he hopes they didn't.

"Who's Harlan, darling?" Josie questions, curiosity lacing her words.

"He's just a friend from school. I saw him at the park the other day when I took the girls to play," Luka supplies, trying to stay as close to the truth as possible.

"Harlan's pretty," Gabby adds, as if that is the most important fact about the entire experience, and she can't believe Luka would have left that out.

"Gabby, honey, boys aren't pretty. They are handsome. Only girls can be pretty, so please never use that word to describe a boy again," Matt chastises, and Luka wants to punch something again because boys can most definitely be pretty. Harlan, for example, is very pretty. Beautiful, even. Handsome doesn't sum up how good Harlan looks, and it would be a travesty of justice for someone to use that word to describe him.

"Lu, you've never mentioned a Harlan. You should bring him around some time for dinner. Where do his parents go to church?" Josie asks, smiling at him. Fuck. What is he supposed to say? 'No, Mom. I don't think Harlan's parents go to church. Harlan's an atheist who doesn't believe in God.'

"Um...we haven't really talked about that," Luka responds, face heating with the lie while thinking of other things they have discussed. Fuck, he needs to get a grip.

"Then what do you talk about?" Matt asks, as if the very idea of talking about anything other than church and God is absurd. To be fair, he and Harlan have spoken about it and on more than one occasion, discussing both of those topics in a way he never could with either of his parents.

"Mostly about classes. He's really smart. He occasionally helps me with my physics homework during our free period," Luka lies again, this one coming much easier. Harlan *is* really smart, so it isn't that unbelievable.

"Oh. Well, maybe he could tutor you or something. I know you have been struggling in that class. Perhaps a study partner will do you some good," Josie tells him. Fuck, now the only thing Luka can imagine is he and Harlan alone in his room, 'studying' on his bed. Harlan's long limbs would make his bed look small, his pale skin a stark contrast to the dark blue of the comforter and sheets. Luka licks his lips, telling his dick to calm down. He shouldn't be thinking these sinful thoughts since his heart is already being punished for them in the first place.

"Yeah. Maybe. Anyways, Willow, these are my sisters: Lizzie, Mary, Becca, and Gabby," Luka introduces them, quickly changing the subject, pointing to each girl as he says their name. He knows that Willow is probably starting to feel awkward with the conversation straying towards Harlan, and he doesn't want that. She is doing him a huge favor, after all.

"Well, sit down everyone," Josie says, motioning for them to take a seat. Willow looks confused when they all begin holding hands as soon as they sit down, preparing to say grace. Luka reaches for her hand, giving her a small smile. Her hand feels weird in his, mostly because it's not large and adorned with rings.

His mind flashes back to the day he wrote his initial on Harlan's hand, remembering how warm and big it felt in his own. That felt right, but this...this feels wrong on so many different levels. It's not the first time he has held hands with Willow, but it will never fail to make him internally cringe. It is nothing against her at all. She is a beautiful girl, and Tabitha is very lucky to have her. He just hates it. Hates that he has to pretend. Hates that he has to force himself to be someone and something that he's not.

"God. We thank you, our Heavenly Father, for providing us with this feast," Matt starts as soon as Willow's hand is in Luka's, and Luka bows his head, praying along. "We also thank you for our health and happiness. Thank you for bringing Willow into Luka's life, so that she may sit down with us for this meal you have provided. We thank you for everything you graciously do for us every day. May we always follow in your footsteps on the path to righteousness. In Jesus' name we pray. Amen."

"Amen," they all mumble, dropping each other's hands as Matt finishes. He hates how much Matt is showing off for Willow's benefit. He normally just says the same prayer before every single meal, but of course he had to include her in this particular blessing. The irony of his stepdad's words seep deep into his bones, making him shiver a bit. If Matt really knew what brought Willow into his life, he would have an aneurysm. Perhaps Luka should break the news after all.

"So, Willow, what church do your parents go to?" Matt asks as everyone starts eating their meal. Of course, he would ask her that, since it seems to be the only thing he cares about.

"Oh...umm...United Baptist," Willow answers, taking a bite of her green beans.

"That's the church we almost joined," Josie says, smiling at Willow's answer, seemingly happy with her choice.

"Yes. I recall. We decided against it, though, since one of the preachers is an Obama sympathizer," Matt tells her, like he is defending their decision not to join her church.

"Oh...umm...I didn't know that." Willow is obviously uncomfortable with the conversation, but Matt doesn't seem to give a fuck, plowing on as if Willow hadn't spoken.

"Tell your parents. They need to know, so they can switch churches. I don't understand why anyone would actually support Obama," Matt continues, and fuck, here he goes again. Luka buckles his imaginary seat belt and bites his tongue, ready for the inevitable. He knew this would happen, but that doesn't make it any less embarrassing.

Matt's face is already beginning to redden with his anger as he continues, "He is the antichrist, I tell you. He wanted to take our guns and disband the military! Give all of our jobs to those *aliens* south of the border. Did you know he refused to swear in on the Bible? Yeah, he wanted to swear in on the Quran because he's a Muslim. Having a non-Christian as President is just un-American. He and Hillary Clinton, I swear, would take this country straight to Hell. Thank God she didn't win the last election." Matt pauses, and Luka thinks he may be done. They got off easy, but no such luck. He is just catching his breath. Damn.

"I just don't understand what people were thinking. Why would anyone think a woman is capable of being the President of the United States? Women are far too emotional and hormonal for that kind of job, and she is no different. Women would much rather talk about their feelings than fight for freedom. A woman doing a man's job is just plain stupidity. It's what's wrong with

America, really, what is wrong with our families. President Trump is a gift sent from God. I am so thankful every single day that a man of faith won the election. I know we all prayed about it." Matt is now red-faced and breathing heavily as his rant comes to an end, looking similar to the preacher during the church service on Sunday.

"Now, Matt, remember your blood pressure," Josie reminds him, patting his arm. Luka almost wishes he wouldn't remember his blood pressure. Saying that stuff about women - right in front of his four sisters, his mom, and Willow - makes Luka's blood boil. They should be built up, not torn down because of their gender.

His mind drifts back to the fact that his sisters have to wear dresses to church while he is allowed to wear pants. It's the same concept, isn't it? According to people like Matt, women are beneath them, and so they should be treated as such. It pretty much even says that in the Bible. He glances at his sisters, noting the look of hurt on their faces from their own father's words. He bites his tongue harder, tasting blood. He hates him. He really fucking does.

"Yes, of course, Josie. I just get so worked up over the stupidity of those liberal snowflakes." Matt spits the last words, saliva coating his bottom lip. Luka almost gags. It's not the first time Luka has heard that term, but it still irritates him to no end.

"I know, dear," Josie responds, patting his arm again, attempting to calm her husband down.

"I tell you what liberals need. They need Jesus and a good beating." Matt points his finger towards the ceiling with his words, then slams one large palm down on the table. The loud bang and the sound of the dinnerware clanging as a result makes the rest of them jump.

Luka doesn't understand what it is with some people and wanting to beat everyone who believes and thinks differently than them. Is violence really the answer? If Harlan started to beat

Matt because he is a Christian, then Matt would cry religious intolerance, making sure everyone heard about the heinous crimes against the nation's Christians.

"So, Willow, tell us. What do you plan to do after graduation?" Josie asks, clearly trying to steer the topic away from politics. Luka could kiss her. Willow looks relieved, her body visibly relaxing as she answers the question.

"I plan on going to college, even though my parents aren't keen on the idea," Willow responds, really smiling for the first time during this whole fucking shitshow of an evening. Willow is smart, just like Harlan.

"Oh? What are you planning to study?" Josie asks, clearly interested. Matt huffs beside her, but doesn't say anything and just continues to stuff his face, which is now becoming a more normal shade. Willow holds up one finger as she chews, politely signifying that she is going to answer once she finishes.

"I would like to major in Civil Engineering," she responds, and Luka smiles proudly.

"Oh, that's a lot of math. Are you sure about that?" Matt asks, clearly judging her for her choice in a future career. He can almost hear him saying 'girls can't do math, silly.'

"Oh, I love math. I am currently taking College Algebra, even though I am in eleventh grade. I hope to finish calculus before I start my freshman year of college," she tells them, taking a bite of food. He wonders why Harlan didn't take any college classes like other students seemed to have done. Some are even taking English 101 now, planning to start English 102 when the semester ends. He makes a mental note to ask Harlan, that is, if he ever talks to him again. Matt grunts at her answer, clearly displeased, which is utter bullshit.

"Are those college level courses? Did your parents have to pay for them?" Josie asks, actually interested in what Willow is saying. Luka loves his mom.

"Yes. They are college level, but I paid for them out of my own pocket. I have a job. My parents, umm..." she pauses, clearly unsure if she wants to finish her thought. Luka knows what she is going to say, so he wonders the exact same thing before she decides to continue. "My parents don't want me to go to college. They say it will be a waste of my time, and that I should concentrate on finding a husband and starting a family." Her voice is sad with the admission. Not as sad as the first time she had told Luka the very same thing.

They had this conversation a few days ago, but she sounds sad all the same. She pretends it doesn't affect her. That she doesn't need her parents' permission or support, but Luka can tell that it really does bother her. Shouldn't they be fucking proud that their daughter is so intelligent and wants to further her education? What kind of backwards way of thinking do these people have?

"I can see where they are coming from. You're their daughter. They just want what's best for you," Matt responds, and what the fuck? It's not necessarily what Matt said that leaves a bad taste in Luka's mouth, it's what he left unsaid. It is the words between the lines of his sentences.

What he *meant* by his statement. They just want what's best for her? Is he fucking serious? As if what is best for her isn't to get a good education. As if what is best for her is to get married and settle down and pop out half a dozen kids. As if she shouldn't *want* to get an education, and her parents are actually correct in their goals for her. What kind of bullshittery is that?

Matt has been telling him to go to college and get an education since the day he waltzed into their lives, so why is he singing a different tune with Willow? In fact, now that Luka really thinks about it, Matt has never once talked to any of his sisters about college. He never even talks to them about school or rewards them for good grades like he does Luka. He just encourages them to take courses like Home Economics or Family Studies. Holy shit. What a fucking double standard.

How has Luka been so blind to it before? He just, fuck, he just thought it was *normal,* and he thought that the girls didn't really *want* to go to college or get an education. Now, though, it makes Luka sick because they are *taught* to not want one, by people like Matt. They are *taught* that their main goals in life are to get married and start a family, to do as their husband says without a thought in their brains. Luka's head is spinning with the realization. He is going to be sick. Holy shit. Not for the first time this week, he just wants to talk to Harlan. Harlan has a way of putting things into perspective, which helps Luka to understand.

"Yeah," Willow agrees, voice small and unsure. She sounds beaten and upset, so Luka reaches a tentative hand over to her, rubbing it down her back in what he hopes to be a soothing gesture. That's something boyfriends do for their girlfriends, right? He hates Matt so fucking much right now, his blood is boiling.

Poor Willow. She just added another person to her seemingly never-ending list of people who don't believe in her, who don't believe she could actually succeed in college. Luka decides right then and there that he will be the support that she needs. He will encourage her to pursue her dreams, and he will help her along the way. She doesn't need family. She can make one of her own. An awkward silence fills the room after that, everyone just eating their food.

"Mom. Dad. I have a question I have been meaning to ask you," Luka starts a few minutes later, finally breaking the tension. He puts down his fork to look at his parents. It almost pains him to call Matt 'Dad', but he does it because he is getting ready to ask a favor and doesn't want to be on his shit list even more.

"Of course, honey," Josie responds, smiling encouragingly.

"Saturday is the Homecoming dance, and I know you all don't usually let us go to dances. I thought that maybe I could go this year with Willow, since it's my senior year. I'm eighteen now, so I think I am responsible enough. I will also be home no later than midnight. Willow just really wants to go, and now that you've met her, I thought maybe you would agree," Luka rambles, wanting to get everything out there before they can start arguing the point.

"I don't know, honey. We have never let you before. What do you think, Matt?" Josie asks, looking at her husband for an answer. Luka hates that so much. Why can't she just give him permission? She is his mom after all, the only one of the two to have any biological relation to him at all, yet Matt is the one that holds Luka's future in his fat hands.

Matt looks like he is considering the question, fork hanging between his thumb and index finger as he chews with his mouth open. Luka bites his lip and prays for an answer in the affirmative, just wanting one night to spend with his friends. He has already planned to sneak out and possibly attend an after party, but they don't need to know that.

"Okay, but you will be home by eleven and not a moment later. Am I understood?" Matt asks, pointing his finger at Luka and nodding. Luka is shocked. This is the first time Matt has ever agreed to let Luka do something that isn't directly related to academics, sports, or church. His mouth is actually dropping open at the allowance, but he quickly recovers.

"Thank you. I will be home by eleven, not a minute later," he stutters out, nodding. The rest of dinner goes more or less smoothly, his parents asking Willow questions, her answers always short and safe. He thinks they like her, even though she isn't a cheerleader or whatever. Josie keeps smiling at him as if to say, 'she's a good one,' while Matt keeps glancing down her shirt even though it isn't low cut. What a disgusting prick.

"Lizzie. Mary. Will you help me clean up?" Josie asks, standing from the table once everyone has finished eating.

"I can, Mom," Luka offers, beginning to stand up from his seat between Willow and Gabby.

"Luka sit down. That's women's work, so let your mother and sisters handle it," Matt orders, and Luka sits down, looking at his mom apologetically. It reminds him of the preacher dismissing the women early during their Homecoming celebration at the church. Josie smiles at him, silently thanking him for the offer. Lizzie and Mary rise from their seats, grabbing the remainder of the dishes from the table before they disappear into the kitchen behind their mother.

"I think I am going to go ahead and take Willow home. It's getting late," Luka says a few minutes later when his mom and sisters reappear, the younger girls going to the living room to find something to watch on television. Willow takes that as her cue to stand, Luka following behind her.

"Okay, drive safe. It was lovely meeting you, Willow," Josie says, pulling Willow into a warm hug, the younger girl returning it easily. They make their way into the living room, Luka freezing as soon as he sees what his sisters accidently left the Netflix cursor on. Please, no. Fuck. Please, no.

"Get that shit off of my TV!" Matt yells, making Lizzie jump and turn her attention back to the television. Her eyes widen when she realizes what she has accidentally landed on in her search. "No house of mine will have fucking trash like that on TV! Wanting us to sympathize with fags and actually be tolerant of their choice in lifestyle. No. In fact, I may just cancel the Netflix subscription since they are nothing but millennial pieces of shit pushing their liberal agenda on our youth."

Matt motions wildly towards the television, his face resembling a tomato. The picture of *Queer Eye* is long gone, now replaced with *Lilo and Stitch*. Luka feels sick at his stepdad's words. His eyes sting with tears, but he blinks them back, knowing that crying will just make it worse. First, they will wonder why he is crying, then he will be called a pansy by Matt for showing emotion.

"Honey, they were just scrolling past it," Josie reasons, rubbing Matt's bicep like the good little housewife Matt wants her to be.

"I don't care, Josephine. That filth will not be on my TV. Their parents should have raised those men better." Matt uses four meaty fingers to put air quotes around the word 'men', making Luka ball his fist up behind his back with anger. Matt acting like they aren't men because they are gay makes bile rise in Luka's throat, burning it. He also doesn't miss the comment about their lifestyle choice, as if being gay is a choice. Luka used to think so, but now he isn't so sure. He isn't sure about anything anymore. "I blame their parents. Their parents should have raised them better, raised them in church. When they started behaving in such an ungodly way, they should have sent them away to fix them."

"Well, I'm gonna get Willow home," Luka interrupts, taking a shaky breath while he and Willow slip their shoes on.

"It was nice to meet, y'all. Dinner was great," Willow compliments, then waves as Luka pushes her out the door.

"Yes! Take care," Josie waves, smiling again as they walk out the door, shutting it firmly behind them. When they get outside, Luka closes his eyes, taking in a few gulps of the cool autumn air. He is physically shaking, feeling as though he may throw up his dinner at any moment. A single tear falls down his cheek, but he quickly wipes it away, hoping Willow didn't see it. He bites the inside of his cheek, willing no more to fall.

"Are you okay?" She asks, voice low and hesitant. Luka cracks his eyes open to look at her. She looks concerned and also slightly shaken by Matt's words. He understands the sentiment completely.

"I'm fine. I'm sorry Matt was such an asshole to you about the college thing. Know that you always have someone supportive in me," Luka tells her, glad to have finally gotten to say it. He told her before, when they talked about it, but he wants to reiterate it after what Matt has just said.

"It's fine. I'm used to it, but seriously. Are you okay? That was... intense," Willow asks again, her red eyebrows drawn in worry. Her brown eyes are wide with concern.

"Yeah. I'm used to it, too. Let's just go," he responds, using a foot to push himself off the doorstep, quickly walking down the stoop.

"Lu," Willow starts, but Luka quickly cuts her off.

"Look, Will, I appreciate the concern, but I don't want to talk about it," he says, not missing a step. He closes his eyes for a moment when he hears her sigh, then follows behind him. He can't. He can't talk about it, or he will cry. He can't cry. Not in front of Willow, and not where his parents may be able to see him.

Matt's words are still racing through his mind at light speed, not giving his brain a moment to fucking rest. To think. For the third time tonight, Luka thinks he hates him but then feels guilty for the thought. One of the Ten Commandments is about honoring thy father and mother. Even though Matt isn't technically his father, he is the closest thing Luka has ever had and probably will ever get. He shouldn't hate him. He should probably hate himself instead, for his choices that have led him to this.

If homosexuality is a choice, then why can't he choose not to be attracted to men or Harlan for that matter? He doesn't want to be. He doesn't want to disappoint his family or for God to hate him. It's the last thing he wants, yet it doesn't stop his body. It doesn't stop his *heart*. Why is it so fucking terrible to love someone?

He feels like his world, that was flipped on its axis by Harlan, is now on a scale, measuring every single detail against the others until there is something quantifiable. Something valid. The whole thing is making his head hurt. He just wants to talk to Harlan, but he shouldn't. He should just move on from his bad choices and pretend Harlan doesn't exist. He just can't. His heart can't do it.

22

"I'm not fucking going, Cadeon. Drop it," Harlan practically growls as they walk down the empty back stairway after school.

"Come on, it's Homecoming!" Cadeon begs, grabbing Harlan's arm to stop him when they get to the bottom. Everyone else in school is currently occupying the gym for the godsforsaken pep rally, and Harlan just doesn't feel peppy at the current moment. Or ever really. Sports are pointless and having school spirit for a place you will be leaving in four years is just fucking dumb.

"No. Luka is going to be there, which means I am not going to be there," Harlan shoots, glaring down at his friend.

"You can't avoid him forever, Haz." Harlan flinches at the nick-name, given to him by Luka. Cadeon's tone is soft, making Harlan that much angrier. He hates pity. "You have all of your classes with him. You need to talk to him."

"No. That's the fucking problem, Cadeon. I shouldn't have talked to him in the first fucking place. Talkin' to him is what got me into this disaster of a situation, so I don't think it's gonna help matters. In fact, I should go the rest of the school year without talkin' to him. Let him spend the rest of his miserable life with his Jesus freak of a girlfriend, their 2.5 kids, and their stupid fucking white picket fence with their three crosses proudly standing in the yard. I don't care about him."

Harlan is breathing heavily from his rant, hoping that saying it out loud will help to convince himself. His accent has gotten thicker, certain letters dropping off the ends of words like they do when he gets irritated or upset. Cadeon's blue eyes are wide with surprise, dark brows shooting into his hairline.

"You're fucking lying through your teeth," Cadeon pokes him roughly in the chest, punctuating the accusation. "If you didn't care about him, then you wouldn't be madder than a wet hen. You have been fuckin' mopin' for a week over him having a girlfriend. Lie to yourself all you want to, Haz, but don't lie to me. I'm your friend, and I just wanna help you. Get off your high horse and talk to him because I think he feels the same way."

Cadeon pats him on the chest then walks out the door, leaving Harlan breathing heavily and astonished. Cadeon has never, ever talked to him like that. When the excited screams of his fellow classmates float into the stairwell from the gym, Harlan screams with them, only in anger. He thrusts his hand out, punching the air, then pulls it back, running his fingers through his curls and down his neck.

"Are you okay?" A soft raspy voice says behind him, and dread immediately fills his veins. He is supposed to be at the pep rally with all the other football players, so what the fuck is he doing here? Harlan wipes his eyes quickly before turning away, not wanting him to even see them water. He will not give him the satisfaction. Harlan ignores him and tries to walk past, but the other man steps in his path. Harlan flinches away, not wanting to be touched.

"I asked if you're okay," he says again, blue eyes soft. Harlan shouldn't have looked at them, knowing full well what those eyes do to him. His hair is soft, and he is wearing his football jersey and jeans, like all of the players on the team do on Fridays. The fact that it is Homecoming week makes it even more of a requirement. It's not the first time Harlan has seen him today, but it is the first time he has really looked at him.

"Move, Luka." Harlan's voice sounds broken and cracked, even to his own ears. He silently berates himself, wanting it to come out firm and strong. He can't let Luka see him upset. He can't give him something else to go and talk to his preppy friends about.

"No. I wanted to talk to you," Luka tells him, crossing his arms in front of his chest, widening his stance even more, the voices from the gym echoing around him. He has a look of determination on his face, lips in a thin line, eyes narrowed. If Harlan didn't hate him so much, it would be hot.

"Well, tough shit, 'cause I don't wanna talk to you," Harlan says, his Southern accent becoming even more pronounced than before with his newfound anger. He moves to go up the stairs, but Luka just stands in his way again, effectively pushing him towards the dark area under the stairs, so all of his exits are blocked.

"Will you please just listen to me?" Luka asks, eyes pleading, his voice going straight to Harlan's heart like a stabbing pain. Harlan takes a moment to really look at his features. Luka looks tired and his voice is just a hair scratchier, like he is upset, too. Harlan doesn't know why he would be upset. His life is fucking fantastic. He has a girlfriend, and he is on the football team. Every single student and teacher in the school loves and adores him, so why the fuck would he be upset?

"Why don't you go find your girlfriend and talk to her?" Harlan spits the words out like they are poison. They make his mouth taste bitter, acid rising in his throat. It isn't fair to be mad at Luka for having a girlfriend. He doesn't even know if Luka is gay. For all he knows, Luka could have been trying to be his friend, and Harlan has taken Luka's friendly actions the wrong way. Or Luka could have been fucking with him all along, flirting with him even though he is straight, just to be a dick. Harlan is going to go with the latter, allowing him to hold onto his anger for a little longer.

"I don't want to talk to her. I want to talk to you," Luka insists, stepping towards Harlan. Harlan takes a step back out of instinct, his mind briefly flashing back to middle school.

Luka is not them. Luka will not hurt you. He reminds himself as he eyes the other man. He really doesn't think Luka will physically hurt him, but old habits die hard. He can't stop his body from responding that way, his mind automatically jumping to the worst possible scenario.

"So, you admit that you have a girlfriend? Gee. Thanks for telling me now, a whole fuckin' week later," Harlan says, sarcasm dripping from his every word. Willow is Luka's girlfriend. Every kid in the whole fucking school knows, but it is still painful to hear Luka actually admit it out loud. His stomach is in knots, his arms and hands shaking.

"It's not like that," Luka responds, shaking his head as another muffled scream surrounds them. What the fuck does that even mean? It's not like that? He either has a girlfriend or he doesn't, there are no other options. He basically just said he does have a girlfriend, so how is it not like that? Harlan isn't sure he cares to find out, not wanting to hear Luka's bullshit.

"Really? Not like that, huh? I would ask if she is just your fuck buddy, but you two probably wear fucking purity rings or somethin', wantin' to save yourself for marriage in the name of God or some shit. Did her meeting your parents not go well? Was she not virginal and demure enough for them?" Harlan asks, watching as Luka flinches at his words. Good. He wants to hurt him. He wants to hurt Luka like he has been hurting all fucking week. Maybe then Luka will understand the pain he has endured. It's not fair, though, since Luka is only responsible for a small fraction of that pain. But, as Harlan always says, life isn't fair.

"You heard that?" Luka phrases it like a question, but it is more of a statement, an observation. Harlan can hear the cheerleaders in the gym doing their routine, the godawful pop music now filling the stairwell and offering a horrendous backing track to an even more horrendous conversation. Harlan just wants it to be over. Everything. This conversation. This month. This school year. His life.

"Yes. I'm not fucking deaf, Luka. I heard you ask if she was ready to go to your house for dinner. I also saw you hanging all over her. May as well have been in each other's fucking skin," Harlan says, taking another step back to try and put some distance between them. He can feel Luka's body heat radiating off of him in waves, and Harlan can't handle it. Not when he is this angry. This hurt. He can feel the cold surface of the wall against his skin now, cooling him down.

"Just let me explain..." Luka starts, but Harlan cuts him off as excited cheers from the gym surround them, a stark contrast to the heaviness of their conversation. The happiness of their fellow classmates does nothing to sooth Harlan's sadness. His own emptiness. In all honesty, this is the most he has felt all week. He was doing such a good job of burying it deep, never letting his emotions see the light of day. Here comes Luka, though, to fuck that up, too. Why can't he just leave him alone to suffer through his misery? Why does he always have to tilt his world on its axis and make him *feel*?

"Explain what, Luka? You want to tell me how fucking stupid and naive I am for ever believing that you would want me? Explain how you decided to fuck with me because I'm the weird kid, and I looked like an easy target? Or maybe you want to describe in detail your elaborate joke about pretending to be my friend, getting me to talk to you, convincing me that maybe you and I aren't that different, then stabbing me in the fucking back? Hmm? Which is it? I'm waiting, Luka. I'm all fucking ears." Harlan's deep voice echoes in the stairwell, mingling with the screams of joy from his fellow students in the gym.

He is breathing heavily now, back pressing against the wall. Luka looks hurt by his accusation, his blue eyes shiny, his firm lips wobbly. Harlan hates himself for not being pleased by his expression. He hates himself for wanting to hug him and tell him he doesn't mean any of it, even though he sort of does somewhere deep inside.

"Do you really think that of me? Really think I would do that?" Luka asks, his voice cracking with the question. Harlan has to look away because seeing Luka appear so upset is making his resolve crumble. He blinks back his own tears, eyes stinging with them. He will not cry. He will not give Luka the satisfaction of seeing him cry or the ammunition to use it against him in the future. He bites down on the inside of his own cheek to stop the tears from falling and embarrassing him further.

"I don't know what to think. I don't even know who you are anymore. Not that I ever really did, it seems," Harlan says, staring at the darkened area under the stairs, so he doesn't have to meet Luka's gaze. His mind is whirring with everything going on in front of him and around him, and he can't fucking concentrate with Luka looking at him like that. The voices of his excited classmates continue to carry through the hallways, only adding to his agitation.

"Harlan, I am your friend. None of that was a lie or a prank. I swear to you..." Harlan thinks Luka's face is getting closer to his; he can almost feel his breath on his lips. He refuses to move away, though, partly because he has nowhere left to go with his back now pressing against the wall and partly because he is just so defeated. Harlan wants to believe him. He wants to believe Luka's words, but he can't. Not after everything he has been through.

"Bullshit, Luka. Fuck off," Harlan spits, finally facing him. His eyes immediately go to Luka's dark pink lips, Luka wetting them with an equally pink tongue. Before he is even able to process what is going on, those same lips are on his. The lips he has been dreaming of since the first fucking day of school. They are wet and firm against his own, as small hands come up to tangle in his curls. Their chests are pressing together with their proximity. Luka is soft and perfect against him. Harlan isn't sure what to do now because for all intents and purposes, this is his first kiss.

He leaves his hands at his sides because what the fuck is he supposed to do with those? Grab Luka's shapely ass? Maybe put them on the small of Luka's back? He isn't even sure this is really happening, so he opts to leave them dangling at his side. He comes to his senses a bit after a few seconds pass, and he finally starts kissing back, parting his lips. Almost as soon as it happens, though, Luka pulls away, cocking his head in the direction of the gym. Harlan thinks he has done something wrong. He is probably a terrible kisser. He has never done it before, and he seems to be terrible at everything else concerning people. He starts to panic as Luka smiles at him.

"And now, to introduce our football players!" A disembodied voice says, echoing in the stairwell. Harlan is stunned. His brain feels like it is short circuiting. He isn't sure what the fuck just happened. Did Luka kiss him? Is this a fucking dream? Because he hasn't slept more than sixteen hours total all week, so he could have very well fallen asleep. Maybe he is hallucinating. He digs his fingers into the now healing marks on his arm, feeling them sting with the pressure. Nope. Not a dream. This is actually fucking happening. Luka kissed him. Fuck.

"Look. I've gotta go. You're coming to the game though, right? Can we talk after? My parents will be there, but I can probably get a few minutes away. We can go somewhere alone, under the bleachers or something, to continue this conversation. Please?" Luka begs, looking frantic now, eyes glancing in the direction of the gym where he is clearly supposed to be. Harlan just nods dumbly, not trusting his voice.

"Great. I'll explain everything then. I promise," Luka says, getting up on his tiptoes, pressing their lips together again, this time quicker, and then he's gone. Harlan touches his lips, not quite allowing himself to believe what just happened. He stares at the door as it closes, the sound echoing around him. Flashes of their conversation float in his mind, the feeling of Luka's lips on his own burning into his memory.

He almost forgets how angry he is at Luka. He isn't even sure if he is angry anymore, not after that. He is more confused than anything else. Luka is definitely into men, but Harlan doesn't want to be his dirty little secret. He doesn't want to be used as a way for Luka to cheat on his girlfriend. He could never do that to Willow. He guesses he is going to the stupid fucking football game after all. He shakes his head and starts walking in the direction of the gym. Holy shit.

23

"Osborne just scored a touchdown for the Pioneers, making the score 15 to 14 with only 30 seconds left on the clock. The Pioneers will kick off and Thomas, number 28, is back deep for the Rebels. He catches the ball, and he's off!" Luka barely registers the disembodied voices as he catches the ball in his hands then takes off into a sprint. His head hasn't been in the game all night, eyes continuously drifting to Harlan in the stands sitting next to Cadeon. Harlan, who has been paying absolutely zero attention to the game all night, instead opting to read. Of course, Harlan 'I-Don't-Do-Sports-Ball' Sharp would read during a football game. Luka has never been more endeared.

As he runs, he glances over to the curly-haired boy in the stands, watching as his dark brow furrows at the book in his large hands, his lips puckered at the words. Not for the first time, Luka's mind drifts back to the kiss they shared in the dark, back stairwell of the school. Luka still can't believe he fucking kissed him. What was he thinking?

He was just so hurt that Harlan would think that of him, and he could tell the other boy was gearing up for another rant. He shut him up the only way he knew how, with his lips on Harlan's. It was the most perfect kiss Luka has ever experienced. The cool air on his lips now provides a stark contrast to the warmth of Harlan's lips against his own from a few hours ago. It was the most daring thing Luka has ever done, and strangely enough, he doesn't regret it.

Luka's attention snaps back to the game as he feels another body collide with his own, knocking the breath out of him. The ball slips from his fingers before he hits the ground. "Oooh, Thomas takes a hit and fumbles the ball, but the Rebels are able to recover! Thomas has seemed out of the game all night. Rebels call a timeout," the announcer says, voice booming over the field and stands.

Luka gets up and shakes his head. He glances over at his family as he makes his way over to the side of the field for the time out. Matt is red-faced and screaming in his direction, hands flailing wildly. Luka grimaces, not even wanting to know what the man is currently saying about him.

"What the fuck is wrong with you, Thomas? You need to get your goddamn head out of your fucking ass and play the game," Coach Stanley screams, gum barely staying in his mouth as Luka removes his helmet. Luka just nods because he really has nothing to say for himself. He has been distracted, but he thinks it is the best kind of distraction.

Matt is still yelling on the sidelines; Luka can hear every other word now. Phrases like 'fucking moron', 'playing like a fucking girl', and 'no son of mine' floating through the air like pollution, making Luka feel even more like a fuck-up. The coach is explaining their next play, but Luka is barely paying attention, just nodding along. He really should be paying attention, since a lot is riding on him, but he keeps glancing toward Harlan. He is now smiling down at his book, his green eyes sparkling in the harsh light of the stadium. His cheeks are bright red from the cool air, making the paleness of his skin stand out even more. He looks so beautiful it physically hurts Luka.

"Alright, get your lazy asses out there and get us that W!" the coach yells, pointing toward the field with one fat finger. Luka would like to see this guy get out there and fucking run for hours on end. The man probably hasn't seen his own feet in years, his belt barely holding his pants up under his large gut. He is just some washed-out player that peaked in high school and has been yelling at younger, more talented people for the past

25 years. Luka would pay big money to see him run across the field or, fuck, even throw a ball. He would probably dislocate his shoulder if he even tried, then have a heart attack from exertion.

Luka puts on his helmet and straps up with the rest of the team, feeling a few of his teammates hit him on his pads as he walks towards the 60-yard line. "And we're back, score 15 to 14 for the Pioneers, with only 15 seconds remaining on the clock. Rebels still have possession of the ball, but Thomas has the chance to deliver something special here to secure the win."

As Luka gets into position, he looks back over at Harlan. Cadeon nudges his friend, Harlan's attention snapping towards Luka, green eyes finally meeting his. He quickly puts his book down, smiles at Luka and shoots him a thumbs up. That is the best encouragement Luka has received all night. Not his coach yelling at him, not Matt screaming about how terrible Luka is, but Harlan smiling and giving him a thumbs up. He hasn't even been paying attention to the game, but he has faith that Luka can do it. Faith from Harlan. That's all Luka really needs.

Luka gets into position and waits for the ball to be snapped. He takes off when it is in the hands of the quarterback, running a few yards and turning to catch the ball as it is being thrown to him. With Harlan's eyes on him, he makes a mad dash toward the end zone, feet flying while dodging anyone that gets in his way.

He glances back to see Ezra block someone that was about to tackle him. Ezra usually has his back, thank God. He can almost feel Harlan's eyes on him as he continues to run down the field, using Harlan as fuel to get to the end zone. He just wants to end the damn game so he can finally clear the air with Harlan. If this is how he needs to do it, then he will dodge fifty fucking players from the other team and God himself to do so.

"Look at Thomas go! When he takes off, nobody can catch him! He's at the 40, 30, 15, and TOUCHDOWN!" the announcer yells, the entire stadium erupting into cheers, sending a chill through Luka's spine as the rest of his teammates grab him and hoist him onto their shoulders. Luka barely registers any of it, though, as he cranes his head to spot Harlan on his feet, cheering along with Cadeon and the rest of the crowd.

His eyes are bright, curls windswept, cheeks and lips even more red, large fists in the air. It looks strange to see Harlan outwardly showing so much emotion, especially happiness, but it looks so fucking good on him. Luka decides then that he wants Harlan to look this happy for the rest of his life because a smiling Harlan Sharp is what dreams are made of, not winning a high school football game.

He never takes his eyes off of Harlan, who is now smiling at him, dimples popping, making Luka want to swoon. He removes his helmet, running his gloved fingers through his sweaty hair and smiles back, barely registering the feel of his teammates hands as each one of them gives him a pat wherever they can reach, several of them smacking his ass. He finally tears his eyes away from Harlan to see his mom and sisters smiling and waving happily. Matt still looks angry, but he will have to get over it. They won, so why does it matter if it was at the last possible second? Luka has always had a flair for the dramatic, after all.

He walks over to the sideline with the rest of his team, not paying attention to a single word the coach says. Again, he looks at Harlan. He nods his head toward a spot under the bleachers, silently trying to tell the other boy to meet him there. Harlan nods back in understanding, then turns to say something to Cadeon, who is practically yelling at him. Luka smiles, wishing he could be in on their conversation. He turns his attention back to his coach, catching the end of his usual 'good job, I knew you could do it' speech. It's funny because not even five minutes ago, the asshole was cussing them out and calling them pussies. Funny how things change when people are successful.

When he looks up next, he finds Harlan has disappeared, with

Cadeon shooting him a confused look. "Hey, Ez, man. I need a favor," Luka says, clapping Ezra on the shoulder. Ezra turns to him with confused eyes, clearly ready to do whatever Luka is about to ask him.

"What's up?"

"I need you to cover for me with my parents. If they ask where I am, just tell them I had to go to the bathroom or something," Luka tells him, trying to convey to his friend with his eyes how desperately he needs this. He quickly glances over at his parents, who are currently making their way down the bleachers toward him. He turns back to Ezra with panicked eyes.

"Yeah, sure. Where ya going?" Ezra asks, also glancing in the direction of Luka's family.

"I can't tell you," Luka stutters out, feeling terrible for asking Ezra to lie for him when he can't even tell him the goddamned truth. He is such a shitty friend.

"Okay. That's fine, man. I understand. You know, you can tell me anything, though. Right? Whenever you're ready," Ezra says, his dark eyes sincere. A jolt of panic goes straight through Luka. Does Ezra know? Fuck, does he suspect? What if he tells Luka's family? Oh fuck, but Ezra looks earnest, as if trying to tell Luka that he cares. Luka just gives him a small smile.

"Go." Ezra claps him on the back, pushing him, right as Luka's parents step onto the field a few yards away. Luka sprints off in the opposite direction. He looks around to make sure no one is watching him, then ducks under the bleachers, giving his eyes a moment to adjust to the dim light. He is suddenly more nervous than he felt the entirety of the football game as he looks around for Harlan. His stomach is in knots, his gloved hand sweaty as he grips his helmet under his left arm.

"Right here," he hears a deep voice say to his left, causing him to jump in the air, almost hitting his head on a low beam. That's just what he needs, a fucking concussion. He places a hand on his chest in hopes of calming his racing heart. He was already nervous, now he can add 'scared shitless' to the endless list of ever-present emotions he is currently going through. It snuggles nicely between 'oh shit, Harlan is looking at me' and 'what if God's not real?'. Those are emotions, right? They have to be because he feels them every single fucking day of his life lately.

"You scared the fuck out of me," Luka says, gripping the helmet he almost dropped and looking at Harlan's dark form. He steps closer, their bodies almost touching, so they can see each other in the dim light. It is perfect.

"Whoops." Harlan laughs, clearly not sorry about it. Luka smiles, so glad to just hear his voice again after a week of being completely deprived. He doesn't think he will ever forget this conversation. For some reason, he knows it is pivotal. The tension between them quickly returns, almost feeling as though a weight has been dropped on them in their dark hole under the bleachers.

"Hey," Luka says, voice barely above a whisper. His eyes trail to Harlan's lips. The same lips he had been kissing just a few hours prior. He still can't believe he did that. He has no idea what he was thinking, but if he is going to commit a sin, it may as well be for Harlan Sharp. He realizes he doesn't regret his decision to kiss Harlan. It felt almost inevitable in some way. Like some indescribable force has been pulling him to Harlan since the very first day of school. Maybe it is his heart. Maybe it is his brain. He is certain, though, it isn't God.

"So, um...wanna tell me what's going on?" Harlan ventures after a few moments of silence, the only remaining noise muted voices from the small number of fans that remained in the stadium. Luka thinks it's odd that they keep having these conversations when there are so many happy and excited people around them. It strangely fits, though. Luka suddenly feels sick again, the elation from hearing Harlan's voice gone in the cool breeze blowing under the bleachers. His stomach is tied in knots, and he searches his brain for the best way to begin.

"I don't know where to begin," Luka says finally, sighing. They haven't even started, and he already feels defeated. He is so scared of fucking this up. He would give up the win of the football game he just played if it meant that this conversation would be successful. He fidgets with the helmet still tucked under his arm, looking down at Harlan's pigeon-toed feet.

"Luka, I don't want to be your dirty little secret. I am not going to help you cheat on Willow just to scratch some fucking itch and get it out of your system. So, why don't you start by telling me what you meant when you said you and Willow aren't like that?" Harlan asks, his deep voice slow and measured. Luka's gaze snaps up to meet Harlan's. He began the statement with a harsher tone of voice, but his green eyes are soft and curious, as if he just wants answers. Luka doesn't blame him. If he were in Harlan's position, he would want answers as well.

"Willow is only my girlfriend by label. We made a deal. She would pretend to be my girlfriend to get my parents off my back, and I would do the same for her," Luka finally answers, looking down again in embarrassment. He has no idea why he is embarrassed, but his cheeks are heating with the admission. His face feels like it is on fire.

"Why do your parents care if you have a girlfriend?" Harlan asks, and Luka was not expecting Harlan to talk so much, nor ask this many questions. It is kind of strange actually speaking to Harlan and not just reading his messy scrawl written on a piece of paper, in mostly capital letters. He isn't sure what he was expecting, but he and Harlan have never really had a long verbal conversation, unless he counts the fight from earlier. The one that ended in the best kiss Luka has ever experienced. His dick twitches in his cup just thinking about it. He somehow made it through the entirety of the pep rally without climbing the bleachers and tasting Harlan's sinful lips again.

This had to be what Eve felt like in the Garden of Eden because

Harlan's taste is the very definition of sin. Like everything Luka wants but knows he can't have. Luka is desperate for another taste, but he can't right now. He has some explaining to do, even though he would much rather go back to allowing Harlan to suck his soul out through his mouth. It doesn't seem like he would have much use for his soul, anyway, given that it will probably be damned.

"Because my stepdad is a bit of a misogynistic pig that measures every man's worth by how many women he's linked to. At every single new school, I am expected to have a girlfriend by the third week, tops," Luka explains, rolling his eyes at the mention of Matt. Harlan nods his head, almost as if he understands.

"Luka, it's October. If that's the case, you should have had a girlfriend weeks ago," Harlan points out.

"I bought myself some time," Luka answers, honestly.

"Why did you need to, though? Why didn't you just do what you seem to have done at other schools?" Harlan asks, his dark brows drawn with the question, causing two little wrinkles to form on his forehead. Luka wants to kiss them. He shakes his head, trying to stay in the conversation.

"Because...umm..." Luka pauses, not sure how he wants to continue. He takes a deep breath and decides to just go with the truth. They are teetering on the edge of something, and he is afraid he will fuck it up by lying. He doesn't want to lie to Harlan. He would lie to himself all day, but Harlan is different. "You."

"What about me?" Harlan asks, eyes widening with Luka's last word. A pang hits Luka in the chest. It's like Harlan can't understand why anyone would even take him into consideration, as though no one has ever cared enough to. Luka wants to change Harlan's mindset about that. He doesn't need to know the details of whatever suffering Harlan has endured, to prove to the other boy that not everyone's the same. Luka doesn't want to

172

hurt him. He has hurt him, this Luka knows, but it was never his intention.

"I met you. I wanted to be with you, so I lied to buy myself time. The very idea of fake dating a girl makes me sick, regardless. Then I met Willow in Bible Club and came up with the plan. At least this time, the girl I am fake dating is in on it, and I don't have to fake an attraction. I don't have to hide what I want to have with you," Luka whispers the last part, like a secret. It is one, though, his biggest secret. He wants more with Harlan, but he can't believe he actually just said it out loud.

"What do you want with me?" Harlan asks, and that's a good fucking question. Luka isn't sure how to answer and definitely doesn't think he could say what he wants out loud. He bites his lip, trying to think of the best way to say it without actually saying it. He is still confused as to what he wants, truth be told. Well, he knows what he wants, but he also knows he *shouldn't* want it.

"I want to be with you," Luka whispers, because he is afraid God will smite him where he stands if he says the words any louder. They already feel so loud to his ears, almost as if he screamed them instead of saying them so low, he is sure Harlan barely heard him over the sound of the excited chatter all around them. Harlan narrows his eyes at him, as if trying to decide if he is lying or not. Luka tries to put as much honesty into his gaze as he can muster, willing Harlan to believe him for once in his goddamn life. To actually believe that he is worth something to someone.

"Is this some kind of joke, Luka?" Harlan asks, and Luka wants to fucking scream. Jesus, he feels like they have had this conversation at least four million seventy-two thousand three-hundred and sixty-eight times in the past two months, but here they are again, back to the fucking definition of insanity. Harlan is going to drive him insane, Luka just knows it, but he is strangely okay with this, as long as Harlan keeps kissing him like he did before.

What the fuck does Luka have to do to convince Harlan that he is sincere? At this point, he has considered writing it in the sky, screaming it from the highest mountain, and his favorite, tattooing that shit on his fucking forehead. Maybe then Harlan will actually understand. He tries not to get too frustrated. Something had to have happened in Harlan's life that has made him believe that no one would ever want anything with him, but instead he loses his cool, letting his frustration out.

"Despite my parents' constant bitching, I avoided getting a girlfriend for you. I put up with your shitty fucking attitude towards me. I have done everything in my power to get you to open the fuck up to me, including making friends with Cadeon so you would be forced to talk to me. I fucking kissed you. I am questioning everything I know, everything I've ever been taught and believed in. For *you*, Harlan. When will you stop asking me that stupid fucking question? Jesus," Luka snaps, because he is so tired of defending his actions to Harlan.

Sure, last week was a total fucking mess, but he thought that kissing him would actually prove something. He seems to be wrong, again. He has the sudden urge to throw his helmet, needing something to do to release the anger that is rising in his chest. He has never in his life met someone that makes him so incredibly fucking frustrated.

Harlan is the epitome of a contradiction to him. He wants to strangle him with his hands, and yet, run his fingers through his dark curls at the same time. He wants to smack his face, all the while resisting the urge to kiss his lips. He wants to tackle him, then either punch him for being so fucking frustrating or hump the apprehension right out of him. Words. He must use his words.

"I don't think Jesus has anything to do with this, babe," Harlan finally responds, a smirk in place, and Luka could fucking cry. He may have finally broken through one of the many fucking walls Harlan has constructed around his heart and soul. Luka wants to howl in joy and dance at the victory. It is more triumphant than their win of the football game just moments ago.

It's like they have been under the bleachers for hours, when in reality, it has only been mere minutes. Time seems to stand still when he is with Harlan, though, which is fine by him since they never seem to have enough of it. As if they will always run out of it, with words unspoken and skin untouched.

Luka laughs because of course Harlan would say something like that. He can feel the tension between them dissipating, floating away in the cool breeze along with the chatter of the crowd. His smile fades when he looks up into Harlan's eyes. There is a seriousness in them that wasn't there a moment ago, as if he is trying to come to a decision. Luka bites his lip, waiting, the old tension being replaced by something completely different. Like charged electricity in the air, similar to what Luka felt when the game had first started. His stomach knots with the anticipation of what's to come.

Luka watches Harlan's light pink tongue dart out to lick his red lips, the same lips Luka was touching with his own hours ago, even though it feels like days at this point. Harlan hesitantly reaches out both hands, placing them on Luka's hips between his football pads and his pants, making the skin below the material heat up.

He uses those same ridiculously large hands to pull Luka to him so that their chests are aligned. He looks into Luka's eyes one more time, seeming to search for something Luka isn't sure he will find. Luka wants to squirm under his gaze, the intensity in Harlan's green eyes weighing on him. Finally, after what feels like a lifetime, Harlan grips Luka's waist tighter, bends down, and brings their lips slowly together.

Luka lets Harlan control the pace of the kiss this time. Harlan kisses like he talks, slow and methodical. As if he is planning every little movement before he actually does it. At first, he keeps it soft and gentle, feeling everything out before deepening it. He licks the seam of Luka's mouth to gain entrance, which Luka quickly grants because tasting Harlan is his new favorite thing to do.

It is like a drug, a very sinful drug, and Luka has no idea how he will kick the habit. He isn't even sure he wants to. Why would God hate something that feels so inherently *right*? How could it be so wrong to feel this good? He moans when Harlan's tongue begins exploring his mouth. He briefly wonders how much experience Harlan has with kissing since he seems to be so hesitant about it. He is probably just hesitant because it's Luka, though. Luka, who is the epitome of everything Harlan seems to hate in life.

Luka drops his helmet onto the grass in favor of putting his arms around Harlan's neck, deepening their kiss even more. One large palm is cupping his cheek, ringed fingers touching his sweaty hair. Luka almost can't believe this is happening. Harlan is actually kissing him.

Harlan, who has done everything he can to avoid any kind of relationship with Luka. Harlan, who has more trust issues than Luka has ever seen in an eighteen-year-old. Harlan, who is very different from himself, but who he feels so drawn to. If this is a dream, Luka doesn't want to ever wake up. He can be safe in his dreams, where he doesn't have to worry about being persecuted by both his family and God. In his dreams, he can be who he wants to be without being ashamed. His dreams are a good place, as long as they don't become nightmares.

They jump apart when they hear a loud bang followed by several loud pops in succession. Luka's heart skips a beat when they are both bathed in red light, shadows dancing across their bodies. Luka and Harlan both look around for the source of the noise. "What the fuck?" Harlan asks, eyes searching the field toward the bright lights and sounds.

"Fireworks. Fuck. I almost forgot they were setting them off tonight for Homecoming," Luka replies, the answer dawning on him, the imaginary light bulb coming on over his head.

"Scared the piss out of me," Harlan says, holding his chest as if to calm his heart down. He looks up at the sliver of sky they can see from their vantage point, his green eyes sparkling in the light.

"Me too," Luka breathes out, also watching the brightly-colored sparks from between the risers. He looks at Harlan in the light, observing the way the rainbow colors dance across his beautiful features. The red over his lips, the blue in his hair, the green over his eyes, and the rest of the colors on various parts of his body, mingling with the shadows and creating an image Luka wishes he could have framed.

Of course, it would be rainbow. No other colors would ever suffice to bathe Harlan's beautiful pale skin. A rainbow is also strangely fitting for the moment, although he is sure the fireworks people would probably shit an entire brick house if they had known what was taking place beneath their colored lights.

"Harlan, umm...I'm sorry to cut this short again, but I have to go. My parents are going to be looking for me. Ezra can only cover for me for so long before they actually send out a search party with floodlights, cadaver dogs, the whole nine yards," Luka jokes, prompting a smile from Harlan.

"It's fine, Lu. I understand," Harlan tells him, letting his small smile bloom into something so bright, the fireworks themselves are muted.

"Okay. Umm...will you be at the Homecoming dance tomorrow night?" Luka asks, voice hesitant. He isn't sure where they will go from here, but he wants something more concrete. He doesn't want them to just find each other to make out and maybe give the occasional hand job. He could find that anywhere.

"I wasn't planning on it. Dances aren't really my thing," Harlan responds, brows creasing in thought.

"Well, I will be there with Willow, without my parents breathing down my neck. Maybe you can make it your thing?" Luka asks, thumbing Harlan's black jacket, the old worn leather catching on the rubber of his gloves.

"Maybe," Harlan shrugs but smirks, giving Luka the indication that he will be there.

"Okay. Umm...bye." Luka is suddenly feeling very awkward. Before he can question himself, he fists Harlan's jacket, gets on the tiptoes of his cleats, and kisses Harlan gently on the lips. Harlan's lips are still warm under his own. He just wants one more taste before he has to go back to reality.

Once they break apart, he stares into Harlan's eyes again, hoping to find his answer there. He doesn't. He waves goodbye, picks up his helmet, and ducks out from the bleachers. He quickly catches Ezra's gaze, smiles, and waves to the other boy who is talking to Matt pretending to be interested in what he has to say. Luka walks up to the group, watching Harlan emerge from the same spot minutes later; he hopes nobody else noticed.

24

"Why the fuck did I agree to this? I'm a fucking masochist," Harlan groans out, placing both hands over his face and rubbing up and down furiously, trying to scrub the memories from last night out of his mind. He opens his eyes, blinking at the light and quickly realizes it didn't work.

He still remembers the fight, the pep rally, seeing Luka score the winning...touchdown...it is a touchdown, right? Or was it like a home run? He doesn't really know nor care. He just knows Luka scored the winning points. Then he remembers everything afterward in vivid detail. Their conversation, the exchanged touches and kisses, his agreement to go to the dance, all burned into his brain like a brand that he will never, ever forget.

"We already knew you were a masochist, and you agreed because you like him." Cadeon sing-songs the last part, wiggling his eyebrows at Harlan, pushing another item of clothing to the side. Harlan told Cadeon that he didn't need help dressing himself, but after Cadeon heard the story of what took place under the bleachers, he insisted on coming over for a chat.

Harlan has no idea why he even told Cadeon. He considers it a brief moment of insanity. He has been having a lot of those lately, like the moment he chose to kiss Luka again. He may as well check himself into a mental hospital because he is definitely fucked up. He's always been a little fucked up though, so he may as well add this to the ever-growing list of proof.

"No, I don't," Harlan insists, watching as Cadeon makes a face at yet another one of his nicer shirts, then pushes it to what he has labeled the 'pasty ass emo kid, so no thanks,' side of the closet. Why does he like Cadeon? Oh yeah, he is literally the only person that will speak to Harlan. Besides Luka. And now Ezra. Fuck. What has Luka done to him? Has he become, dare he say, sociable? If so, he wants to go back to his previous existence because this is maddening.

"Then why are you going to...what were the words you used?" Cadeon places his finger up to his chin, looking up and pretending to be in thought for a few seconds. Harlan glares at him and goes to interrupt before he strangles him, but Cadeon continues, "Oh yeah, 'an antiquated sexist dance where everyone's aim is to spike the punch and lose their virginity'. I believe you said only people with less than five brain cells are going."

"I said three," Harlan corrects.

"Six one way, half a dozen the other," Cadeon dismisses. When Harlan glares, he explains, "Three is less than five, so my point still stands." Cadeon points a finger at Harlan triumphantly. Yes. Harlan is for sure going to strangle Cadeon before the afternoon is over.

Why Cadeon wanted to come over now when the dance doesn't start for another four hours is beyond him. Probably to drive him crazy. It's working. He's succeeding. Give him a fucking trophy and not even a useless one, like the kind they give for participating. He needs an actual trophy with a little version of him on the top crushing Harlan's brain in his hands and his name engraved into the golden plate at the bottom: Cadeon James Hart, 1st place in Driving his Best Friend Crazy.

"Cadeon, why do you hate me?" Harlan sighs, because that has to be it. Cadeon hates him. It is the only plausible explanation as to why this entire fucking conversation is currently taking place.

"Stop deflecting. Just admit you like him. You fuckin' kissed the guy. He was your first kiss, Haz. You can't pretend you don't like him. I know you do, and the first step is admitting it," Cadeon says, his features stern as if he is scolding a child.

"Jesus, Cadeon, I'm not an alcoholic. This isn't a twelve-step program," Harlan quips. He can't help it. It's far better than the alternative, which is actually saying what he is feeling out loud. Saying it out loud makes it seem more real, more believable, and Harlan still isn't sure how much he wants to believe. He knows what Luka told him, but his brain still finds that incomprehensible for many reasons. He is still uncertain of Luka's motives, especially after the bullshittery that was last week. He does, however, feel a shit ton better knowing that Willow is in on it.

He didn't help Luka cheat on his actual girlfriend. He helped him cheat on his pretend girlfriend, which is better, he supposes. Who is he kidding? In which realm is that any better? Harlan wouldn't want to take their relationship, or whatever this is, out into the open for the world to see anyway. Getting stoned to death or being burned at the stake does not sound like his idea of a fun Saturday afternoon, so a secret relationship would be key for survival purposes.

"Deflecting," Cadeon sing-songs, pulling out the only pair of skinny jeans Harlan owns that do not have holes in them and throwing them on the bed. "I feel like we have had this conversation at least a dozen times and my patience is wearin' thin. Why don't you just fuckin' admit it, so we can move on with what you're goin' to wear."

"Fine. I like him," Harlan grits out through clenched teeth, feeling like he has been backed into a corner. The words sound weird coming from his own mouth, as if they weren't meant for the outside world to hear. He doesn't think they are. They were supposed to stay in his mind, never to be released for a single person on earth to hear and repeat. Admitting it out loud is the first step to believing it. Harlan wants to believe it; he just doesn't know if he can. Not with his past. He knows Cadeon has a point, but that doesn't stop him from wanting to kick his ass for it.

"Awe, H! I'm so proud of ya! This must have been what my mom felt like when she birthed me," Cadeon exclaims, tackling Harlan onto his bed in a hug. Harlan manages to keep his laugh in, not wanting to reinforce Cadeon's new touchy behavior toward him. Well, he has always been touchy with him, but he has never been tackled-on-the-bed touchy. Harlan has only ever really been tackled by one person, and it's the same person that currently haunts his dreams.

"Fuck off," Harlan says, pushing at Cadeon, but Cadeon makes himself a dead weight, not allowing him room for much movement.

"You've come so far. Making out with boys in the back stairway, then again under the bleachers during the fucking Homecoming game no less, where anyone could see ya. Admitting you like said boy and possibly starting a secret relationship with him. This shit is the high school drama you see in movies. I'm tellin' ya, Haz, they are gonna write a book about it someday. Well, let's hope they make it into a movie, 'cause books are borin'. Who do you think they'd get to play me? Maybe Leonardo DiCaprio?" Cadeon asks, crooking his head to the side in thought.

"Yeah, right. My story would never be interesting enough for that, and Leonardo DiCaprio is too good-looking to play you, not to mention he's like forty-five and could never pass for a high schooler," Harlan says, wiggling his arms to try to free them out of Cadeon's tight hold.

"Semantics," Cadeon dismisses, finally getting off Harlan and sitting on the bed facing him, with an excited grin and a wicked glint in his eyes. "So, tell me about your first kiss. I need details. Don't leave anything out."

"No," Harlan responds flatly, but Cadeon just crosses his arms and raises his eyebrows, waiting. Cadeon will literally stare at him all night if that's what it will take to get Harlan to talk. He has done it before. It's annoying but seemingly effective. "Fine. It was nice."

"Nice?" Cadeon looks unimpressed with the information. "Nice is how you describe a car or your fucking day. You don't describe your first kiss as nice, unless it sucked."

"It didn't suck," Harlan says, allowing his mind to travel back to the empty stairwell. "It was amazing, actually. Luka's lips were soft, even though he was clearly angry and frustrated with me. It was like a dream. As if I was watching it from outside of my own body, but I could feel every little thing. The very air around us felt electrifying, like it does before a big storm."

"Only you would describe your first kiss in such a grossly poetic manner," Cadeon chuckles, covering his mouth with his hand.

"Why the fuck did you ask then?" Harlan punches Cadeon on the arm, effectively getting Cadeon to stop giggling.

"Anything else? Was there tongue?" Cadeon asks, bobbing his eyebrows suggestively.

"You know, for someone who claims to be straight, you sure are interested in how two boys kissed," Harlan muses, punching Cadeon again, this time not as hard.

"I am straight, but I'm also curious," Cadeon defends, rubbing the spot on his arm that Harlan has now hit twice. His smile is still there, amusement twinkling behind his blue eyes. Harlan hates him. Harlan needs new friends. Scratch that. Harlan needs zero friends. That seems to be a way better alternative.

"Didn't curiosity kill the cat or something?" Harlan asks, squinting at Cadeon, hoping the other man takes the bait.

"It had nine lives, so...about those tongues. Where were they?" Cadeon asks, shit-eating grin spreading across his face. Harlan goes to punch him again, but Cadeon dodges this time, cackling loudly.

"Fine. If you must know, we didn't get a chance to really use tongues the first time. He had to go to the pep rally. Tongues happened under the bleachers," Harlan informs, smiling at the memory. He still can't believe it fucking happened, and he has no idea *how* it even happened.

He is trying to tell himself that it's okay that it happened. That Luka really is interested in him and doesn't want to hurt him. It's just difficult to rewire his brain toward positivity after so much negativity. Luka just seems so sincere. Then again, so did Logan. Harlan shakes his head, trying to dislodge the image of that boy from his mind, not wanting to taint the good memory of Luka.

"Now we're getting somewhere," Cadeon says, rubbing his hands together and grinning like the cat that ate the canary. Why is he so excited about this? Is this what girls feel like when they have sleepovers? He is sure it is nothing like in the movies with sexy pillow fights that end in kissing. He has never seen the appeal of two women kissing. That should have been his first clue that he was gay. Very, very gay. His second clue probably came when the boys started putting pictures of naked girls up in their lockers in middle school, while Harlan wanted to display pictures of David Bowie.

"Seriously, why is my sex life so interesting to you? I never ask you about the girls you bang or want to bang, for that matter," Harlan points out, shuddering to think of Cadeon with a girl. Cadeon isn't a virgin by any stretch of the imagination, but that doesn't mean Harlan really wants to envision it.

Picturing Cadeon naked would be like seeing his brother naked. And a girl? No, thank you! Harlan would much rather stick to dudes. They are much more fun to look at. He wonders what Luka would look like naked. In porn, he has definitely seen his fair share of cocks. Luka probably has a nice one, but his ass. Holy shit. His ass. Harlan wants to grab it. Maybe he will find the nerve to actually do so next time.

"So, you wanna fuck Luka!?! I *knew* it!" Cadeon exclaims, like it's the best discovery since sliced bread. Thank the Gods Harlan's mom isn't home to hear this. He's always thought she would throw a shit fit, but she probably wouldn't actually care. Harlan groans, dropping his face in his hands again. Yes. Harlan definitely needs less friends.

25

"Do I look okay?" Luka asks Lizzie, holding his hands out to his side. He feels stupid. He refuses to get overly dressed up for the Homecoming dance, despite his mother's wishes to rent him a suit. He is wearing dark red trousers, a white dress shirt with a black collar that has a single button, and a pair of black and white suspenders. He has the sleeves rolled up, wanting it to look even more casual. Matt is going to give him shit for the suspenders, but he likes them; therefore, Matt can fuck off.

"You look great. Willow is going to love it," Lizzie says, sitting on his bed and assessing his outfit. Luka doesn't really care what Willow thinks of it; she will be happy with anything he wears. He isn't going to the dance to impress her. He wants to impress Harlan. Of course, he can't say that out loud. He still can't believe he actually made out with a boy, under the bleachers of their high school, with his parents within yelling distance. He doesn't know what has gotten into him. He isn't reckless by nature, but something about Harlan makes him want to throw caution to the wind.

It wasn't his first time kissing a boy, but all of the other times were in the dark with a loud party going on around them. Those instances were alcohol-fueled and urgent, with one goal in mind: to get off. Kisses that happened in the dead of the night, when both men tasted like alcohol, their minds fuzzy with need and inebriation. None of them felt that...innocent.

Funny he uses the word innocent to describe it because it was also filthy and sinful. It wasn't something that could easily be swept under the rug and dismissed as drunken shenanigans. No.

He has no excuse for this, which makes him feel uneasy. At least before, if he ever had to explain himself to God, he had an excuse. He could chalk it up to the alcohol and teenage rebellion while begging for mercy. This time, though, he doesn't have one other than he simply wanted it.

It felt so right. So, fucking perfect, yet he *knows* it is wrong. It is wrong to feel this way about a person of the same sex. He knows this. He just can't seem to stop himself. He wants Harlan. Why is that wrong? Oh yeah, the Bible says so. Not to mention the fact that if his parents ever found out, they would probably send him away to never be seen again. So yes, he wants Harlan, but he also should probably keep his feelings at bay, at least until the school year is over and he can work out in his head if being attracted to the same sex really is all that bad.

It's wrong, but he also has his fair share of doubts at this point. Stupid Harlan. He never questioned things before him. He always just planned to eventually stop hooking up with men, find himself a nice, normal girl to marry, and convince himself that he would be happy. He would keep going to church on Sunday, and then maybe God would have mercy on him to relieve him of his impure thoughts. God hasn't done that yet because all he can think about is Harlan.

Harlan, with his long legs and pale skin. Harlan, with his curly hair and ridiculously green eyes that he sometimes lines in black. Harlan, with his big hands, long ringed fingers, and black painted nails. Harlan, who is aware of everyone's disapproval but doesn't seem to give a fuck and continues to just be himself. So yes, as much as he doesn't want to admit it to himself, it is Harlan he wants to impress. He really hopes Harlan's 'maybe' from the night before really meant 'yes'. He told Willow what had happened with Harlan in the stairwell and then again after the game, and she seemed genuinely happy for them, which made him feel relieved.

"Luka! You better hurry! You're supposed to be picking Willow up in fifteen minutes!" Luka's mom is yelling from downstairs, effectively snapping him out of his thoughts about Harlan.

"Come on, Liz. Thanks for helping me, by the way," Luka says, gesturing for his sister to follow him out of the room, shutting the door behind him. She nods in response, trailing right behind him. As they walk down the stairs, he allows himself to wonder what Harlan will be wearing. He could go for something a bit dressier, like the shirt he was wearing that day in the park.

Knowing Harlan, which Luka feels like he is starting to, he will show up in a pair of jeans and a t-shirt. Fuck. Luka hopes he is wearing eyeliner. That's not a sentence Luka ever would have expected to think, but it's true. He likes it when his boy wears eyeliner. *His* boy? Luka likes the sound of that, too. Well, maybe not the sound exactly, since he hasn't said it out loud, but he likes the way it sounds in his head, at least.

"Oh Lu, you look so handsome! Your first dance!" His mom exclaims, blinding him with the flash on her phone as soon as he reaches the landing. He blinks a few times, trying to get his eyes to adjust again, then smiles at her because she looks so happy.

"Thanks, Mom. I should be going, though," Luka says, praying that he will get out of there without a Matt lecture.

"Wait, young man," Matt interrupts, walking into the living room from the kitchen. He stops, eyes raking over Luka's appearance with a look of disgust. Luka stands there quietly, thinking this has to be what Judgment Day will feel like. He prays again, this time, that he will be allowed to leave in the foreseeable future, and Matt won't change his mind. "Those suspenders make you look like a fucking fairy. Ridiculous."

"I think they look great," Josie disagrees, placing two fingers under the aforementioned piece of clothing and tugging once, then giving Luka a reassuring smile. Luka is happy that his mom seems to be on his side for once.

"Thanks, Mom," Luka says quietly, trying to keep his head up and his gaze level with Matt. Showing fear would only make matters worse. It would only mean that Luka would have to change, even though he very much likes his outfit.

"Well, I think you look stupid, and you should change. I don't want my son going to a dance looking like the fag in a boyband," Matt huffs, eyes slanted at Luka. Luka grits his teeth when Matt refers to him as his son. Luka isn't his son. He isn't even sure he wants to be, although Matt did legally adopt him. When that happened, he was thankful, but now, he hates the very idea of calling Matt 'dad'.

"Matt don't be like that. He is probably dressed like a lot of boys his age. Let him go and live," Josie responds, placing her hands on her hips. Luka can't believe his mom is actually standing up to Matt for him. This rarely happens, and if it does, his mom usually loses because Matt pulls the 'I'm the man of this house' card. His mom doesn't seem to be backing down right now, though. He holds his breath and waits for Matt's response.

He really should have just worn something he knew would make Matt happy. Well, not happy, but that he would approve of. It would have saved an argument and possibly Matt being unhappy with his mom. He should know better than to try to be the slightest bit himself in the presence of Matt.

Over the years, he has learned to suppress his typically flamboyant side, instead going for something more stilted and less natural for himself. He hates it, but he has to. He has to do it to keep the peace and to keep his family together. So, what if he has to sacrifice himself and his happiness? He would give it up for the happiness of his mom and sisters in a heartbeat, which Matt seems to provide.

"Fine. If he wants to go looking like that, then he can. I just hope nobody I know sees him," Matt says finally, gesturing towards Luka and then stomping back into the kitchen, probably to grab another beer. Luka sighs in relief, glad it didn't cause more of an argument than necessary. Well, he doesn't see why it was necessary to argue about his choice in clothing at all, but he supposes it is inevitable with someone like Matt around.

"I think you look pretty, Lu," Gabby says with a small voice and wide eyes. Luka likes that she chose the word 'pretty', even though Matt told her not to refer to men that way. He is proud of her.

"Thanks, Gabby, and I think you look pretty, too." She beams at the compliment, Luka messing up her hair a bit. She doesn't seem to mind, just runs her small fingers through it and smiles.

"You're gonna be late. Better get going," Mary says, looking at the clock above the television. Fuck. She's right. He is going to be late if he doesn't get going. He takes a deep breath, steeling his nerves. His mom gives him another reassuring smile, which he appreciates, but a pang of guilt hits his chest because she has no idea about the real reason he is nervous. Luka kind of hates himself for lying to her, but what else can he do? He can break things off with Harlan, but that doesn't feel like an option.

26

"Have you seen Harlan?" Luka asks Ezra, two hours into the dance. He feels like time is slipping away from him. He can actually hear the seconds tick by and still no sight of Harlan. Maybe Harlan lied to him and had no intention of attending. Luka's heart sinks at the thought. He thought he may have actually broken one of Harlan's walls down, gotten through to him, but maybe he was wrong. Maybe Harlan is still second guessing everything. He probably still doesn't trust Luka, but Luka doesn't know what else he can do. He really thought he had made a breakthrough.

"No. Honestly, this isn't really his thing. I haven't seen him at a dance since..." Ezra's sentence trails off, his gaze going into the air as if trying to actually think of the last time he had seen Harlan at a dance. Was it *that* long ago? "Come to think of it, I don't think I've ever seen him at a dance," Ezra finally finishes, looking back at Luka. Luka takes a drink of his punch, which has clearly been spiked with vodka. He hasn't drunk that much, so he is fine. Mostly it is just making him warm and loose.

"He just told me he would be here," Luka says, trying to keep the disappointment from his tone. He doesn't think he succeeds, given the look of confusion marring Ezra's features.

"He did? That's weird. I'm still shocked he even talks to ya. Before you came into town, he tended to keep to himself," Ezra says conversationally, but Luka can hear the smallest hint of curiosity in his tone.

"Yeah..." Luka allows his thoughts to trail off as he glances around the room again, spotting Cadeon walking towards them. He smiles at the other man.

"Where's Willow?" Ezra asks, snapping Luka's attention away from Cadeon. Fuck. That's a good damn question. He hasn't really seen her since they had gotten to the school. She went off with her friends when they arrived. They planned to meet back up before his curfew so he could drop her off at home like the good boyfriend he is supposed to be.

"Umm…" Luka starts, trying to buy some time as he looks for her flaming red hair and black dress on the dance floor. He spots her a few seconds later and smiles when he sees who she is with. "She's dancing with her friend, Tabitha." Luka points to the two girls with bright smiles as they laugh when Willow almost trips in her heels, Tabitha steadying her.

"Hey, guys!" Cadeon greets, finally joining them, fist bumping Ezra and clapping Luka on the back.

"Hey. Harlan here?" Luka asks impatiently, cutting straight to the point. He knows he asked it too quickly, though, because Ezra is giving him a funny look while Cadeon's features have morphed into a smirk and there is definitely a glint in his eye. Could Cadeon know Harlan's preference? Harlan doesn't strike him as the type to tell people, but Cadeon is definitely not at all confused by Luka's insistence.

"Yup," Cadeon answers, rocking on his heels and popping the 'p'. When Luka gives him an impatient look, he just points towards the entrance. Luka looks in the direction Cadeon's finger is pointing to find Harlan standing awkwardly, eyes scanning over the room, finally falling on Luka.

Harlan, of course, is wearing a pair of ripped skinny jeans and his signature black band t-shirt that looks like it may actually be older than Harlan. In the darkness of the room, he can't really make out the logo on the shirt. Luka really needs to start writing these bands down, wanting to listen to them. Maybe it will help him gain insight into Harlan's mind. Harlan has one large hand shoved in his pocket, the other clutching a Solo cup, probably full of spiked punch.

"He looks nervous," Ezra observes, eyes following Luka's.

"As a long-tailed cat in a room full of rocking chairs," Cadeon adds, and what the fuck does that even mean? Why would a cat be nervous in a room full of chairs? Is it because it has a long tail? Do cats even get nervous? They can be curious, but he has never heard anyone refer to them as nervous. He'll just add it to the list of 'weird as fuck' phrases he has heard Cadeon say. He swears he is doing it on purpose.

Fuck. Harlan has begun walking towards them, his long limbs almost gliding across the floor. People in his path part, letting him through while simultaneously gawking. Harlan is like Moses or some shit, parting the crowd like the fucking Red Sea. Luka tries not to get irritated by the stares Harlan is gaining just by being at the dance, but Luka wants to punch them and tell them all to mind their own fucking business. Harlan is allowed to be wherever he fucking wants to be, and if they don't like it, they can shove it.

Just as Luka takes a drink from his own cup, Harlan is close enough for him to see that his eyes are lined with black, making the green stand out. His nails are also freshly painted black, no chip or mark in sight. Luka almost chokes on his punch, inhaling the liquid as it burns his lungs. Cadeon laughs and claps him on the back a few times to help clear his airways, as if he knows why Luka almost died. Fuck. He might. Did Harlan tell him? Oh, God. What if he did? They didn't really rule out telling their friends, he just thought it was an unspoken request. Fuck. Cadeon might *know*.

"Hey," Harlan greets the group as he comes to a stop beside Luka. He is looking down, not making eye contact with any of them. Luka thinks that Ezra's presence may be making him feel anxious, along with the overall effect of having everyone in the room stare at him. He wants to reach out and hold his hand and squeeze, letting him know that it will be okay, but he can't.

It is so frustrating not being able to openly comfort him, and it makes Luka want to scream. He never intended for Harlan to feel nervous and if he had known, he would never have asked him to come. He is suddenly struck by the realization that whatever they have must mean a lot to Harlan because this is a big step for him. This is forcing Harlan out of his comfort zone completely, and Luka wants to hug him even more. Fuck.

"Hey. It's good to see you here, Harlan," Ezra responds, smiling at Harlan. Well, Harlan isn't actually looking so much as smiling in Harlan's direction. There is an awkward silence that falls over them as they all sip their punch and look out at the dance floor. Harlan is becoming increasingly more tense as the seconds tick by, and the loud pop music blaring in the room almost feels deafening. Luka wants to sling his arm around him but can't. Fuck. Maybe this was a terrible idea. Maybe Harlan's right, and they are just too different.

"Mr. Hart, Mr. Carter, Mr. Thomas and...ah, Mr. Sharp. Interesting seeing you here," Mrs. Marcum, their pre-calculus teacher says, with her pointy nose up in the air, as she looks down on Harlan through her silver-rimmed glasses.

"Evenin', Mrs. Marcum," Cadeon waves, smiling at her. She ignores him, taking in Harlan's outfit with a critical eye. It almost makes Luka feel as though Matt is looking at him, and he hates it.

"Harlan. I don't think that is appropriate apparel for a school dance," she chastises, eyes finally landing on his face, looking appalled by his eyeliner. It's not like she hasn't seen him in eyeliner before, since they all have her class during fourth period, right before lunch. Perhaps she is just pissed because it is at a school dance, where everyone went out of their way and spent far too much money to look nice.

"I don't think the girls walking around here with their asses showing and their boobs hanging out while wearing stripper heels is appropriate either, so I guess we all have our grievances," Harlan responds, not even cracking a smile. Luka literally has to bite his tongue to keep from laughing.

Cadeon is smiling into his cup, while Ezra has the most adorable, surprised expression on his face, as if he can't believe Harlan just spoke to a teacher that way. Luka thinks it serves her right for being a bitch. Luka suspects that Harlan may not be able to *afford* nice clothes, but he can't be sure. Harlan hasn't really talked about it, but it would explain why all of his clothes seem either too small or like he got them from a thrift store; however, it could also just be how he chooses to dress.

"Mr. Sharp, do you kiss your mamma with that mouth? She should wash it out with soap. It would do you well to remember who you are speaking to; I could kick you out for that," Mrs. Marcum responds, anger making her tone sharp, but he didn't understand half of what she just said. Kiss his mamma? Wash what out with soap? Was she referring to his mouth? Because that sounds unhealthy. Soap has a bunch of chemicals that shouldn't be ingested; surely a teacher would know that. He holds his breath as he watches Harlan roll his eyes, a rebuttal clearly on the tip of his tongue.

"Mrs. Marcum, I think what Harlan means is that people seem to be able to wear whatever they want to these dances, so he shouldn't be any different. He isn't dressed inappropriately. He may be a little casual, but he isn't wearing anything offensive," Ezra chimes in, effectively cutting off Harlan's most likely biting reply. Harlan doesn't bother to mask the surprised expression on his face at Ezra coming to his defense. Luka, on the other hand, just wants to cheer for him because fuck yeah. Ezra is a really fucking good person and has never talked badly about Harlan, but it is still nice for Harlan to finally see it. See that maybe the entire school isn't against him. That maybe he could have more than one person who cares for him.

"I'm sure that is what he was trying to say. I will be watching you boys," Mrs. Marcum says, pointing at each one of them as she walks off toward whatever bitch cave she flew out of.

"Jesus, that woman puts the cunt in country," Cadeon quips once she is out of earshot, prompting the other three boys to laugh, even Harlan.

"Thank you for umm...sticking up for me, Ezra," Harlan says quietly once the laughter has died down. He is back to looking at his feet, but Luka is so proud of him for actually being the first to say something to Ezra.

"You're welcome, man. You were right. It's not fair, and she clearly just wanted to be a bitch about it," Ezra responds, and Harlan finally looks up to meet his eyes, giving him a small smile. Another feeling of pride sweeps through Luka, threatening to crack his rib cage and overflow onto the dance floor. He can't help the fond expression that takes over his features as he watches Harlan and Ezra continue their conversation.

27

"Do you wanna, maybe, find somewhere to hide?" Luka whispers in Harlan's ear, his raspy voice sending chills down his spine. Harlan almost chokes on his drink. He was not expecting that, at all. He sputters and coughs a bit, trying to catch his breath, feeling Luka's small hand patting and rubbing him on the back. Luka touches him often, but he still isn't used to it. He has to mentally remind himself that he doesn't need to pull away.

The four boys had made their way to a table, spending the last hour talking and laughing. Maybe Ezra isn't such a bad guy after all, but Harlan still doesn't trust him. They haven't really talked to each other exclusively, just keeping it within group conversations. Willow checked in periodically, probably trying to keep up appearances for the sake of Ezra and the other people in attendance. Harlan still hates it, but he can tell that Luka is keeping their interactions to a minimum, only touching her when he thinks he has to. She has just excused herself, again, disappearing with her friends onto the dance floor.

"What?" Harlan chokes out, making sure he heard the other boy correctly.

"Do you wanna disappear for a little bit?" Luka asks again, blue eyes gleaming in the low light, his straight white teeth showing with his easy smile. Fuck. Does he know how pretty he is? Luka places his hand on Harlan's knee, the warmth seeping into his skin. He doesn't move his knee and gives himself a mental pat on the back for not even flinching. Once he gets used to it, the touch makes his stomach do a little flip, warmness pooling in the pit.

"Um...sure...yes...but, um...how?" Harlan stumbles out, his cheeks heating in embarrassment from his stuttering. He needs to get a fucking grip when he is around Luka. He is usually perfectly fine at never showing any type of emotion at all, but Luka does something to him. Makes him let his guard down, and he doesn't like it.

"Meet me in the hallway by the chemistry classroom in five," Luka whispers, glancing to make sure Ezra and Cadeon are still engrossed in their conversation. They are.

"Won't someone find us?" Harlan asks.

"No one will be there, trust me," Luka responds, winking and fuck. Harlan trusts him. How could he let this happen? He does, though. Somewhat.

"I am going to go dance with Willow since she has been begging me all night," Luka says to the rest of the table then, standing up and smiling at Harlan.

"Alright, man, see you around," Ezra responds, while Cadeon just waves. Harlan watches with an amused expression as Luka disappears into the crowd, hips swaying as he walks. Holy fuck. It should be illegal for Luka to wear dress pants and suspenders. Seriously. He almost gave Harlan a heart attack with that outfit when he first arrived. The suspenders act like arrows, pointing down to the prize, which is the dark red trousers that cling to his shapely legs and plump ass like a second skin.

Harlan tries to pay attention to the conversation between his...friends? Well, he isn't one hundred percent sure they are his friends. Cadeon is, but Ezra is questionable still. That just seems like the best word to use to describe the two men he is currently sitting at the table with.

His cock is already stiffening with the idea of being alone with Luka again. He tells it to calm down and cut that shit out because they will probably just kiss or something equally innocent. He looks at his watch for the fifth time and realizes that it has been exactly three minutes. It will take at least a minute to get to the designated hallway, not even factoring in excusing himself from the table and all of that. Well, at least that is what he tells himself as he stands.

"I have to go to the bathroom. Excuse me," Harlan tells them, watching as a grin bloom across Cadeon's face. The bastard. He has probably figured it out. Ezra looks suspicious for .5 seconds before he shrugs, waving to Harlan.

"Alright. Have fun," Cadeon says with a wink. Harlan almost flips him off but doesn't want to seem suspicious in front of Ezra, so he refrains. He just rolls his eyes, waves at Ezra, and makes his way through the crowd. Most of the people around him don't stop and stare at him this time, thank fuck. He just wants to sneak out in peace.

He looks around for any teachers, finding it clear, then sneaks through the door quietly. As soon as the door shuts behind him, he is met with a deafening silence. He closes his eyes for a moment, leaning against the door and taking a deep breath, letting the stillness wash over him. He can still hear the dull thump of the music through the doors behind him, but after being in a loud environment for so long, it is nice to just relax for a minute. He has been out of his comfort zone all night, so taking a minute just to relax and breathe is exactly what he needs.

After a few more deep breaths, he straightens himself back up and begins walking down the empty hallways of the school. Harlan is used to them being filled with fluorescent lights, voices, and footsteps, but they are dark and eerie in the late-night hours. His own footsteps echo down the corridor as he makes a right, then a left, trying to get to his destination quickly and quietly.

When he rounds the last corner, he is confused to see that Luka isn't there. His heart drops, thinking that Luka has changed his mind and didn't want to show. Maybe he will find a note or something that says he doesn't want to do this anymore. He slowly walks down the hallway, looking around for Luka. He almost screams when he feels small hands grab him and shove him into the corner where the wall meets the lockers.

"You have got to stop doing that," Harlan breathes out, panting as he looks down at the smiling face of Luka. The light in this particular hallway is dim, but not so much that Harlan can't see the crinkles by his eyes. He can still see the way Luka's chest is rising and falling with his breaths, a small giggle escaping him at Harlan's words.

"Why? You scared *me* last time," Luka pouts, his bottom lip pulling down with it. It doesn't last long, though, because a few seconds later he is smiling again. Harlan wants to die. How could someone so pretty and happy want to be with him? He is so weird and moody. It is ridiculous, really. Luka is like the sun and Harlan, well, Harlan isn't sure what he is, but he is definitely not the sun. Maybe the moon? Harlan doesn't have time to consider it because Luka wedges himself between Harlan's legs then and gets up on his tiptoes to kiss him. "I've been wanting to do that all night," Luka murmurs against Harlan's lips.

"Did I tell you that you look amazing tonight?" Harlan asks, and he has no fucking clue where that came from. He would have never thought, in a million years, he'd say something like that, but things fucking change, he supposes. They sure have changed quite a bit in the past three days. He hopes he doesn't sound like a total fucking nerd with the compliment, but it's true. Luka does look amazing.

"You did not but thank you. You look beautiful tonight as well," Luka tells him, blue eyes roaming over his face in the dim light. Harlan thinks he is lying, but he isn't giving out any of his normal tells to show he is doing so, like using the words 'obviously' and 'literally' while emphasizing them. He actually seems genuine.

"I look the same as I look every day," Harlan counters, glancing down at his outfit. He would have bought something fancy, but that requires actual money that he doesn't have yet. He is going to get his first paycheck soon, though he doubts he will spend it on clothes. He isn't sure he actually cares. He does care what Luka thinks, for whatever reason, but he doesn't care what he looks like to everyone else.

"You put a fresh coat of polish on your nails, and you're wearing eyeliner. You are also wearing an extra ring on your left pinky. While you do wear eyeliner on occasion to school, you never care if it is put on with a steady hand. This time, it's clear that you took your time, so no, you don't look exactly the same." Harlan doesn't bother to mask the shock on his face, his mouth forming a small 'o'.

What the fuck? Luka notices that stuff about him? Nobody else has. He doesn't even know if his own mother knows he came to the dance tonight. She had to work, so probably not. Cadeon doesn't notice shit like that, and others were too busy staring at his arrival at the dance to bother taking in his actual appearance. A warmness spreads in his chest when he comes to the conclusion that someone may actually pay attention to him. Luka pays attention to him.

He doesn't say anything, just grabs Luka's suspenders because honestly, he has been wanting to do that all fucking night, pulls the other man toward him and kisses him again. Luka's small hands immediately come around Harlan's neck, tangling in his dark curls. This kiss isn't quick and innocent like the others have been. This one is intense and heated, making Harlan's cock stiffen in his jeans. He moans at the feeling of Luka's own erection against his, rubbing through the fabric, and it feels so fucking good.

"Fuck, Harlan." Luka's voice is high and needy, not quite a whine, but not a whimper either. He trails kisses down Harlan's jaw, biting and nipping the skin there. Harlan's eyes roll into the back of his head when Luka kisses, then bites, and finally sucks on the spot where his jaw meets his ear because, holy shit. Har-

Ian is embarrassed when a moan escapes from deep within his chest, but it seems to urge Luka on. He grinds his hard cock against Harlan's, releasing a high raspy sound into the spot he has claimed as his own on Harlan's neck.

"You feel so good," Luka says in his ear, grinding harder. The coil in the pit of his stomach tightens with the words. Fuck. He is getting close, but he is literally stuck between a rock and a hard place. His back is pressed against the locker and the wall, Luka pinning him in. He couldn't pull away even if he tried, and he isn't sure he wants to because the sensation is so good, he may faint. Luka's lips are back on his, swallowing his next moan.

Without thinking, Harlan releases Luka's suspender straps. He had no idea he was even still holding them, to be honest. Before he can second guess himself, he places his hands on Luka's lower back, pulling the other man impossibly closer. Luka continues the slow grind of his hips as he kisses him, wet and sloppy, tongues delving deep. It all feels like too much but not enough. His entire body is on fire, and Luka gripping his hair tightly isn't helping matters. Each nerve ending is shooting off in different directions, but they all find their way back to his hard cock.

Harlan's hands are subconsciously working their way toward Luka's round ass. He has been dreaming about that ass for far too long, so who could blame them. He will call them traitorous later, but right now they have a mind of their own. When they finally come to rest on Luka's ass, the smaller boy moans into Harlan's mouth, prompting him to squeeze the firm muscles.

Luka seems to like that because he grinds harder, his movements becoming quicker. Holy fucking shit. Harlan has never felt this good in his entire life. His hand would never compare to Luka fucking Thomas grinding their cocks together through the fabric of their pants while kissing the life from him. It's pathetic, but it's the truth. Harlan doesn't know how he will ever go back to his hand after tonight.

"Oh, God," Luka moans when Harlan squeezes his ass firmly.

Harlan would usually have some sort of 'no God here or anywhere' remark, but he can't fucking think when his balls feel like they may explode any second now as Luka's tongue is massaging his own. Harlan begins grinding back, just needing to come. He is so close; he is out of his mind with need. He just needs to come, and Luka grinding on him quickly now is exactly the friction he needs. He calls out Luka's name as he comes in his own jeans, squeezing Luka's ass so hard he is probably going to leave bruises.

Luka breaks their kiss, eyes wide, mouth open, looking down in surprise. Fuck. Shit. What the fuck just happened? Harlan creamed his jeans like a horny fourteen-year-old, that's what fucking happened. Harlan can feel his cheeks and chest burning with the realization. Luka must think he is a stupid fucking virgin. Fuck. He is a stupid virgin, isn't he? He didn't want Luka to know that, but now he must. Harlan doesn't look Luka in the eye as he pushes him away, looking down at his come stained pants for a few seconds. Letting the shame sink in even more. Jesus, the first real makeout session with a boy, and Harlan fucking comes in his pants. He is so stupid. He hates himself.

He doesn't say a word to Luka, ignoring his calls and running down the dimly-lit hallway and into the darkness of the next one. He quickly locates an exit that won't sound an alarm, breathing in the fresh air as he pushes through the thankfully unlocked doors roughly. He blinks back tears as he continues to run in the direction of his home. All he can hear is the echo of his boots and the blood rushing to his ears. The air is cold on Harlan's too warm face, helping him cool down a bit and dry the tears in his eyes as they form.

He tries to breathe as deeply as he can while he runs, but it's difficult. All he wants to do is collapse on the dirty ground and cry, but he can't. He needs to make it home, to his bed, before he lets the panic take over him. His breaths are coming out in short huffs. He doesn't know if he will make it, but he has to try.

He doesn't even want to consider the embarrassment he would suffer if someone from school found him mid-panic attack on a dirty sidewalk in town.

28

Luka runs after Harlan's retreating figure, following him out of the school. He thinks he loses him to the night when he exits but spots a glimpse of him going around the corner. He quickly follows him. Harlan doesn't run that fast, and even in his dress clothes, he knows he will catch up with him sooner rather than later. He has no idea where Harlan is going, he just follows blindly as he continues to beat himself up over his reaction.

He had been surprised. That's all. He hadn't been expecting Harlan to come. He didn't mean to make Harlan think he was upset with him in any way. He was just so fucking surprised. In fact, a feeling of pride swept through him right after. Being able to get Harlan off just by kissing and grinding did something to his ego. Of course, Harlan didn't see that. His cheeks had already begun turning a bright shade of red, his large hand going to cover the wet spot on his crotch. He didn't even say anything to Luka or look him in the eye, he just fled.

Harlan looks like he is struggling to breathe ahead of him, hand going up to cover his chest, judging by the angle. Luka is barely breathing hard as he begins to catch up, just a few steps behind Harlan now. Luka takes his opportunity when Harlan turns to walk into a driveway. He grabs Harlan's elbow, spinning him around. "Harlan, please don't run from me. Please," Luka begs, suddenly feeling like he and Harlan are back to square one. He certainly hopes not because that would suck major ass, but Harlan isn't making eye contact, much like the first day. Harlan ignores him and tries to turn around again, but Luka stops him with another firm hand on his elbow.

"Let go," Harlan says, rubbing his chest with his other hand. He is blinking a lot, biting his lip, and Luka thinks he may actually be holding back tears. Luka hates himself for making Harlan feel this way. It was never his intention. He just...he was just so surprised. He, himself, was about two minutes away from coming in his own pants, if he is honest, but Harlan apparently didn't see it that way.

"Not until you talk to me," Luka responds, tightening his grip even more when Harlan tries to pull free. Harlan is breathing hard, probably from the sprint. His green eyes are cast down and his curls are disheveled. His pale skin almost glows in the moonlight, making him seem ethereal. Luka just wants to reach out and touch his face, pull his lip out from between his teeth, but he doesn't. He is afraid one wrong move will scare him even more.

"What is there to talk about? I fucking came in my pants. You happy? Wanna make fun of me? Remind me of how I am a virgin who, up until two days ago, had never kissed anyone, let alone had someone grind against me?" Harlan accuses, his tone raw, voice cracking on the last two words.

At first, Luka is angry at yet another accusation, but his heart breaks when he comprehends what Harlan has just admitted to him. Harlan must have just realized it too, because his eyes get wide as saucers, his cheeks turning an even deeper shade of red, if possible. Harlan is a virgin? Holy shit. Luka had no idea. He thought that maybe he was inexperienced, but never imagined that hot as fuck Harlan Sharp would be a virgin at eighteen. Just like that, another piece of the puzzle known as Harlan has fallen into place.

"Oh, love, no. It's not like that," Luka insists, trying to keep his eyes kind and his tone earnest. Anything to make Harlan understand. Luka takes his fingers and uses them to lift Harlan's chin up. Harlan's eyes are still mostly downcast, but he glances up at Luka making eye contact for a split second. That is all Luka needs to keep going. "I was just surprised, that's all."

"I just...I can't, Luka," Harlan starts, but Luka is quick to cut off that sentence.

"Can't what? Harlan, I need you to listen very carefully. You ran off before you could see the look of pride on my face. Do you have any idea how fucking hot it is to know that I made you come in your pants? That you got so turned on by what we were doing that you came? Fuck. I almost came just knowing I got you so turned on. In fact, I will probably go home tonight and get off at the mere thought of it. Holy fuck, Harlan, don't you understand what a compliment that is?" Luka asks, and at some point, during his speech, Harlan finally meets his eyes. He is looking at Luka as if trying to decide if Luka is telling the truth. Luka most certainly fucking is.

"I feel like an idiot," Harlan mumbles after a few excruciating minutes of silence. His eyes are shining in the moonlight with unshed tears, and Luka's heart breaks a tiny bit more for him. Harlan takes a deep breath, looking up at the sky and blinking a few times. Luka bets Harlan looks beautiful when he cries. He looks beautiful doing everything else, including but not limited to, breathing, sitting still, and sucking a goddamned straw.

"You're not an idiot, love. It's actually normal. The first time I did something like that, I also came in my pants. The guy was a total asshole about it, though. He made me feel like shit for it, and that wasn't fair. I think it's a compliment," Luka tells him, thinking back to the time he snuck out of his house on New Year's Eve when he was sixteen. He ended up getting drunk and dry humping this random dude, that he doesn't even remember the name of, until he came.

"I'm sorry he was an asshole about it," Harlan responds, finally meeting Luka's gaze and keeping it. Harlan does seem genuinely sorry, but Luka just shrugs. It really isn't that big of a deal now, but Luka promised himself that he would never ever make someone feel bad for coming.

"Are you okay?" Luka asks, placing his hand on Harlan's chest, feeling his heartbeat erratically beneath his fingers.

"Yeah. 'M fine," Harlan answers, but Luka isn't entirely sure he believes him. Now that his focus isn't only on Harlan, Luka begins to finally take in his surroundings. Harlan has led them to a part of town Luka didn't know existed. Behind Harlan is a small and very run-down house. The white paint is dingy, chipping off in several places. One of the dark shutters is broken, the other is crooked. The windows look grimy, spider webs woven through the dirty white banister.

"Harlan, is this your house?" Luka asks before he can think better of it. Fuck. He feels Harlan stiffen below his hand, his heart rate picking back up. The look on his face has gone back to panic. Luka is just a major fuck-up tonight. That's the only explanation for any of this. Luka shouldn't be allowed to talk anymore. Talking gets him into trouble and makes him say things to cute boys that could be taken the wrong way. So stop talking? That should be easy, right? It's not like he ever says anything important.

"Um...yeah," Harlan responds, voice barely above a whisper. His body has turned back in on itself, feet pigeon-toed, gaze firmly planted on them. "I know it's just a glorified shack and probably not nearly as nice as yours, but...yeah, this is where I live. You probably have already gathered that I am poor. I guess you were gonna find out about the shithole I call home at some point." Harlan laughs soberly.

"Love, I don't give a fuck what your house looks like or if you're poor. None of that matters to me," Luka tells him, taking his large hand in his own. The rings are cool on his skin, but Harlan's hand is warm.

"Fuck, this whole night has been a disaster," Harlan says, cheeks red with his embarrassment. Luka thinks he has seen Harlan show more emotion tonight than he has in the last two months combined. He would be happy if the emotions weren't shame and embarrassment.

"I wouldn't say that," Luka replies, smiling a bit. It hasn't been a total disaster. He got to make out with Harlan. He got him off and has plenty of wanking material for later. He knows way more about Harlan now than he ever thought he would. He feels...closer to him somehow. "I think this night has been perfect, full of doing things we shouldn't do and having a secret little rendezvous."

"You need to stop studying all of those stupid vocabulary words Mrs. Perry keeps assigning as SAT prep." Harlan laughs, the sound deep and musical.

"Probably," Luka says, returning Harlan's smile and getting on his tiptoes to kiss Harlan on the lips.

"I'm sorry I flipped out," Harlan sighs, Luka feeling the hot breath on his lips. Luka doesn't want him to apologize.

"No need to apologize, love. I don't mind, as long as you keep the things I said in mind for next time."

"Next time?" Harlan asks, as if he can't believe Luka would still want to continue this. Luka wishes he could smack some sense into him, but he needs to keep proving himself to make Harlan understand.

"Of course," Luka answers, glancing down at his watch and sighing when it reads 10:30 pm. He is slightly panicked, his chest constricting at the idea of being late for curfew. His parents never let him do anything, so being late this one time is sure to mean he won't be allowed to do anything ever again. "I'm sorry, Harlan, but I have to go. My parents are expecting me home at eleven, and I don't want to know what will happen to me if I am even a minute late. I still have to drop Willow off."

"It's fine, Lu. I understand," Harlan says, giving him a small smile, and that is really all Luka could ask for. Luka hates doing this. Hates leaving him when he feels like he has cracked through another wall. He may have many more to go, but the moment seems fragile somehow. In such a way that Luka is afraid that as soon as he turns his back, Harlan will put cement over the cracks and pretend they never happened. He supposes if he wants Harlan to trust him, he is going to have to trust Harlan, too. Trust that their blossoming relationship won't be a continuous cha-cha of one step forward and two steps back.

"Gimme your number," Luka says then, the idea popping into his head suddenly. He doesn't want another week like the one before, wanting to speak to Harlan but having no way of contacting him. Having his number would at least give him another avenue of communication. Sure, Harlan could ignore him, but he also knows where he lives as well. He then pulls out his phone and hands it to Harlan. Harlan does as asked, using too large thumbs to type in his number, then sends a quick text to himself so that he has Luka's.

"Text me, if you want," Harlan adds the last part, as if he isn't sure Luka really wants to text him. If it takes forever, Luka will get him to understand that he does want to text him, and talk to him, and kiss him, and do all sorts of other things with him.

"Of course, love. Alright, I better get going. Bye," Luka says, kissing Harlan softly on the lips with the word. "Oh, and by the way, I love the flowers." Luka gestures at the flowers planted in the bed alongside the chipped painted siding. He catches Harlan blush the prettiest shade of pink before he turns on his heels and begins to run off, smiling from ear to ear.

There are still so many unanswered questions about the mystery that is Harlan Sharp, but this is a wonderful start to what Luka hopes is a beautiful ending. His heart is light in his chest at the prospect of the future for once. Now more than ever, he realizes just how much he is dreading his destiny of the white picket fence, the loveless marriage, and the 2.5 kids. If this is just an itch, Luka is afraid he will never stop scratching it. He doesn't know if he cares to. What does that say about his belief? Luka pushes that thought aside, refusing to think about God for the night. That will be a conversation for a different day.

ACKNOWLEDGEMENT

I just want to take a moment to thank some very important people. First and foremost, Dana and Linda who have been my support system through all of this. They also had a huge part in editing it and always pushed me to achieve my goals. They are my closest friends, and I do not know where my writing would be without them.

Mindy and Sarah have also edited this and read through it before it was published. A huge thank you to Bibi and Daria who created the book cover and back. They all provided something invaluable to this team. I also want to thank Zoe. She was a huge part in editing this series when this was first being written. Then Veronika, Morgane, Melanie and Ashley for always being my cheerleaders and believing in me.

Finally, last, but certainly not least, my husband, Michael, and girlfriend, Taren, for always supporting me in everything I do in life.

I also want to take a moment to thank everyone who buys and reads this. It means more to me than you will ever know.

ABOUT THE AUTHOR

L. M. Archer

 I was first drawn to writing as a way to express my feelings when oftentimes, I found that I couldn't say them out loud. That's why my writing is more on the dark side of the romance spectrum. I tend to write in a way that showcases real scenarios and events. My books tackle mental health, moral values, religion and many other topics that are raw and real.

I'm not afraid to make my readers look at the darker side of humanity and question the very foundation of life and existence. The topics in my books can be triggering, but I am a firm believer that you need to shed light on certain situations. Keeping them in the dark only hurts more.

TAKE ME TO CHURCH SERIES

The Take me to Church series is a real depiction of falling in love as a gay teen amidst the rampant homophobia of the south and the mental health issues many people face. It's explicit in the way that life is. It's raw, beautiful, and real. Readers will scream in anger and cry in pain, but also laugh in joy and healing as they grow with these characters.

Sweetness In Innocence

Luka Thomas is leading a double life. Publicly, he is a God-fearing Christian with a loving girlfriend. What happens in the shadows of his reality tells a different story. Because of one boy, he has begun to question everything.

Harlan Sharp promised himself he wouldn't fall for Luka, but he doesn't know how to stop it. Each kiss, each touch, each gentle caress they share only leads him further toward revealing the secrets of his past and bearing his scars.

The nature of their relationship must be hidden from everyone. Luka's family will disown him. His God will never forgive him.

It's a sin that Luka isn't ready to confess, but Limbo can't last forever.

Born In Sickness

Luka Thomas is a God-fearing Christian. When his family moves to the Bible Belt right before his senior year of high school, he knows he'll blend right in. Sort of. Being gay is a sin, so he's not gay. He's just...experimenting.

Then he meets Harlan Sharp and begins to question everything he knew to be true.

Harlan stopped believing in fairytales when the darkest days of his past left him scarred, angry, and questioning God's motives. He doesn't trust anyone, let alone Luka, who reminds Harlan of the very same person who hurt him.

When blatantly ignoring all of Luka's attempts at conversation doesn't deter him, Harlan begins criticizing the one thing that Luka seems to believe wholeheartedly: his faith in God.

With Luka's incredibly strict step-father pressuring him to date a girl, he desperately makes a deal, but at what cost to his budding relationship with Harlan?

BOOKS BY THIS AUTHOR

Cool For The Summer

Unlike the average American college student, Gabriel Walker is not looking forward to his summer break from college. All of his friends are gone, with the exception of his roommate, Darien. He plans to spend the summer working to pay for his off-campus apartment, but all of that changes when Darien drags him to a house party held to kick off the summer break. There he meets a tattooed man with long hair and golden boots who completely turns his world upside down.

Xander Bennett is comfortable with his sexuality, and he isn't afraid to show it. His biggest flaw is the fact that he seems to have a thing for straight men. When he meets Gabriel at a party hosted by mutual friends, he knows he should keep his distance, but what he knows and what he feels are two different things.

Gabriel thought he was straight, but Xander is making him question everything he thought he knew about himself. They spend the warm months getting to know each other, but the question plaguing both of their minds is ever-present. Is this a relationship that will last beyond the summer?

The steamy scenes paired with the self discovery of these characters will touch your heart, and the bit of drama will have you celebrating their happy ending.

Printed in Great Britain
by Amazon